The Fair Maid of Bohemia

In the Nicholas Bracewell series

The Laughing Hangman
The Roaring Boy
The Silent Woman
The Mad Courtesan
The Nine Giants
The Trip to Jerusalem
The Merry Devils
The Queen's Head

In the Domesday Books series

The Lions of the North
The Dragons of Archenfield
The Ravens of Blackwater
The Wolves of Savernake

The
Fair Maid
of
Bohemia

[A NOVEL]

Edward Marston

ST. MARTIN'S PRESS ❧ NEW YORK

Map by Mark Stein Studios

Library of Congress Cataloging-in-Publication Data

Marston, Edward.
  The fair maid of Bohemia : a novel / by Edward Marston.— 1st ed.
    p. cm.
  ISBN 0-312-15606-5
  1. Theater—Czechoslovakia—Prague—History—16th century—Fiction. 2. British—Travel—Czechoslovakia—Prague—History—16th century—Fiction. 3. Bohemia (Czech Republic)—History—1526-1618—Fiction. 4. Lord Westfield's Men (Fictitious characters)—Fiction. 5. Bracewell, Nicholas (Fictitious character)—Fiction. I. Title.
PR6063.A695F34   1997
823'.914—dc21   96-53925
                                                                                   CIP

First Edition: June 1997

10 9 8 7 6 5 4 3 2 1

In loving memory

of

Harriett Hawkins Buckley

Friend, Scholar and Shakespearean Heroine

'I am to go over the seas wi' Mr Browne and the company . . . now, good Sir, as you have ever byne my worthie friend, so helpe me nowe. I have a sute of clothe and a cloke at pane fo three pound, and if it shall pleas you to lend me so much to release them, I shall be bound to pray fo you so longe as I leve; for if I go over, and have no clothes, I shall not be esteemed of.'

—Letter from Richard Jones to Edward Alleyn, 1592

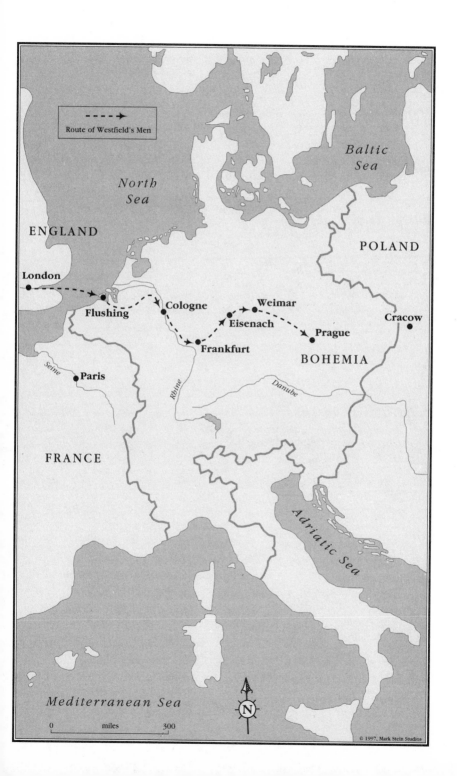

The Fair Maid of Bohemia

[CHAPTER ONE]

They all saw her. Sooner or later, every eye in the company was drawn ineluctably up to the place where she sat in the lower gallery. The yard of the Queen's Head was filled to shoulder-jostling capacity, as the eager citizens of London converged on Gracechurch Street to see a performance by Westfield's Men of *The Knights of Malta,* yet she still stood out clearly from the mass of bodies all around her. She was like a bright star in a troubled sky, a fixed point of illumination from which all could take direction and reassurance. A sign from above.

What was remarkable was the fact that she evidently did not set out to become a cynosure. There was a natural poise and a becoming modesty about her which forbade any deliberate attempt to court attention. Not for her the vivid plumage which some ladies wore or the extravagant gestures with which some gallants sought to make their presence felt. Her attire was sober, her manner restrained. That was the paradox. Here was a young woman whose desire to be invisible somehow made her strikingly conspicuous.

Owen Elias was the first to notice her. When he came out in a black cloak to deliver the Prologue, he was so dazzled by her that he all but forgot the rhyming couplet which ended the speech. The ebullient Welshman swept into the tiring-house at the rear of the makeshift stage and passed the warning on to Lawrence Firethorn.

'Beware!' he whispered.

'Why?' asked Firethorn.

'An angel has come to look down on us. Avoid her, Lawrence. Gaze up at her and you will not even remember what day it is, still less which role you are taking in what play.'

'Nothing can distract me!' asserted Firethorn, inflating his barrel chest. 'When I marshal my knights in Malta, the sight of Saint Peter and a whole choir of angels would not lead me astray. My art is adamantine proof.'

'She sits with Lord Westfield himself.'

'Some costly trull he keeps for amusement.'

'No trull, Lawrence, I do assure you.'

'Stand aside, Owen.'

'A heavenly creature in every particular.'

'They *want* me.'

As the martial music sounded, Firethorn, in the person of Jean de Valette, Grand Master of the Order, strutted imperiously onto the stage, with four knights in rudimentary armour at his back. It was a majestic entrance and it brought a round of applause from the throng. Lawrence Firethorn was the company's actor-manager, a man of towering histrionic skills with an incomparable record of success on the boards. He could breathe life into the most moribund character and transmute even the most banal verse into the purest poetry. Declaiming his first speech, he convinced his audience that he had a whole army at his behest and not a mere quartet of puny soldiers in rusty helmets and dented breast-plates.

Fie upon this siege! Defiance is my cry!
How dare the base and all-unworthy Turk
Presume to touch this island paradise
And crush its treasured liberties to death
Beneath the blood-soaked heel of Ottoman.
No tyrant from the east will conquer here.
The Knights of Malta will protect the isle
And fight with God Almighty at their side
To bless their cause and urge them on to feats
Of valour, acts of noble note, triumphing
At the last o'er Turkish hordes, whate'er their
Strength and purpose.'

Firethorn was not simply establishing his hold over the spectators and giving them a brief summary of the plot of the play, he was using the speech as a means of surveying the female faces in the galleries, feeding off their wide-eyed admiration and searching for a new conquest for his capacious bed. When his roving eye settled on Lord Westfield's young companion, it roved no further. She provided firm anchorage for his scrutiny. Like Owen Elias, he was struck by her beauty but it did not threaten to deprive him of his lines in the same way. Instead, the Grand Master of the Order of Saint John Jerusalem worked the bellows of his lungs to put more fire into his bold words and left flames of defiance crackling in the air when he quit the stage.

Nicholas Bracewell had the actors ready for the next scene. As the Knights of Malta made their exit, a booming drum announced the entry of the Turkish army. When the book-holder had ushered them into action, he had a moment to observe the bemused look on the face of the Grand Master.

'What ails you?' he asked with concern.

Firethorn beamed. 'He is right, Nick. He has hit the mark.'

'Who?'

'Owen. He first witnessed the miracle.'

'Miracle? What miracle?'

'The one beside Lord Westfield.'

Nicholas understood. 'A young lady, I think?'

'No, Nick,' said Firethorn, kissing his fingertips with expressive emotion. 'An alabaster Venus. A saint in blue apparel. Virginity made manifest.'

'Look to your defences,' advised the other, one ear on the progress of the play. 'Scene Three finds you inspecting the fortifications at Fort Saint Elmo. Stand by, for you will soon be called.'

Firethorn heaved a sigh. 'My walls have already been breached. Not by the Turkish soldiers or by any ordnance that man can muster. But by that divine creature in the lower gallery. Her eyes are cannon-balls that leave no stone of my heart still standing. I lie in ruins.' A beatific smile lit his countenance. 'Behold a Grand Master brought to his knees by a virtuous maid.'

'Edmund will not applaud your capitulation.'

'Why so?'

'He has worked long and hard to repair this play,' reminded Nicholas. 'To make an old theme sound new-minted, he has rewritten the last two acts in their entirety. He will not thank you for surrendering Malta without even putting up token resistance.'

Firethorn's pride was stung. 'You mistake me, Nick. I do not yield to the enemy because I have seen a gorgeous apparition out there in the yard. Nothing will separate me from the part I play. I am Jean de Valette, lately Governor of Tripoli and Captain General of the Order's galleys, now elected Grand Master. Nobody will change that. But she will inspire me to greater heights. Edmund Hoode will have no complaint about *The Knights of Malta*. Under the spell of that demi-god beside our patron, I will give the performance of a lifetime. Besiege my island! Storm my fortresses! This indignity will not be borne. I'm in a mood to conquer the entire Ottoman Empire with my bare hands. Set me loose!'

When the fanfare sounded, Firethorn went bursting onto the stage to take command once more. Though he dedicated his lines to one select pair of ears, all the spectators were moved by the power and sincerity of his acting. Where he led, most of the company could not begin to follow. Firethorn was scaling mountain peaks that left them dizzy with fear. While he was helped by the sight of the mysterious young lady with Lord Westfield, they were fatally handicapped.

Even the dependable James Ingram was stricken.

'She is bewitching, Nick,' he said as he left the stage.

'Is that why you stuttered on your first line?' chided Nicholas. 'Is she the reason you dropped that goblet?'

'I was careless.'

'You are never careless, James.'

'Then my mind was elsewhere.'

'Our spectators will be elsewhere if we give such a poor account of ourselves. There's hardly a member of the cast who has not stumbled over his role.'

'The lady has unnerved us.'

'Will you let one solitary person affect you thus?' said Nicholas, loud enough for his reprimand to reach everyone in the tiring-house. 'I begin to think she has been planted on us by Banbury's Men to drive you all to distraction and make our rivals seem the finer company. This is a poor way indeed to serve our patron and our play.'

Ingram accepted the rebuke with a nod and vowed to make amends for his lapse of concentration during the next scene. But the list of casualties lengthened steadily. One by one, the actors succumbed to the subtle impact of the face in the lower gallery. Even the apprentices were not immune. Schooled to portray maiden modesty themselves, they became its hapless victims. Nicholas was shocked to see Richard Honeydew, the youngest, most talented and reliable of them, falling prey to the charms of the singular spectator and gabbling his words as if they were hot coals in his mouth that had to be spat out as soon as possible.

George Dart was the most spectacular casualty. The assistant stage-keeper, a reluctant actor at the best of times, was too busy in the early scenes trying to remember his lines and his moves as a Turkish soldier to notice any of the spectators. It was only when he saw the growing wonderment of his colleagues that he thought to look up at its source. It was a disastrous mistake. Instead of rounding up Maltese prisoners, Dart was an instant captive himself and gazed up at the gaoler of his heart so steadfastly that he lost his bearings completely and wandered off the edge of the stage and into the arms of the standees in the front rank.

The smallest soldier ever to serve in the Turkish army now became the funniest, and the audience roared with laughter. By the time that Dart was thrown back onstage, the next scene had started and he found himself marooned in the middle of the enemy stronghold. Not knowing whether to stay or flee, he did both alternately, and his madcap indecision drew fresh hysteria from the crowd. It was only when the Grand Master lashed at him with a sword that Dart realised that a hasty retreat was in order.

Scurrying into the tiring-house, he fainted with relief at his escape and fell into the book-holder's arms. Nicholas winced. A tale of heroism was in danger of becoming a farce. He would have stern words for George Dart when the latter recovered to participate in the siege of Malta.

Predictably, there was only one survivor. Barnaby Gill, the company's acknowledged clown, was impervious to feminine beauty of any kind, treating all women with a police disdain as a necessary evil put upon the earth for the sole purpose of procreation. Gill's darker passions led him in another direction. When he first spied the lady who was causing such commotion among his fellows, he accorded her no more than a cursory glance. However, his attention soon returned to her when he realised that she was admiring his performance above all else on stage.

Gill took the role of Hilario, jester to the Knights of Malta, a man whose songs and dances brought welcome comic relief to a fraught situation. Hilario was also a key figure in the romantic sub-plot which enlivened the play. Whenever he appeared, the young woman clapped her gloved hands with polite enthusiasm and his jig in Act Three had her trembling with mirth. Gill responded by directing much of his performance at her, coaxing smiles, laughter and, eventually, tears of delight. In pleasing an honoured guest of their patron, he would earn Lord Westfield's gratitude and that was always to be sought.

Lawrence Firethorn was galled by his rival's success. As Hilario skipped nimbly offstage to sustained applause, the Grand Master was waiting to intercept him.

'There was no dance set down for that scene, Barnaby.'

'I invented one to satisfy my admirers.'

'The only admirer you have is the one who gazes back at you from the looking-glass. Play the scenes as they are written.'

'Save your strictures for our fellows,' said Gill with a dismissive wave. 'They deserve them, I do not. It is they who are enslaved by that creature beside our esteemed patron. While she has bewitched every man in the company, I alone have enchanted *her*. She rose to her feet after my last jig.'

'To break wind in disgust, no doubt.'

'The lady is a shrewd playgoer. She recognises genius.'

'That is why she hangs on every word I say.'

'Only hangs, Lawrence? She *drools* over mine. Your Knights of Malta may defeat the Turk, but Hilario is victor over both armies. Ask of the creature in blue. She worships me.'

Firethorn blustered impotently. The hideous truth had to be faced. Barnaby Gill was stealing the play from its leading player. The gorgeous young lady in the lower gallery somehow preferred a licensed fool to the Grand Master of the Order. Smarting from this blow to his professional pride, Firethorn blazed even more gloriously in the ensuing scenes. The rest of the audience were beneficiaries of this extraordinary display of his talent but he could still not win over the one person who mattered to him. Patently fascinated by his portrayal, she did not sigh at his setbacks or stir at his heroism. When he sent twenty lines of exquisite poetry winging its way up to her, all she could do was to watch him with quizzical interest. Then the clown stepped back into the action and her little hands were clapping once more.

It was humiliating. For once in his career, Firethorn was made to feel that he was failing both as an actor and as a man. Yielding the palm to Barnaby Gill—of all people—made the pain almost unendurable. The spectators at the Queen's Head saw none of his personal suffering. What they were witnessing was a stock play from the company's repertoire being turned into a small masterpiece by the spirited performance of the Grand Master and the comic genius of Hilario. Between them, the two men rescued the drama from its string of early mistakes and inspired the whole company to do itself justice.

Nicholas Bracewell was relieved that *The Knights of Malta* was now recognisably the piece which they had rehearsed. As the drama moved with gathering force into its final scene, he could sense the power it was exerting over its audience. It was then that Edmund Hoode made his only appearance. Having laboured so strenuously to refine and improve the play, the resident author of Westfield's Men made sure that he himself had a small but decisive role. Where better to impress himself upon the spectators' minds than at the very close? What part could be more ideal for this purpose than that of Don García de Toledo, Viceroy of Sicily and the man who finally raised the siege by coming to the aid of the gallant knights?

When Hoode made his triumphant entry, spontaneous cheers and applause broke out in the yard. It briefly turned a competent actor into an accomplished one and he declaimed his first few speeches with a panache worthy of Firethorn himself. When the Grand Master embraced him with thanks, however, Don García got his first glimpse of the face in the lower gallery. It took his breath away so completely that he could barely get his tongue around his lines. Eventually, after an interminable pause to collect himself, Hoode put tremendous feeling into the finest speech in the play.

Unfortunately, *The Knights of Malta* was not the play in question. Jolted out of character by the vision before him, he ended up in *Love's Sacrifice,* one of his own pieces. When it slowly dawned on the audience that Don García de Toledo, a military hero, was not celebrating his victory but declaring his undying passion to someone in a totally different play, the chuckles began in earnest. They soon turned to raucous jeers, and two hours of unremitting work upon the stage were in danger of being sunk beneath a sea of mocking laughter.

Firethorn saved the day with commendable speed. Pulling Don García into a second embrace, he spun him around so that Hoode was no longer able to see the lady whose beauty had ensnared him so utterly. With deft fingers, the Grand Master picked his pocket of all his remaining lines and delivered them himself, investing the words with such awesome authority that the sniggers were soon cowed into silence. Control had been reaffirmed. *The Knights of Malta* was able to end on a high note and the company left the stage to deafening acclaim.

While the players came out to take their bows, Nicholas peeped through the curtain at the rear of the stage to take his own first look at Lord Westfield's guest. She had posed a far greater threat to Malta than the whole Turkish army, but it had been no deliberate attack. Any damage had been unwittingly caused. Nicholas could see that and his annoyance at once faded into admiration.

What surprised him most was her youth. The flamboyant Lord Westfield had a predilection for Court beauties, mature ladies who were seasoned in the arts of coquetry and who added a lustre to his entourage. The newcomer did not conform to the archetype in any detail. Nicholas decided that she could be no more than sixteen or seventeen at most. And with her tender years came the bloom of pure innocence.

Sparkling blue eyes were set in a face of delicate loveliness that needed no cosmetics. An inner radiance seemed to shine out of her. She wore a dress in the Spanish fashion with a corseted bodice in dark blue. A heavy, jewelled stomacher-front dipped to a point over her stiff farthingale skirt. A gown of a lighter-blue material fitted the shoulders and waist neatly. It was fastened from the high-standing collar to the hem with large jewelled buttons and loops. The wide lace ruff was a series of white petals around her face. Her fair hair was swept up under her tall-crowned, brimless hat, which had ostrich feathers held in place by precious stones.

Nicholas was viewing a child on the cusp of womanhood. He was impressed with her aristocratic mien but not so overwhelmed by her that he was unable to take a full inventory of her charms. In doing so, he saw things which had eluded the actors. Where they had stolen hungry glances, Nicholas was able to feast his eyes. Applause was long and loud. She was on her feet to contribute to it with ardent clapping. There was an air of astonishment and regret about her, as if she had just discovered something truly remarkable, only to have it snatched away from here when the players made their exit. The gaze which she fixed on the Grand Master was full of frank yearning.

Lawrence Firethorn rushed to place the most flattering interpretation upon it. When he had bowed a dozen times towards her, he waved a farewell and led his troupe from the stage. After berating them for their lapses during the performance, he took Nicholas aside to share in what he felt was another personal triumph.

'She loves me, Nick! That angel is *mine!*'

'Do not bank on that,' suggested Nicholas discreetly.

'She stood to honour my performance.'

'Indeed, she did, and justly so. You and Master Gill were supreme this afternoon and kept the play from falling apart.'

Firethorn gave a haughty snort. 'That was nothing of Barnaby's doing! I had to rescue the piece from his depredations as well as from the idiocies of the rest of the company. What was wrong with the fools? I had to carry the entire play on my own shoulders.'

'And you did so superbly.'

'Why, then, did she not give me my due reward during the performance itself? I was Jean de Valette to the life, yet she gave her readiest attention to the cavortings of Hilario. Can she really set Barnaby's stale clowning above my passion and my eloquence?' He gestured towards the stage. 'Had she not just shown me that I was the true object of her desire, I tell you, Nick, I would have been deeply wounded. All is forgiven. She has been heaven-sent to me. In the art of wooing, I am still a veritable Grand Master.'

Nicholas let him preen himself for a few minutes before he introduced a note of reservation. He first made sure that nobody else was within earshot.

'The young lady did not prefer Hilario's performance,' he said. 'It was simply easier for her to understand.'

'That boring array of dull songs and dreary dances?'

'The songs were accompanied by comic mime.'

'What is comic about Barnaby Gill pulling hideous faces and waving his arms around?'

'Gesture surmounts all language barriers.'

'Barriers?'

'Yes,' explained Nicholas. 'That was why the young lady did not give your portrayal its due reward. She does not speak English. She liked best what she comprehended most, and that was mime and dance. They need no translation.'

Firethorn gulped. 'Not speak English? Can this be so?'

'It would be my guess.'

'On what basis?'

'Observation of the lady,' said the other. 'Those high cheekbones do not belong to an Englishwoman. And though she dresses in the Spanish fashion, that fair hair has not travelled here from Spain. There is another clear indication, and that is our patron's attitude towards her. Lord Westfield usually indulges in badinage with his female companions. He treated this one with great respect and spoke no word to her while I watched. The lady is a foreigner.'

'By Jove, this may be true! Of what country, Nick?'

'Some part of Germany, perhaps. Austria, more likely.'

'And of high birth?'

'Without question.'

Firethorn slapped his thigh. 'By all, this is wonderful! I have conquered the heart of an Austrian princess! No wonder my jewelled speeches fell on deaf ears. Bring her to me and I'll talk the universal language of love. I'll teach her gestures that she will never see from Barnaby and we'll dance a jig together, she and I, that will last a whole night.' He punched Nicholas playfully on the shoulder. 'Fetch her to me, Nick. I'll meet this princess in a private room. And if she speaks no English, I'll be a lusty tutor for her lips. Bring her to me presently. I must have her.'

Nicholas accepted the charge reluctantly. With dozens of urgent chores confronting him, the last thing he wanted to do was to act as Firethorn's messenger. He knew, also, that his journey would be in vain. This was one admirer whom the actor would never possess. She was infinitely beyond his reach. As he set off on his errand, his protective instincts came to the fore. Nicholas was the guardian of Westfield's Men and he could always recognise a threat to the company. Her mere presence at a performance had inadvertently inflicted harm on them. Further contact with her would bring more serious and lasting injury. Nicholas felt it in his bones. In pursuing his alabaster saint, Lawrence Firethorn was leading his troupe towards certain catastrophe.

Alexander Marwood swam against the tide of humanity that was pouring out of the Queen's Head. It gave the testy landlord no satisfaction to observe that his innyard had been filled with paying customers, many of whom bought ale or food from his servingmen to swell his coffers. Westfield's Men were troublesome tenants to him. He lived in constant fear that their occupation of his premises would bring the ire of the city authorities down on him, lead to wild affrays, cause damage to his property, and—notwithstanding the eternal vigilance both of himself and his Gorgon wife—result in the seduction of his nubile daughter, Rose, by one of the rampant satyrs who called themselves actors. Marwood's suffering found no relief in the marriage bed. His wife, Sybil, had long since converted that into an instrument of torture.

Delighted playgoers who streamed out into Gracechurch Street were met by no genial host. What confronted them was the grim little figure of the landlord buffeting his way towards his inn and cursing his fate with even more than his usual relish. A hat concealed the balding pate that was harrowed with anxiety, but the haggard face, with its haunted eyes and its twitching lips, its deathly pallor and its expression of cold terror, was a drama in itself. Manacled to misery, he took a perverse pleasure in rattling his chains.

When he finally fought his way to a side-door, he let himself into the inn. Marwood was scuttling along a narrow passageway when he saw a familiar figure coming down a private staircase that led to the lower gallery. The landlord pounced on Nicholas Bracewell and sank skinny fingers into his arm.

'The end is in sight!' he moaned.

'Yes,' agreed Nicholas. 'The spectators have all but dispersed and they have done so in a happy mood. Your servingmen have made you a tidy profit, Master Marwood.'

'That is small consolation.'

'A full yard. The numbers ought to please you.'

'They strike at my heart.'

'Westfield's Men continue to bring custom to the Queen's Head. Can you not find at least a crumb of comfort in that?'

'No,' said Marwood, releasing his arm to bring both hands up in a gesture of despair. 'Because it will not last. My yard may be packed today. Tomorrow or the day after, it may as easily be deserted.'

'Not while Westfield's Men offer their plays.'

'And how much longer will that be?'

'As long as we keep our reputation in good repair.'

'The law will not permit it, Master Bracewell.'

'What law?'

Marwood seized on his cue. 'While you performed here, I watched another tragedy unfolding. While you rejoiced in the numbers of spectators, I quailed before numbers of a different order. Do you know where I have been, sir?'

'Tell me,' encouraged Nicholas.

'To Clerkenwell. To visit a sick aunt of mine. Word came that she was grievously ill and like to die. I thought that old age had at last caught up with her and went to pay my last respects.' The memory activated two more nervous twitches on his face. 'Do you know what I found?'

'The lady was already dead?'

'Her house was boarded up.'

Nicholas blenched. 'Another plague victim?'

'One of three in the same street,' wailed Marwood. 'I ran away on the instant lest I should contract the disease myself. It is closing in on us again. When plague victims reach the required number, the edict will be signed. All theatres, bear-baiting arenas and other places of public assembly will be closed down so that the infection will not spread.' He snatched off his hat and beat his thigh with it. 'I will be ruined, Master Bracewell. No plays, no profit. This plague will sever the Queen's Head like an executioner's axe.' He bared his blackened teeth in a fearsome grin. 'You are looking at a corpse.'

Nicholas was at once alarmed and relieved, dismayed at the news but grateful that he had intercepted Marwood before the landlord could rush into the taproom to blurt out his doom-laden intelligence. Plague was an ever-present menace for the London theatre companies, and it had more than once swept Westfield's Men from their stage and sent them touring the provinces in search of an audience. Nicholas was only too aware of the latest outbreak, but he did not realise that it was already reaching such proportions. Summer lay ahead and the warmer weather would only exacerbate the problem.

There was genuine cause for concern, but Nicholas would at least be able to pass on the warning to his colleagues in a calm and reasonable way. Alexander Marwood would only scatter panic and despondency among them. They needed to be spared that. The book-holder took the trembling landlord by his bony shoulders.

'Say nothing of this to my fellows,' he insisted.

'But they have a right to know that they will soon be flung into abject poverty.'

'That is a possibility they live with every day. This profession has enough hazards without your adding another prematurely. Besides, it will not advantage your purse.'

Marwood started. 'My purse?'

'Yes,' continued Nicholas. 'Charge in there to publish your tidings and you will empty the taproom at once. Is that your intention? To deprive yourself of custom before such a circumstance is forced upon you? Your good lady would not approve of that.'

Seized by a paroxysm of fear, Marwood twisted out of his grasp. Nicholas reinforced his argument.

'Make hay while the sun shines,' he urged. 'Do not wish black clouds upon us before they are ready to come. While our plays are still free of any plague edict, do all you can to entice more people into your yard and your taproom. What you take from them now will serve to see you through leaner times ahead. Exploit the goodwill of your customers. Nurture them.'

Marwood pondered. 'This is wise counsel,' he said at length. 'But my wife must be told the truth.'

'Save it for the privacy of the bedchamber.'

'That has already been afflicted with the plague,' said the landlord under his breath. He spoke aloud. 'I'll break the news to my wife but school her to keep it close for the few days that may remain to us. Master Firethorn must also hear this dire intelligence. I'll to him straight.'

'That will be my office,' said Nicholas firmly. 'I am on my way to him even now. Leave Master Firethorn to me and simply convey your message to your good lady.'

The prospect made Marwood emit a mad laugh before he went trotting off down the corridor. Having come from an aged aunt whose house had been boarded up, he was now going to a flinty wife whose heart, mind and body had been shut tight against him for many a long year. His marriage was murder by slow degrees.

Nicholas faced a less daunting interview, but it was one that he was dreading. He now had a double blow to deliver.

Lawrence Firethorn paced the room restlessly, ducking under its central oak beam every time he passed it. Having divested himself of his armour and helmet, he had left his sword with George Dart so that the pig's blood could be washed from its blade. A few minutes before, a mirror had enabled the actor to comb out his beard and adjust his apparel to best effect. He then adjourned to the private room and awaited the visitation of an angel from a foreign land.

A tap on the door made him strike a dramatic pose.

'Enter!' he cooed in his most mellifluous tone.

The door opened and he bowed submissively low to greet the newcomer, reaching out to take her hand in order to bestow a kiss upon it. When he found himself staring at the broad fingers of Nicholas Bracewell, he jumped back with such a start that he banged his head on the low beam.

'Where is she, Nick?' he howled.

'I will come to that in a moment,' said Nicholas, closing the door behind him. 'First, there's more important news.'

'Nothing is more important than her. And me. And us!'

'I met with the landlord on my way back to you.'

'That ghoul?'

'He brings sad tidings.'

'When did the vile rogue bring anything else?' snarled Firethorn. 'Away with that leprous knave! I'll have none of him. Why talk of a cadaver like Marwood when I wish to hear about my beloved?'

'There are other cadavers to make us pause.'

'What say you?'

Nicholas was brisk. 'Our landlord visited a sick aunt in Clerkenwell and found her dying of the plague. The third victim in her street. In diverse parts of the city, there have been several more. The numbers climb towards an edict.'

'Close the theatres! That is sacrilege.'

'It is a sound precautionary measure.'

'Where is the soundness in throwing us out on the streets to beg? I'll not be silenced, Nick. I'll not have my company smothered to death by process of law! Lord Westfield will intercede on our behalf.'

'Even his intercession will not preserve us.'

'A plague on this plague!' roared Firethorn, pounding the oak table with his fist. 'Has it not already taken sufficient toll of us? It has hounded us out of London before. And I have not forgotten the time when it lay in wait to expel us from Oxford. They actually paid us not to play. It was insulting!'

'I took it as an act of consideration.'

'They must not close the Queen's Head to us again. It is robbery with malice. Stealing our audience from us by official edict and leaving us without any means of support.'

'Pray God it may not come to that!' sighed Nicholas.

'But you sense a likelihood?'

'I have been concerned for some weeks. We have had some isolated plague deaths in Southwark, but they may well be but precursors of a wider epidemic. Marwood saw the evidence with his own eyes in Clerkenwell. Other wards are also hearing the rattle of the death cart in their streets.'

Firethorn was dejected. 'Is there no hope for us, Nick?'

'A little. A little. The plague has abated before when it seemed set to tighten its hold. But we cannot rely on that happening again. My advice is this: Hope for the best but prepare for the worst.'

Firethorn slumped onto the stool and looked into a bleak future. Touring the towns and cities of England was a laborious and often thankless business. It would take him away from his wife and children for an extended length of time. It would also deprive him of the joy of lording it on the stage at the Queen's Head, where he could woo and win some of the most gorgeous women in the capital. That thought made him leap to his feet again.

'What of *her*, Nick?' he demanded. 'Give me some medicine to ward off this disease. If I am to lose my occupation, at least let me taste one of its sweetest joys first. Why did you not bring her to me, as I requested?'

'That was not possible, I fear.'

'Did you not speak to her?'

'Alas, no.'

'Not even through an interpreter?'

'By the time I reached our patron, his guest had departed.'

'Then why did you not fly after her?' cried Firethorn. 'Why did you not overtake the lady and urge my suit? I won her heart. She would have come to me post-haste.'

'I was too late,' said Nicholas. 'A coach was waiting to take her to London Bridge, where she is boarding a boat that will take her to Deptford. The young lady will sail from there on the evening tide. She is returning home.'

Firethorn was aghast. '*Home?* She has spurned the chance of being alone with me in order to go home? This news is worse than the plague and it infects me with rage. She went *home?*'

'The young lady had no choice in the matter. Her passage was booked. Her great-uncle expects her.'

'What great-uncle?' growled the other. 'Some fat fool in Brandenburg? Some leering Bavarian oaf? Some cross-eyed count in Austria? Who is this great-uncle that she must reject me to speed back to his side?'

'Rudolph the Second, Holy Roman Emperor and King of Bohemia.'

Firethorn's jaw dropped in amazement and his hands spread in disbelief. Nicholas had to suppress a smile at his reaction. It was a full minute before the actor could speak.

'Did you discover her name?'

'I did. She is called Sophia Magdalena.'

'Sophia! Sophia!' repeated the other, rolling the name around in his mouth to savour it. 'Yes, it had to be Sophia. I should have guessed. She was every marvellous inch a Sophia.' He gave a philosophical smile. 'You were right as ever, Nick. A foreign beauty who did not understand our tongue. Related to an Emperor, no less. That accounts for her noble bearing.' He shook his head slowly. 'Sophia! So that is the name of the fair maid who caused such commotion among us today. Can we be surprised? She is a paragon. She is Nature's most sublime piece of work. A true Saint Sophia.'

'Yes,' added Nicholas. 'The fair maid of Bohemia.'

[CHAPTER TWO]

At his death, Jacob Hendrik bequeathed his English wife far more than just a house in Bankside and a thriving hat-making business. Anne also inherited her husband's belief in the dignity of work and his readiness to fight hard against any adversity. Whenever she recalled how a Dutch immigrant had prospered in a country whose language he did not at first understand and whose trade guilds had ruthlessly excluded him and his kind, Anne Hendrik was filled with admiration for his tenacity and dedication.

There was another bonus. While she had been helping to improve his command of English, he had been teaching her Dutch, and—since she showed an aptitude for languages—he had schooled her in German as well, a tongue he had himself mastered in Holland for commercial purposes. A happy marriage had been a constant education for both partners. The attractive teen-age girl who had fallen in love with Jacob Hendrik was now a handsome widow in her early thirties with moderate wealth and an independent streak that set her completely apart from her female friends and neighbours.

Anne was able to keep her Dutch in excellent repair by conversing with her employees. Preben van Loew, the veteran hat-maker, was always delighted to slip back into his native tongue. Old and emaciated, he still retained his superlative skills at his craft. When Anne stepped out of her house and into the adjoining premises where her employees worked, she found Preben bent over his latest commission, a woman's hat with a tall, elegant crown. After greeting them all in English, she spoke to the senior man in Dutch.

'Could you spare me a few minutes, please?'

'Of course,' he said, putting his work aside and rising at once from his stool. 'What is the problem?'

'It is a private matter, Preben. Follow me.'

The sadness in her voice and the shadow across her face were bad omens. After a glance at his colleagues, he padded obediently behind her until they reached the parlour of her house. Anne closed the door behind them, then took a letter from the little table.

'This came this morning from Amsterdam,' she said.

'Bad news?'

'I fear so, Preben. My father-in-law is dying.'

'Frans!' he said with a sharp intake of breath. 'Dear old Frans Hendrik! Tell me this is not true.'

'If only I could!'

'Frans is as strong as a horse. He will live forever.'

'Not according to his brother. He writes to tell me that it is only a matter of weeks. Here,' she said, offering the missive to him. 'Read it for yourself. As you will see, Jan asks that I show you the letter because you knew my father-in-law so well.'

'I knew the whole family,' said Preben fondly. 'Frans Hendrik, his poor wife—God bless her!—his brothers, Jan and Pieter, and his children. Jacob, your late husband and my good friend, best of all. *Know* the Hendrik family? I was part of it, Anne.' He began to sway unsteadily. 'They were the kindest people in the world.'

'I learned that for myself,' said Anne, taking him gently by the arm to guide him to a seat. 'Rest there a moment. When you have got over the shock, read the tidings for yourself.'

The old man gave a nod of gratitude and buried his face in his hands. Memories flooded back into his mind and it was a long time before he was able to shake them off. He made an effort to brace himself, then held out his hand. Tributaries were soon trickling down from his already moist eyes as he read the letter, but it was not only the imminent death of Frans Hendrik which prompted them. Preben van Loew was being forcibly reminded of the loneliness of exile. Cut off from his native country, he was reading words in his own language about friends he had been forced to leave behind.

[18]

Anne felt a surge of sympathy for him. He was clearly torn between grief and helplessness, shocked by the impending loss of someone he loved, yet powerless even to pay his last respects before Frans Hendrik slipped out of the world. Relieving him of the letter, she glanced through it again herself.

'I must go,' she decided.

'Jan does not ask you to do so.'

'Not in so many words, Preben, but it is there between the lines. It is my only chance to see my father-in-law again and I must take it. When Jacob died, the whole family came to England to comfort me even though the cost of the visit was crippling. For my husband's sake—and because I love his father as if he were my own—I must find a way to get to Amsterdam.'

'Would that I could go with you!'

'Your place is here, looking after the business.'

'Carrying on the Hendrik tradition.'

'Nobody could do it better.'

He gave a faint smile. 'It is an honour,' he whispered. Then a thought struck him. 'I must make contact somehow. I will write to Frans. Let him know that he is in my thoughts. Will you carry my letter to him, please?'

'Willingly.'

'When will you go?'

'I need to discuss it with Nicholas first.'

'Ah, yes!'

'He is the sailor among us,' reminded Anne. 'Nick will tell me all that is needful. And it is reassuring to know that while you see to the making of hats, he will be here to mind the house itself.'

Nicholas Bracewell had come to lodge in the house again, but the old Dutchman knew that he was much more than just a paying guest. Anne and the book-holder were close friends and occasional lovers. After a long period apart, they had finally drifted together again, and nobody had been more pleased by that development than Preben van Loew. He could see what each gave to the other. The household had a buoyant feel to it once more and it rubbed off on the employees in the adjacent building.

There was, however, one serious danger in the wind.

'How long will Nicholas be able to remain?' he asked.

'As long as he wishes.'

'He would wish to stay forever, I am sure, but that decision may be taken out of his hands.'

'In what way?'

A forlorn shrug. 'Plague deaths mount every day. If the disease continues to spread so fast, it is only a question of time before they close all the theatres. Where will Nicholas go then? He can hardly stay here in Bankside with no occupation. Westfield's Men may have to leave London in order to find work, and they will certainly take their book-holder with them.'

'That is true,' she admitted ruefully. 'He has already warned me that the Queen's Head may not open its doors to them for much longer. The plague is one of the hazards of a profession that has more than enough to contend with already.' She made an effort to brighten. 'But the disease may yet loosen its hold, as it has done in the past. Nick may be able to stay in the city. Even if he does not, I will still travel to Amsterdam. It is a call that I cannot refuse.'

'A thousand pities you cannot take Nicholas with you!'

'It is not his place to be there,' she corrected gently. 'This is a private family matter. Besides, Nick has problems enough of his own. If a plague order is signed, Westfield's Men will be in complete disarray. Nick will have to pilot them through some very rough water or they will founder.'

The exodus had already begun. There was foul contagion in the air. Nervous aristocrats turned their backs on the joys of Court intrigue and stole quietly away to the safety of their country estates. Worried professional men and anxious merchants removed themselves and their families from the danger area. Others soon followed, and every road out of London became a busy escape route for citizens fleeing in terror from a ruthless and undiscriminating enemy.

Those unable to leave were forced to stay and risk a lonely death. Plague was a hideous bedfellow. With a grim sense of humor, it liked to tickle its victim under the arms and on the feet, leaving marks that were no bigger nor more irritating than flea-bites at first. Except that these bites developed quickly into sores which in turn swelled up into ugly black buboes. Some doctors lanced the buboes to draw the poison out of the body. Others used a warm poultice made of onions, butter, and garlic to perform the same office, or held a live pullet against the plague sores until the poor creature itself died of the venomous poison.

When the victim was beyond help, he or she was abandoned to a grisly fate. Infected houses were sealed and a placard bearing–within a red circle–the words LORD HAVE MERCY ON US was displayed outside. Other inhabitants were condemned to isolation for twenty days or more, their wants being supplied by the wealthier members of the parish. Imprisoned in their own homes, some of the miserable wretches did not dare to climb the stairs to the bedroom to relieve the agony of their dying family member lest they caught the plague themselves. In the largest city in England, victims found themselves left cruelly alone. Even their servants would not answer their summons. Only the grave enfolded them in an embrace.

Adversity converted many back to the Christianity that they had either neglected or renounced in their hearts. Churches were full of eager congregations who knelt on the cold, hard stone to pray for divine intercession against the sweeping menace, but God seemed to be preoccupied with other affairs and in no position to come to their aid. The torment had to be borne. And so it was. As the weather grew warmer, the plague became more virulent and the shallow burial pits were filled with grotesque corpses at an ever-increasing rate. Anguish walked through every ward of the city. Elizabeth might be queen in name but pestilence ruled London.

Plague orders were inevitably signed and many restraints put swiftly in place. Great efforts were made to clean up the stinking thoroughfares of the capital, and the populace was forced to burn or bury its rubbish instead of just casting it out through the door to rot away beneath a pall of buzzing insects. Butchers were compelled to abandon their habit of casually dumping animal entrails and blood in the streets. Barber-surgeons were forbidden to dispose in the same way of any human viscera or limbs, removed from their owners in the heat of crude and often fatal operations, and encouraging packs of mangy dogs to sniff among the gory bones and add their own excrement to the general slime.

Theatres and other places of entertainment were summarily closed to check the possible spread of infection among large assemblies. The Queen's Head was allowed to continue to function as one of the many capacious inns, but it was no longer the home of a leading dramatic company and thus a popular attraction to which citizens and visitors to London alike could flock six days a week. Westfield's Men were forcibly ejected and their repertoire cast into the plague pits along with all the other random casualties.

This was no minor epidemic that would burn itself out in a few weeks.

The pestilence was evidently set to stay throughout the summer and beyond. Poverty would come hard on the heels of unemployment. Many were doomed to starve. At the Queen's Head, there was a mood of utter despondency in the taproom. Four men sat on benches around one of the tables.

'It is a death sentence!' groaned Thomas Skillen, the ancient stagekeeper. 'My natural span is over and the sexton is ready for my old bones. I have served Westfield's Men for the last time.'

'Not so,' said Nicholas, vainly trying to cheer him. 'Those sprightly legs of yours have outrun the plague many times before, and so they will again. You are armoured against the disease, Thomas. It has not left a mark upon you.'

'It has, it has,' sighed the other. 'Each outbreak has left the deepest scars on my memory because it has robbed me of my loved ones and my fellows. You are all too young to remember the worst visitation, but it fills my mind whenever the plague begins to stalk once more.' He wheezed noisily and placed a palm against his chest. 'In the year of our Lord 1553, I was living here in London when over seventeen thousand of its hapless citizens fell victim. Seventeen thousand! Hardly a street or lane was untouched. The whole city reeked with contagion.' He turned to Nicholas. 'And you tell me that I outran it. No, my friend. I lost a mother, a father, and two sisters in that terrible year. No man can outrun a nightmare like that.'

George Dart shuddered. 'Seventeen thousand plague deaths!'

'This visitation may kill even more.'

'Then we are all done for!' wailed Dart.

'Only if we are foolish enough to stay,' said Owen Elias. 'We will quit this infected city and stage our plays in healthier places. Banbury's Men begin their tour tomorrow.'

'It is true,' confirmed Nicholas. 'Other companies will soon do the same, Westfield's Men among them. If we are to keep our art in repair and ourselves in employment, we must ride out of London and try our luck in the provinces.'

There was an awkward silence as each man weighed up the implications for himself. Thomas Skillen was close to despair. When the company went on tour, there was no chance that they would take him with them and it might be six months or more before they returned to the capital. What hope had he of surviving the rigors of the plague? Even if he did, how could an old man with no income keep well-fed and warm during the harsh winter that lay ahead?

George Dart had his own quandary. Terrified to be left behind, he feared the consequences of going. When the company went on tour, it cut its number to lower its operating costs and made greater demands on its individual members. The young assistant stagekeeper was routinely pressed to the limit by Westfield's Men when they performed at the Queen's Head. On tour, as he knew from experience, he would be burdened with additional duties and taxed with greater responsibilities. Staring into his ale, Dart was beset by a crisis of confidence.

Owen Elias was the least vexed by the notion of travel. A sharer with the company, the resilient Welshman was certain to be included in the touring company and would make the most of the situation, adapting easily to the different audiences and performance conditions they might find in each town and taking his pleasures along the way with his usual jovial lechery. Elias was a born actor and nothing could dampen his enthusiasm for his craft. But he was also a caring man who was very conscious of the prospects faced, respectively, by Thomas Skillen and George Dart. For the sake of his two colleagues, he did not talk excitedly about the compensatory joys of touring because the former would not experience them and they would be a continual ordeal to the latter.

Nicholas Bracewell was quietly resigned. Westfield's Men faced the stark choice between flight from London and complete extinction. Now that he and Anne Hendrik were happily reunited at last, he hated the idea of having to part from her again and he was all too aware of the fact that it was a previous tour to the West Country which had split them apart and evicted him from his lodging in Bankside. But it was not only personal considerations which saddened Nicholas. Everyone in the company would suffer. Those who embarked in pursuit of the uncertain rewards of a provincial tour would also be tearing themselves away from families and loved ones. Those who were discarded by Westfield's Men—and it would fall to Nicholas to inform them of their dismissal—were effectively being thrown into penury. Thomas Skillen was among them, and Nicholas knew in his heart that his dear old friend and colleague would begin to wither once his beloved theatre company had left him behind.

Nicholas finished his ale and looked around at the others.

'We must count our blessings,' he said softly. 'Many have already succumbed to the disease. We may have lost our home here; still, we have our health and strength.'

'How long will *that* last?' murmured Skillen.

'In your case—forever!' said Elias with a forced smile.

'I will be lucky to reach the end of the month.'

'Is there no remedy against the plague?' asked Dart.

'None that has yet been found,' admitted Nicholas. 'We do not even know whence it comes or why it has been sent.'

Skillen was bitter. 'Its purpose is all to clear. It is God's instrument for the punishment of sin. A brutal justice that carries off the innocent as well as the guilty.'

'You are wrong, Thomas,' argued Elias. 'This pestilence is caused by a poison in the air. It strikes hardest when the weather is at its warmest. Heat and contagion have ever been yoke-devils.'

'Master Gill has another explanation,' said Dart meekly. 'He told me that our destiny is written across the heavens in the stars. If we want to know whence the plague arises, we should consult an astrologer.'

'Go shake your ears!' exclaimed Elias with scorn. 'Do not listen to a word that Barnaby tells you. He is just as likely to persuade you that the cure for this disease lies between your boyish buttocks, and he will urge you to unbutton so that he may conduct his search. Stars in the heavens! Ha! There are only two orbs that interest Barnaby Gill, and they lie close to the earth. Every pretty youth has a pair inside his breeches.'

George Dart blushed a deep crimson and Thomas Skillen forgot his misery long enough to emit a loud chortle. Before the Welshman could get into his stride, Nicholas jumped in to take control of the conversation.

'This is idle speculation,' he said firmly. 'The plague is a mystery that has yet to be divined. Some believe you may ward off infection with onions, cloves, lemons, vinegar or wormwood. Others seek a remedy in tobacco, arsenic, quicksilver or even dried toads. In times of distress, people will grasp at any false nostrum that is offered. Every quack and mountebank has his own useless treatment to foist upon desperate victims. This one sells you some lily root boiled in white wine while that one purveys a draught concocted of salad-oil, sack, and gunpowder.'

'Gunpowder!' repeated Dart in astonishment.

'There are worse remedies than that,' warned Elias.

'Indeed, there are,' continued Nicholas. 'The sovereign cure is one that only the very rich and the very gullible may sample. It is a specific that draws out the poison and provokes a violent sweat in the patient. Its chief ingredient is that rarest commodity—powdered unicorn's horn.'

'Is there such a thing?' gasped Dart.

'Only if you are ready to believe in it.'

'Nick is right,' added Elias. 'The only true relief from the disease is a compound made from holly leaves, horse dung, and the testicles of a tiger, cooked slowly over the flames from the mouth of a Welsh dragon!'

'Has that been known to work?' asked a wide-eyed Dart.

'Infallibly.'

'A Welsh dragon?'

'I saw the wondrous beast myself.'

'Owen is teasing you,' said Nicholas with a smile. 'Pay no heed to him, George. There is no remedy. Take my word for it.'

'*Someone* must have caught the disease and survived.'

'None that I know of,' muttered Skillen.

'Nor I,' agreed Elias.

The three of them turned to look at a pensive Nicholas.

'There was one survivor,' he recalled at length. 'I have met him myself, so I know it to be true. His name is Doctor John Mordrake and he lives in Knightrider Street. By all accounts, he is a noted physician, philosopher, and alchemist. Doctor Mordrake contracted the disease and cured himself.'

'Impossible!' announced Skillen.

'He is living proof to the contrary, Thomas.'

'How did he do it?' asked Dart. 'What was his remedy?'

'That remains a secret,' said Nicholas. 'All I can do is to repeat common report. People who witnessed his miraculous recovery came to the same conclusion. There was only one way that Doctor Mordrake could possibly have done it.'

'And how was that?'

'By magic.'

Margery Firethorn was one of the most hospitable women in the whole of Shoreditch, but her customary open-armed welcome was tinged with regret when Barnaby Gill and Edmund Hoode arrived at the house in Old Street. The two were conducted into the parlour with a faint air of reluctance. They understood why and sympathised with her. Margery was not simply inviting some close friends into her home. She was admitting the two men who were—along with Lawrence Firethorn—the principal sharers in Westfield's Men and therefore responsible for all major decisions affecting the company. They were there to discuss the projected tour of the provinces. The visitors had come to take her husband away from her for an indefinite period.

Waving them to seats, she called for the servant, and a pitcher of wine was brought in on a tray. Margery dismissed the girl with a glance and filled two of the three cups which stood on the table. Gill and Hoode expressed their gratitude before sipping their wine.

'This is a sad day for us all,' she began.

'It is, Margery,' said Hoode with a sorrowful smile. 'We are swept from our stage like unwanted dust. London ousts us.'

'Nobody can oust me,' boasted Gill, striking a petulant pose. 'I leave of my own free will. Neither tempest, flood, nor fire will drive me away when I do not wish to go.'

Hoode shrugged. 'Even you cannot defy the plague, Barnaby.'

'People are still leaving in droves,' said Margery. 'There are wards of the city where the disease is rampant. Shoreditch has so far been spared the worst effects, but we have victims enough here. Would that we could all flee!'

'I am not fleeing,' insisted Gill. 'I merely choose to exercise my right to go.'

'This is no time to stand on your dignity,' said Hoode with irritation. 'Choice does not come into it, Barnaby.'

'It does for me.'

'Plague orders compel us to set off on a tour.'

'They may compel you, Edmund. I am above compulsion.'

'What do you mean?'

'Simply this,' said Gill with a lordly sniff. 'You may be content to drag yourself around England in search of an audience of smelly oafs who cannot even tell the difference between a tragedy and a comedy. But I am not. Why should I demean myself? Why should I suffer the indignity of walking at the cart's-tail with a ragged band of players?'

[26]

misery of another tour and that you would consider other offers which you had received.'

'Tempting offers,' said Hoode. 'That is what you called them, and you have clearly been tempted. If you have already sold your soul to another buyer, why bother to come here in the first place? What point is there in discussing a tour in which you have no intention of taking part?'

Margery indicated the door. 'There is the way out,' she said. 'Leave while you may. When Lawrence hears about this treachery, he'll tear you limb from limb. What greater disgrace is there than abandoning your fellows in their hour of need?'

'I am not abandoning them,' denied Gill.

'You are,' confirmed Hoode. 'We both heard you.'

'Nothing is yet settled.'

'Even to countenance the possibility is a crime against Westfield's Men. Put the company first for once.'

'And waste my talent in front of country bumpkins?'

'An audience is an audience.'

'I deserve the best!'

Margery was scathing. 'If you leave the company now, you deserve to be boiled in oil,' she said. 'And I will be happy to stoke up the fire with my own bare hands.'

Barnaby Gill flared up angrily, Margery Firethorn struck back at him, and Edmund Hoode tried in vain to calm them down. The argument was still at its height when they heard the swift approach of a horse. It made Gill freeze and stilled Margery in mid-expletive. Hoode crossed to the window.

'Lawrence!' he announced. 'At last!'

Firethorn brought his mount to a halt, dropped from the saddle and tossed the reins to the servant who came running out of the house. The gallop had put a glow into the actor's cheeks. His face was streaked with perspiration and his beard flecked with dust. As he crossed the threshold of his home and doffed his cap with a flourish, there was no mistaking the air of excitement about him. He looked as if he had just quit the stage at the end of one of his most towering performances.

'What means this sudden return?' Margery wondered.

'The strangest news that ever you heard, my love.'

'Good news, I trust?'

'Good news but mingled with bad,' he confessed, putting an affectionate arm around her. 'Lord Westfield sent for me to put a proposition to us that still makes my head reel.'

'He bestowed money on us?' said Hoode optimistically.

Gill was cynical. 'Disbanded us, more like!'

'Far from it, Barnaby,' explained Firethorn. 'A signal honour has been conferred upon us. We will be the envy of the London theatre. But honour, alas, comes at a high price. While some will prosper, others will have to suffer their absence.' He placed the softest kiss on his wife's forehead. 'We are to leave the city, my angel, and that right soon.'

'I expected no less,' she said with a brave smile. 'Marry an actor and you are a hostage to fortune. There will be hardship without you, but I will bear it nobly.'

'As ever, my pippin.'

Firethorn pulled her to him and gave her another gentle kiss. Disgusted by the sight of marital tenderness, Gill became increasingly impatient.

'Why did our patron summon you?' he asked.

'To show me the invitation,' said Firethorn.

'What invitation?'

'The one that set my blood racing, Barnaby. The one that made me gallop hell-for-leather back to Shoreditch to acquaint you with its import.'

'Then do so without further delay.'

'My mind is still bursting asunder.'

'Why?' demanded Gill. 'Why, why, why?'

'Will the company still go on tour?' asked Hoode.

'Oh, yes!' affirmed Firethorn. 'And such a tour as we have never been on before. It will be a supreme challenge, but it may also be the crowning achievement of Westfield's Men.'

'Skulking from town to town like beggars?' sneered Gill. 'You call that a crowning achievement? It is an insult to ask of a man of my abilities to play before the dullards of the English countryside. I refuse to lower my high standards.'

'You will need to raise them,' warned Firethorn. 'We must give the very best account of ourselves, Barnaby. But not for the benefit of English eyes and ears. We are to sail across the sea on a glorious adventure.'

'The sea!' gasped Margery, clutching at him. 'Will you go so far away from me, Lawrence? Why? When? For how long?'

'And *where?*' asked Gill.

'To Holland, Germany, and thence to Bohemia.'

His wife was aghast. 'Bohemia!'

'That is our principal destination,' he said. 'We have received an invitation to play for two weeks at the Imperial Court in Prague. What higher accolade could there be for Westfield's Men? The company has performed for Her Majesty on more than one occasion. An even mightier sovereign now recognises our worth. We are going to Bohemia at the express wish of the Emperor Rudolph the Second. This is one of the proudest moments of my life. We are set to conquer a whole new world.'

Firethorn was positively glowing but his wife was fighting to hold back tears. All that she knew about Bohemia was that it was a distant country which would deprive her of her husband for a long and arduous period. Travelling around England with his company, he could at least keep in regular contact with her by letter. If he went to Bohemia, she feared that she would lose all track of him. Firethorn himself was enough of a husband to regret his forced departure, but he was even more of an actor and thus eager to respond to the call for a command performance in front of an Emperor.

Barnaby Gill was equally thrilled by the invitation. He could already hear the applause at the Imperial Court as he displayed the full repertoire of his theatrical talents. He was quick to endorse acceptance of the invitation.

'We must go!' he asserted. 'By heaven, we must!'

Edmund Hoode could not resist some gentle mockery.

'We will, Barnaby,' he said. 'Without you, alas.'

'*Without* me?'

'You will be too busy with your other tempting offers.'

Anne Hendrik lay naked in his arms while he stroked her hair. Conscious that they would soon be separated for a lengthy period, they were sharing a bed for the night while they still could. It gave their love-making an extra urgency. Panting from their exertions and glistening with perspiration, they lay there in silence for several minutes and listened to the beating of each other's hearts. It was Nicholas Bracewell who finally put quiet words to sad thoughts.

'I will miss you,' he whispered.

'Mine will be the greater loss,' she said. 'I will to Holland and back as swiftly as I may, but your journey will last an eternity. While you are being honoured in a foreign court, I will be pining for you in an empty bed.'

'It does not have to be that way, Anne.'

'What do you mean?'

'I do not have to leave you.'

'But you told me that it was all arranged. You were at the Queen's Head this evening when Lawrence Firethorn sent for you to tell you of the invitation and to seek your advice. The decision to go to Bohemia had already been taken.'

'It had. Westfield's Men will soon set sail.'

'Then there is an end to it.'

'Only if I go with them.'

Anne stiffened in surprise and pulled away from him so that she could look into his eyes. 'You *have* to go, Nick,' she said. 'They would be lost without you. Westfield's Men have come to rely on you totally.'

'That may be another reason to stay behind.'

'Stay behind! I do not believe that I heard you say that. To visit other countries and play at foreign courts. This is an opportunity that may never come again. Any man of the theatre would grab at it.'

'And so would I if it were not for the circumstances.'

'Circumstances?'

'You, Anne,' he said, pulling her to him again. 'I yearn to go with the company, yet I am loath to leave your side. This invitation is like a blessing from on high. It will take us from a plague-ridden city to the capital of the Holy Roman Empire, where we will be honoured guests. My head urges me to join the company on this wonderful adventure, but my heart tells me that my place is here with you.' He cupped her chin in his palm. 'Say the word and I will remain behind.'

Anne was profoundly touched. 'Would you really do that, Nick? Bid farewell to Westfield's Men for my sake?'

'I would!' he affirmed.

'That pleases me more than I can say.'

'Then choose for me, Anne. Do I go or stay?'

'It is a decision that only you can make,' she said, 'and it would be unfair of me to influence you. Weigh duty against inclination here. All that I will offer is this comment. I would much rather welcome a happy Nick Bracewell back from his foreign travels than live in Bankside with an unhappy one. The mere fact that you were willing to make such a sacrifice is enough for me. Do not feel obliged to go through with it.'

Nicholas lay there in the dark and wrestled with his problem. There was no comfortable solution to the conflict of loyalties. Any decision he made would involve pain, loss, and deep regret, but the election had to be his. Anne was right. It was unjust to make her either give him permission to go or entreat him to stay. Nicholas had to take account of all the possible consequences of his actions. The one saving grace of joining Westfield's Men on their tour was that Anne Hendrik would be waiting for him on his return. If he left the company at such a moment, there would never be a joyous reunion with his fellows. Close friendships would perish. An occupation that was a labour of love would become a sour memory.

'I will go with them,' he said.

'That is where you belong, Nick.'

'But I'll not spent a day longer apart from you than I have to, Anne. You must sail for Holland, and so must we. Let us at least travel together as far as Flushing. The sea is in my blood, as you know, and I would love to share its mystery with you even on so short a voyage. Shall you sail beside me?'

'Always!' she vowed.

They sealed their love with a surge of renewed passion.

[CHAPTER THREE]

The next few days were among the most hectic that Westfield's Men had ever known. Preparations which should have taken a month were made with wild haste in a fraction of that time. Decisions which needed the most careful consideration were reached with undue speed. Mistakes were inevitably made but their consequences would not become clear until a later date. Eager to escape the plague, the company was about to rush off on a headlong adventure which had implications that they had not even begun to see, let alone to appraise properly.

News of the impending departure struck the players in a variety of ways. Some shared the excitement of Lawrence Firethorn and indulged in grandiose fantasies about triumphs in foreign courts. Others thought less about where they were going than what they would leave behind in a perilous city. Married actors feared for their families while their wives and children in turn grieved for them. Westfield's Men were about to set off on a journey into the unknown. While that prospect might inspire a questing spirit like Owen Elias, it daunted a more cautious creature such as Edmund Hoode, and it left a lesser mortal like George Dart positively gibbering with terror.

The first and most important task was to determine the composition of the touring company. Preference was given to the sharers—those with a financial stake in Westfield's Men which gave them certain rights—and to the apprentices. Only a few of the hired men could be taken, and versatility was the key factor.

'My choice falls on Clement Islip,' said Barnaby Gill.

'We all know that!' murmured Lawrence Firethorn.

'Clement is a gifted young man.'

'So he should be, Barnaby. You have showered enough gifts on him these past few months. Has he been duly grateful?'

'Clement is a musician,' reminded Edmund Hoode, 'and not a player. We need someone who can play an instrument *and* take his share of the smaller parts.'

'He can do both,' insisted Gill. 'He lacks instruction in acting, that is all. Clement will quickly blossom into an actor if I take him in hand.'

'Have you not already done so?' teased Firethorn.

'That is a gross calumny!' exploded Gill.

'We are met to choose the best company we can muster. Not to find some simpering bedfellow for you, Barnaby.'

'Clement Islip would be an asset to us.'

'He is a male varlet who plays a viol tolerably well.'

'This is unendurable!'

'Let us forget Clement,' said Hoode tactfully. 'He is not the man for this occasion. A fine musician, I grant you, but too young and of too delicate a constitution to withstand the stresses that a long tour will place upon us. I am sorry, Barnaby. My vote is cast for Ralph Groves.'

'My mind inclines that way, too,' said Firethorn.

'Well, mine does not,' snapped Gill. 'Ralph Groves is a disgrace to this noble profession of ours. I'll not take a blundering fool like him to the Imperial Court.'

'Ralph can both act and sing,' argued Hoode.

'But he can do neither with any distinction.'

'Let's hear what Nick has to say,' suggested Firethorn.

Nicholas Bracewell had remained silent throughout the long and acrimonious debate. As the book-holder, he was merely a hired man with the company, and its decisions lay in the hands of the three major sharers. He only gave his advice when it was sought. The four men were sitting around a table in one of the Eastcheap taverns. Firethorn's house in Shoreditch was the usual venue for meetings about company policy, but the actor-manager had considerately moved it well out of earshot of his wife on the grounds that a prolonged discussion of his departure from the country would only cause further anguish to Margery. Eastcheap had also been chosen in preference to Gracechurch Street because the hovering presence of its landlord would have made the Queen's Head a difficult place in which to talk in private.

'Well, Nick?' prompted Hoode. 'What's your opinion?'

'Clement Islip or Ralph Groves?' asked Firethorn.

'Neither,' said Nicholas quietly. 'Both have their virtues and both have served us well in their own ways at the Queen's Head. But this tour will make special demands on every one of us and test our resources to the full. I do not believe that either Clement or Ralph would be equal to the challenge.'

'Then who is to come in their place?' said Gill.

'Adrian Smallwood.'

'Smallwood!' sneered the other. 'Can this be serious counsel? Adrian Smallwood has only been with Westfield's Men for five minutes. And will you promote him over a more worthy and long-serving contender than Clement Islip?'

'Yes,' returned Nicholas. 'It is true that Adrian has been with us for less than a month, but in that time he has proved himself beyond question. Not only is he a fine actor, he can also sing, dance and play the lute. He is the most complete man we have and it would be folly to leave him behind.'

Firethorn nodded. 'I see your reasoning, Nick, and it is as sound as ever. Because he is such a newcomer, I had not even taken Adrian Smallwood into my calculations. Now that I have, I begin to appreciate his merits.'

'So do I,' said Hoode thoughtfully. 'A lutanist will be sorely needed on this tour and I have heard Adrian upon the instrument. He is a trained musician who will give us all that Clement would have given us.'

'That is not true!' countered Gill.

'No,' agreed Firethorn. 'Adrian will certainly not give you what that prancing viol-player would have offered. But his contribution to the company as a whole will be far greater.'

'Not merely on the stage,' said Nicholas. 'There is another factor we must weigh in the balance here. We are all so keen to reach Bohemia itself that we have forgotten how long and how dangerous the journey there may be. Holland and Germany have their robber bands and masterless men just as we have here. When we travel through open country, we will seem like easy prey to outlaws. We must be able to defend ourselves.'

'My sword is ready,' asserted Firethorn. 'And so will yours be, Nick.'

Owen Elias is a doughty fighter as well, so that gives us three weapons we may call upon.'

'More than that,' said Nicholas. 'We have others who can handle a rapier and dagger. James Ingram, for one. Even Edmund here, in extremity. But in Adrian Smallwood we have someone as strong and capable as any of us. There may be situations in which those qualities turn out to be vital.' He glanced across at Gill. 'With respect to Clement Islip, I do not believe that he would render the same help in an emergency.'

Firethorn chuckled. 'All that Clement could do would be to beat off an ambush with his bow or play a sad melody on his viol while the rest of us were being butchered. No,' he decided, thumping the table with an authoritative palm, 'we do not even have to look at Clement Islip or at Ralph Groves. The man of the hour is assuredly Adrian Smallwood.'

'I accept that willingly,' said Hoode, 'and we should be grateful to Nick for discerning the value in a man whom we had all overlooked.'

'I am not grateful!' said Gill sourly.

'Your ingratitude is of no concern here, Barnaby,' said Firethorn with a dismissive wave. 'Edmund and I both embrace Nick's recommendation. Our two voices silence your lone and ridiculous protest. Smallwood is our man, and there's an end to it.' He beamed with satisfaction. 'Now, what's next to be settled?'

'Our repertoire,' reminded Nicholas. 'Until I know which plays we mean to offer, I cannot assemble the costumes and properties which need to travel with us.'

Firethorn was peremptory. 'That is easily resolved. We will play *Black Antonio, Vincentio's Revenge, Hector of Troy, The Corrupt Bargain* and *The Knights of Malta.*' When he saw Gill spluttering with rage, he threw in a concession. 'To please the rougher palates, we might also perform *Cupid's Folly.*'

'No!' howled Gill. 'I'll not permit such an outrage!'

'Then we'll omit *Cupid's Folly* altogether.'

'This is monstrous!'

'I am bound to agree, Lawrence,' ventured Hoode boldly. 'Every play you listed is a tragedy in which you take the leading part. Comedy will be more welcome to an audience which may not speak our language, and even a Titan of the stage such as Lawrence Firethorn needs to take a secondary role at times in order to rest himself in readiness for his next great portrayal of a tragic hero.'

'Bohemia must see me at my best!' boomed Firethorn.

'Why, so it shall. But it also deserves to see Barnaby Gill at his best, and Owen Elias and James Ingram. Even a player of such modest talents as my own has the right to shine a little, and your repertoire forbids me. *Cupid's Folly* would be high on my list and not tossed in as an afterthought.'

'It would be first on my list,' added Gill.

'What!' cried Firethorn. 'That low, despicable, rustic comedy stuffed with songs and dances?'

'Those songs and dances are the very reason that it must be included,' reasoned Nicholas, taking up the argument. 'They carry their own meaning with them. Stirring rhetoric will be lost on foreign ears. Edmund is correct. Comedy is a surer way to success. Where tragedy is called for, choose a play that already has a significance for the spectators. They will certainly know the story of *Hector of Troy,* but I fear that *Black Antonio* will confuse them, and *Vincentio's Revenge* will lead to even deeper bewilderment. Simplicity must be our watchword. The more they understand, the more our audiences will enjoy.'

'Well-spoken, Nicholas!' said Gill approvingly. It was praise indeed from one who so often maligned the book-holder. 'You have given us true guidance.'

'I say Amen to that,' supported Hoode.

Firethorn sulked. 'I must be allowed to share some of my glorious roles with our hosts. They will expect it from me. That is why the Emperor invited Westfield's Men in the first place. He heard of my reputation.'

'*Our* reputation, Lawrence,' corrected Hoode. 'You are not the company in its entirety.'

'Indeed, no,' said Gill, seizing on the chance to laud it over his rival. 'Let us be candid. Why have we been invited to play in Prague by a sovereign who has never been within a hundred miles of our work? Because he has been told about us. And by whom? Why, by his great-niece. By that dear creature who so applauded my performance in *The Knights of Malta* that her palms must have smarted for a week.' He sat up straight and preened himself. 'I am the reason this honour has befallen us. She begged this favour of her great-uncle because she is so desperate to see my art sparkle on a stage again.'

'Any woman who is desperate to see you will only meet with further desperation,' said Firethorn pointedly. 'I know full well that it is the beauteous Sophia Magdalena who is the source of this invitation to the Imperial Court. But it is not your Maltese capering which has stayed in her mind. It is my portrayal of Jean de Valette. A Grand Master fit for this grand mistress.' He inflated his barrel chest. 'Whatever we omit, it will not be *The Knights of Malta*.'

'Perforce, it must be,' said Nicholas.

'Never!'

'The decision is already taken.'

'By whom?'

'By you, by Edmund, and by Master Gill. In reducing the size of the company, you make such a piece impossible to stage. We do not have enough actors to do it justice. Besides,' said Nicholas, 'it is not a suitable play for our audiences. It touches on religious and political themes that may give offence to our hosts if they manage to understand them. We are guests in foreign courts and that imposes discretion upon us. Mock their religion or pour scorn upon their government and our visit would swiftly be curtailed.'

'I had not thought of that,' admitted Firethorn.

'Choose our plays with the utmost care,' said Hoode.

Gill nodded. 'Let *Cupid's Folly* take pride of place.'

Lawrence Firethorn lapsed into a brooding silence. Nicholas Bracewell was his most trusted colleague, yet it was the book-holder who had dealt him the blow to his pride. When the company embarked on its tour abroad, some of the actor's finest roles would be left behind in England. Firethorn felt like a gladiator who is deprived of his weapons as he is about to encounter the most testing adversary of his career.

'Sophia *wants* me,' he sighed. 'She has persuaded her great-uncle to summon us to his court so that she may feast on my genius. I must have something remarkable to set before her gaze. She must see Lawrence Firethorn in his prime.'

'And so she shall,' reassured Hoode.

'Not in some base, barren piece like *Cupid's Folly*.'

Nicholas intervened. 'I have a suggestion that may answer all needs,' he said. 'If we are to be guests at the Court of the Holy Roman Empire, we should at least take an appropriate gift with us. What better gift from a theatre company than a new play? And what better play than one which celebrates one of the illustrious spectators who will be present?'

'Rudolph himself?' asked Gill.

'No. The generous lady who has made our visit possible. Sophia Magdalena, the great-niece of the Emperor. A play in honour of her would delight our hosts and enable us to give our due thanks for the honour accorded us.'

'A wonderful idea!' said Firethorn, reviving as he saw the potential benefits. 'A sprightly comedy written to enchant her and to give free rein to my superlative skills upon the stage. God bless you, Nick! This meets all needs. Edmund will write the play and we will lay it at her feet as our offering.'

'You are more likely to lay me at her feet,' moaned Hoode. 'If I am to spend the journey to Prague in the devising of some new drama, I will be exhausted by the time we get there. It is a hopeless commission. There is no way that I may accomplish it.'

'There is, Edmund,' said Nicholas evenly.

'A new play would take me months to write.'

'That is why it will not be entirely new.'

'But that was your argument.'

'What I spoke of was a play that celebrated the kind lady who has looked so favourably upon us. It already exists.'

'Who is its author?'

'Edmund Hoode.'

'You are talking in riddles, Nick.'

'Am I?' said the other with a grin. 'Have you so soon forgotten *The Chaste Maid of Wapping*?'

'But that has no bearing upon Bohemia and no relevance whatsoever to Sophia Magdalena.'

'It could have. A subtle pen like yours could make the necessary changes in a matter of days. Your chaste maid is brought up in the belief that the humble folk of Wapping with whom she lives are her true family. It is only at the end of the play that she discovers she is really the daughter of an earl, stolen from her cradle at birth but reunited with her real father at the end.'

'Go on,' encouraged Firethorn. 'There's matter in this.'

'Move from Wapping to Prague at a stroke and the story takes on a new meaning. Change this chaste maid into Sophia Magdalena and make her undergo all the trials that she does in the original drama.' He put a hand on Hoode's shoulder. 'It can be done, Edmund. You are a most proficient cobbler. Put a new sole and heel on this play and we have a drama that will dance joyfully across the stage in Prague.'

'Nicholas may have hit the mark,' said Gill.

'It might be done,' conceded Hoode, thinking it through. 'Changes of name and place. A new song or two. The girl brought up as a peasant in the countryside outside Prague. Yes, it might indeed be done.'

'It *shall* be done!' insisted Firethorn with a ripe chuckle. 'About it straight, Edmund! Dick Honeydew will play the girl and I will be her rightful father, the Earl. This is a brilliant notion, Nick. All we need is a new title.'

'I have thought of that already.'

'You have?'

'Yes,' said Nicholas. '*The Fair Maid of Bohemia.*'

A perverse contentment had settled on Alexander Marwood. He now had something about which he could be truly unhappy. Instead of circling the Queen's Head like the lost soul, fearing the worst at every turn and viewing even the intermittent moments of good fortune as warnings of some future evil, he had a genuine cause for grief. Plague had not only emptied his innyard of playgoers, it had drastically reduced the number of visitors to London and thus depleted the traffic which came his way. Stables were bare, ostlers stood idle. Servingmen had little to occupy them in the taproom. Many regular patrons of the inn had either left the city or were keeping away from a public place where the lethal infection might conceivably lurk.

Personal inconveniences added to Marwood's professional difficulties. His wife, Sybil, and his daughter, Rose, had joined the flight from London and were staying in Buckingham with his sister-in-law. Sleeping alone was only marginally less painful than sharing a bed with a cold, indifferent partner, but he missed Sybil's commanding presence in the taproom, where she could quell unruly behaviour with her glare and ensure that nobody consumed ale without paying for it. Rose's departure caused him greater sorrow because she was the one person in his life who brought him a spectre of pleasure and whose uncritical love stayed him throughout the recurring miseries of his lot.

He was in the cellar when he heard the commotion above and it sent him scurrying up the stone steps. The taproom was only half-full, but the atmosphere was taut. In the far corner, six or seven men were engaged in a violent argument which just stopped short of blows. They were actors from Westfield's Men and there was an element of performance in their rowdiness but that did not lessen its potential danger. Such an outburst would never have happened when Sybil Marwood was in control. Lacking her authority, her husband looked around for the one man who could restore calm among his fellows.

Marwood saw him on the other side of the room. Nicholas Bracewell had his back to him, but the broad shoulders and the long fair hair were unmistakable. The landlord trotted over.

'Stop them, Master Bracewell!' he bleated, tapping the other man on the arm. 'Stop them before this turns into a brawl.'

'They would not listen to me, my friend.'

'It is your duty to prevent an affray.'

'I do that best by staying clear of it, sir.'

The burly figure turned to face him and Marwood realised that it was not Nicholas Bracewell at all. It was Adrian Smallwood, a younger man but with the same sturdy frame and the same weathered face. Smallwood's vanity led him to trim his beard while Nicholas allowed his own more liberty, and the book-holder's warm smile was not dimmed by two missing teeth, as was the case with his colleague. Seen together, the two men would never be taken for each other. When apart, however, the resemblance seemed somehow closer.

Their voices separated them completely. Nicholas had the soft burr of the West Country while Smallwood's deeper tone had a distinctively northern ring to it.

'Stand aside, sir,' he advised Marwood. 'These are only threats they exchange and not punches.'

'I'll not have fighting in my taproom.'

'Then tell them as much. It is not my office.'

'They are your fellows.'

'They were, sir, but no longer. Our occupation is lost. Hired men such as we were the first to go. That is what this quarrel is about. The company is to sail to the Continent to play before foreigners. Only a few of us will go with them. The rest will be left behind. Each man here thinks that he should be taken on the tour. Attesting their own worth, they feel they must malign that of their rivals.'

'Why do you not join them in their dispute?'

'Because I already know my fate,' said Smallwood with a philosophical smile. 'There is no hope that I will travel with the company. I am a newcomer. Some of them—Ralph Groves there, for instance—have been in the employ of Westfield's Men for years. They have a much better claim than me and I would dare not to gainsay it.'

Smallwood was now almost shouting to make himself heard above the hubbub. The argument was taking on a new and more reckless note. When the first punch was thrown, others came immediately and the whole group was drawn into the brawl. Marwood emitted a cry of alarm and jumped out of the way of the flailing arms. Adrian Smallwood stood his ground and watched with growing distaste. When one of the combatants fell heavily against him, anger stirred. He could remain apart from it all no longer. Hands which could coax sweet music out of a lute were now put to coarser usage.

With a single punch, Smallwood felled the man who had cannoned into him. Grabbing two of the others by the scruff of their necks, he banged their heads together so hard that they dropped to the floor in a daze. A fourth man was detached from the mêlée and flung ten yards away. Smallwood snatched up a bench and held it menacingly over the heads of the three actors who were still grappling.

'Stop this!' he ordered, 'or I'll crack open your skulls.'

The men froze in horror. Normally placid, Smallwood was a fearsome sight when roused. As they cowered beneath the bench, they knew that his threat was a serious one. It was at that precise moment that Nicholas Bracewell came into the taproom. He looked around the scene of carnage with frank disgust. When he saw that Adrian Smallwood was involved, he was gravely disappointed.

'What is going on here?' he demanded.

Shamefaced actors turned away in embarrassment and nursed their wounds. Smallwood lowered the bench to the ground. Nicholas turned apologetically to the landlord.

'They'll pay for any damage that has been caused,' he promised. 'And they'll pay a larger amount in other ways. Westfield's Men will not have brawling in its ranks.' He looked at Smallwood. 'It grieves me to see that you are part of this, Adrian.'

'But he was not,' Marwood piped up. 'He refused to be drawn into the quarrel that led to the fight. When you walked in just now, he had just stopped the affray.'

'Is this true?' asked Nicholas.

'I did what I could,' said Smallwood.

'He saved my taproom from any real damage,' said Marwood. 'Do not blame him for this. He is another Nicholas Bracewell. Had you been here, this would never have happened. I was lucky to have such a man here in your stead.'

Nicholas looked around the seven actors who had been embroiled in the fight. All were the worse for wear, and a couple slunk out under his stern gaze. When Nicholas studied the tableau with more care, it yielded up a clearer meaning.

His faith restored, he turned back to Adrian Smallwood.

'Can you be ready to sail in a day?' he asked.

The broad grin on Smallwood's face was an answer in itself.

Anne Hendrik went into the workshop to take leave of her employees. They were deeply sorry that she was off on such a sad errand, and the fact that she was visiting their native country made her departure even more poignant for them. After separate farewells to all four, she was conducted outside by Preben van Loew. He pressed a letter into her hand.

'Deliver this to Frans Hendrik,' he said quietly.

'I will, Preben.'

'Let us hope he is still alive to read it.'

'Yes,' she sighed. 'We can but pray.'

'Give my warmest regards to Jan and to the rest of the family. They will remember old Preben.'

'With affection.'

'They are always in my thoughts.'

'I will tell them that.' Anne became brisk. 'As to my house while I am away—'

'Forget it,' he interrupted, holded up a blue-veined hand. 'You will have enough to think about in Holland without worrying about your property here. Put it from your mind. It is safe enough in our keeping. So is the workshop. Stay as long as you wish, Anne,' he urged. 'We have commissions to keep us busy until Christmas, and more will surely come in. London will not go bare-headed while you are away.'

She squeezed him by the shoulders and kissed him softly on the cheek. A faint blush attacked his pallor. No more words were needed. With a grateful nod, she turned away from him.

When she went back into the parlour of her house, she found Nicholas

Bracewell sitting pensively on a chair beside their luggage. He was so preoccupied that he did not even notice her at first. It was only when Anne stood over him that he became aware of her presence.

'Oh!' He sat up with a start. 'I did not see you.'

'You were miles away, Nick. We both know where.'

'Do we?'

'Bohemia.'

'No, Anne,' he explained. 'You are wrong. My thoughts certainly touched on Bohemia but they had not raced ahead to the country itself. I am still troubled about something much nearer home.'

'Troubled?'

'Sit here and I will tell you all.'

'Do we have time before we leave?'

'This is something for which we must make time. I have tried to talk to Master Firethorn about it but he brushes the matter away. And I may not even mention it to Edmund because I have sworn to divulge the secret to none of the company.'

'Secret?'

Surrendering his chair to her, Nicholas pulled the stool across so that he could sit beside her. Anne could see from his knotted brow that his mind was vexed. She took his hand.

'Are you not breaking your oath in confiding in me?'

'No,' he said. 'You are not one of Westfield's Men and I know that I can trust you implicitly. Besides, I need a pair of sympathetic ears so that I can talk about the problem.'

'What problem?'

'This tour on which we are about to embark. It arose out of an invitation to visit the Imperial Court in Prague and to play there for two weeks. The invitation came with the suggestion of the route we should take so that we might acquaint others with the work of Westfield's Men. Hospitality has been arranged for us on the way to these places. Someone has gone to great trouble on our behalf.'

'Is this not a matter for celebration?'

'Indeed, it is.'

'Then where is the problem?'

'Here,' said Nicholas, taking a pouch from the inside of his buff jerkin. 'It was given to Master Firethorn by Lord Westfield himself with express orders. It contains documents to be delivered to one Talbot Royden, an

English doctor at the Court of Rudolph the Second. We are to be couriers, it seems.'

'That is not unusual, Nick,' she said. 'I am a courier myself for Preben. As soon as he heard that I was travelling to Holland, he asked me to bear a letter for him.'

'Did it come with an appreciable amount of money?'

'Not a penny.'

'This did,' he said, holding up the pouch.

'Payment for carrying the documents.'

'Nobody is that generous,' he said sceptically. 'There is enough money here to support us for most of the journey. And when we land in Flushing, two wagons with fresh horses will be put at our disposal. Who is providing all this help?'

'Your host in Bohemia.'

'He makes promise of payment when we arrive, but that will be for the entertainment we provide. Who is ensuring that we will eat well and travel in comfort on the way to Prague?'

'Lord Westfield.'

Nicholas laughed and shook his head. 'He is as deep in debt as ever, Anne. Our patron has neither the resources nor the inclination to assist the company so generously. When he handed over this pouch, he did so in someone else's stead.'

'And who might that be?'

'That is what has been exercising my mind.'

'Does Lord Westfield have close friends at Court?'

'Dozens.'

'Could not one of them have supplied the money?'

'Why did he not present it in person?' asked Nicholas. 'And what is so important about these documents that their very existence must be kept secret?' He replaced the pouch inside his jerkin. 'Why all this mystery?'

'I have no explanation.'

'Nor did I expect one. I merely wished to bring the matter out into the open to see if it really is as curious and alarming as I feared.'

'Alarming?'

'Westfield's Men are being used, Anne,' he decided. 'By whom and for what purpose, I do not yet know. That fact is disturbing enough in itself. But there is another possibility to consider.'

'What is that?'

'Someone is so anxious to see these documents safely delivered to this Talbot Royden in Prague that we are being handsomely paid to take them there. Why hide them in the baggage of a theatre company when they could travel more swiftly by other means?'

'It does not make sense, Nick.'

'Unless letters sent by messenger are intercepted before they reach the person to whom they were directed. Documents which would be confiscated from other couriers may be sneaked through by us. Supposing we are caught in possession of them?'

'By whom?'

'I do not know,' he confessed, standing up. 'That is part of the problem, Anne. I am hopelessly in the dark. But I sense danger here. In carrying those documents, we are not just performing a favour for a friend of Lord Westfield. We may be making ourselves a target.'

London Bridge was one of the busiest thoroughfares in the City. It was the one means of crossing the broad back of the River Thames on foot or on horseback, and it was also a place where many lived and where people came to buy from the shops that lined both sides of the narrow road. While the plague was claiming its victims from every ward, it seemed unable to touch the inhabitants of the bridge, and this guarantee of safety brought the crowds in their usual abundance. Carts and wagons rolled constantly to and fro to increase the bustle and the general pandemonium.

From a vantage point on the bridge, it was possible to take in the whole vast panorama of London, a higgledy-piggledy mass of houses, shops, taverns, ordinaries, prisons, civic buildings and churches, held in place by the high City wall, dominated by the soaring magnificence of Saint Paul's Cathedral and guarded with grim solidity by the impregnable Tower. The multifarious sights and diverse sounds of London were supplemented by the noisome smells of the capital. Billingsgate sent up its abiding stink of fish, but it was mixed with many other pungent aromas and garnished with the sharp odour of the Thames itself.

Anyone looking down from the bridge that day would have seen one spectacle that was unique. Westfield's Men were giving an impromptu performance on the wharf below. No stage was set up and no audience had paid to watch, but a dozen minor tragedies were being played out with great intensity. The company was about to set sail for Deptford, where they would transfer to the larger vessel that would cross the sea to Holland. Tearful wives and howling children had come to send their beloved off with a forlorn hug. Distraught mistresses clung to bodies with which they had been entwined throughout the night. Whole families surrounded some of the actors, with parents, uncles, aunts, cousins, and even doddering grandparents in attendance for a last sighting.

No parting was more touching in its sincerity nor more agonising in its pain than that between Lawrence and Margery Firethorn. Both arms around his children, the actor wept bitterly and gave his wife the same advice after each relay of kisses planted upon her upturned face.

'And Margery, my good, sweet wife . . .'

'Yes, Lawrence?'

'Keep your house fair and clean, which I know you will.'

'Yes, husband.'

'Every evening, throw water before your door and have in your window a goodly store of rue and herb of grace.'

'I am well-provided with them.'

'They help to purge the air and keep disease at bay.'

'This departure of yours is worse than any disease.'

Another flurry of kisses stopped her mouth.

A few friends were there to wave Edmund Hoode off and a bevy of wenches from Bankside were bidding a raucous farewell to Owen Elias. The tall, thin, sensitive Clement Islip was wishing Barnaby Gill a safe voyage, and the bruised Ralph Groves had overcome his disappointment at being left out of the party and arrived to shake hands with Adrian Smallwood and admit that the latter would be a more worthy traveller than he himself.

Amid the tragic scene, there was one touch of unintentional comedy. George Dart was weeping copiously because nobody had turned up to send him off with a kind word. When he saw Thomas Skillen hobbling towards him, he was so delighted that he burst into hysterical laughter and the old man boxed his ears out of sheer force of habit. Dart backed quickly away from the attack and dropped ridiculously into the cold, dark water of the Thames. As they hauled him ashore again, he did not know whether to cry at the humiliation or laugh with relief, but he did both simultaneously when Skillen enfolded his sodden body in a paternal embrace.

Nicholas Bracewell was in his accustomed role as the stage manager to the drama, gently detaching the players from their trailing loved ones and easing them aboard the boat one by one. When all but Firethorn had been shepherded away, the book-holder was suddenly accosted by a weird figure who seemed to glide out of the throng of well-wishers.

'Nicholas Bracewell, I think?' he said.

'Yes,' confirmed the other.

'We have met before.'

'I recognised you at once, sir.'

'Doctor John Mordrake. Come to crave a boon.'

'Of me?'

'You are the only man who can serve me. Step aside.'

Mordrake was a big, heavy, round-shouldered man, his spine curved by a lifetime bent over his experiments. He had long, lank silver hair and a wispy beard. The gold chain around his neck was thrown into relief by his black gown. Nicholas was familiar with his reputation. He was both hailed as a master-physician and denounced as a necromancer, but the balance of opinion tipped heavily in favour of the former. Not only had Mordrake been retained to treat Queen Elizabeth herself on occasion, he had also outwitted the plague.

The old man ushered Nicholas aside for a private conference.

'You are journeying to Prague, I hear,' said Mordrake.

'That is our farthest destination.'

'Could you carry something with you for a friend?'

'We already have cargo enough,' said Nicholas pleasantly.

'This will take up no room at all and may be lodged in your purse without anyone knowing that it is there.' He slipped an object into the other's hand. 'Carry that to its rightful owner and you will be well-rewarded.'

'What is it that I am to carry?'

Nicholas held out his palm and examined the small wooden box which had been put there. It was exquisitely carved. When he tried to ease up the lid, he found the box locked.

'There is no key,' he observed.

'He will know how to open it.'

'Who will?'

'The man to whom I send it—if you accept my charge.'

Nicholas hesitated. 'I need to know its contents.'

'They would be meaningless to you. Here,' said Mordrake as he dropped two crowns into Nicholas's other hand. 'There's proof of how important it is for that to reach Prague. Two more crowns await you on your return if you do me this kindness.'

Nicholas looked into the watery blue eyes. Their keen intelligence was dimmed by a wistfulness and a sense of pleading. Doctor John Mordrake was a distinguished man of science, yet he was imploring a humble book-holder from a theatre company to do him a favour. The reward seemed absurdly out of proportion to what Nicholas was being asked to do.

'You do not even know me,' he protested.

'We met once before,' said Mordrake. 'That told me much about you. I made enquiries. Nicholas Bracewell is a man of good repute. I know that I may trust him.'

'Who is the fellow?' asked Nicholas.

'You'll help me?' gasped Mordrake with a glint of joy.

'If I am able to find the man.'

'Oh, you will find him easily enough, Nicholas. If you play at the Imperial Court, you are bound to meet him, for he serves the Emperor just as I once served him myself.' Mordrake pointed to the box. 'Put that into his hand and your errand is done. No more remains, I do assure you.'

'What is the man's name, sir?'

'Come close and I will whisper it.'

Nicholas inclined his ear. 'Well?'

'Talbot Royden.'

'Royden?'

'Do not forget the name. Doctor Talbot Royden.'

Nicholas mastered his surprise and nodded his head.

'There is no chance of that, sir.'

As the craft edged its way slowly downriver, the passengers waved until the figures on the wharf were dwarfed in size and obscured by other traffic on the water. There was no sense of adventure to spur them on. That would come later. They were still too caught up in their personal griefs and regrets. Firethorn tried to enliven them with fulsome boasts about the triumphs that beckoned them, but even he was only half-hearted in his enthusiasm. It was left to Nicholas to move quietly among his fellows, talking to each one in turn and reminding them that they had abandoned one family in order to be part of another. They were all children of the company now.

Anne Hendrik waited patiently until he had done his rounds. She was never short of companionship. Years of watching Westfield's Men at the Queen's Head had helped to forge a number of friendships with its members. She was especially fond of Edmund Hoode and Owen Elias, but it was with the personable young James Ingram that she was talking when Nicholas finally rejoined her. After exchanging a few token niceties, Ingram slipped away to leave them on their own.

'There is a lot of sorrow aboard this vessel,' she said.

'It will lift in time, Anne.'

'Who was that man with whom you spoke at the quayside?'

'I spoke to several.'

'This one drew you apart. An old man in a black cloak.'

'That was Doctor John Mordrake.'

'You speak his name with a sense of wonder.'

'So I should,' said Nicholas. 'He has wondrous gifts.'

'What did he say to you?'

'He told me how to cure the plague.'

'How?' she asked. 'We all wish to know that.'

'The good doctor advised me to sail out of London in the company of a beautiful woman,' he said with a fond smile. 'So here am I—and there she stands before me.'

Anne smiled. 'Is that all that he said to you?'

'It is all that is of consequence.'

He slipped an arm around her and stared out over the bulwark. London was receding into the gloom. He wondered how long it would be before he returned to the City and how many of the discarded hired men would still be there. Theatre could be a cruel master at times.

When they reached Deptford, they disembarked to the sound of hammering in the shipyards and to the plaintive cries of sea-gulls. Nicholas took a moment to look nostalgically across at the *Golden Hind*, the ship on which he had once sailed around the world with Francis Drake. Moored in perpetuity, it was now an object of veneration and he was hurt to see how much of its timbers had been chipped away by those eager for souvenirs. It now seemed far too small for the interminable voyage it had survived and the large crew it had carried. As unhappy memories flooded his mind, Nicholas turned his attention to getting the company aboard the other vessel.

The *Peppercorn* was a three-masted craft with a reputation for safety, but this was a relative term at sea. When they left the protection of the Thames estuary, Nicholas knew that they would encounter high winds and surging waves. Many of his fellows would feel both queasy and frightened when they lost all sight of land. Moving amongst them again, he warned them of what was to come and suggested precautions they might take. As Anne watched him striding confidently around the deck, she was struck by the consideration he was showing to the others and she was forcibly reminded that she would not be able to call upon that consideration herself for much longer.

'Is all well, Mistress Hendrik?' asked a voice.

'Yes, Adrian,' she said with a weary smile.

'Nicholas asked me to keep an eye on you.'

'That is very kind.'

'He is trying to instil some courage into us,' said Adrian Smallwood. 'We are poor sailors and need all the help we can get. My stomach is already telling me that I should have stayed behind in London.'

'Where do you hail from?'

'York.'

'That is not so far from the sea.'

'It never tempted me,' he confessed. 'I prefer to have dry land beneath my feet and not this tilting deck.'

Anne chatted happily with him. Though Smallwood had only been with the company a short time, he was a gregarious man who got to know everyone very quickly. She liked him. On the few occasions they had met, he had always been polite but effusive. Adrian Smallwood had the same bubbling vitality which she admired in Owen Elias, and even more in Lawrence Firethorn.

As Anne was talking, two men brushed past her and stood a yard or so away. Her brief glance told her that they looked like foreign merchants but she paid them no further attention. It was only when Smallwood excused himself to go below that she was able to take a closer interest in the men. There was a sinister air to them. They were studying the members of the theatre company with great curiosity, as if trying to identify someone.

A throaty chuckle from one man somehow alerted her. Anne moved an involuntary step closer so that she could overhear what they were saying. They were talking in German and she needed a moment to translate the snatches that she picked up. When she edged closer still, only one more sentence was spoken but she was able to understand it at once. The smaller of them, a short, stocky individual with a gruff voice, indicated Westfield's Men with a hand.

'Which one must I kill?' he asked.

The relish in his tone made her blood run cold.

[CHAPTER FOUR]

The first betrayal came from the sea itself. It offered one thing to their faces while plotting another behind their backs. When the estuary broadened out, the *Peppercorn* came round the headland and sailed out into open water. The wind freshened to beat noisily at the canvas and the waves made the vessel twist and undulate, but most of the passengers felt no real discomfort. To the bolder souls who remained on deck, the spray was invigorating and the creaking rhythm of the ship was oddly reassuring.

Standing fearlessly in the prow, Lawrence Firethorn scanned the empty horizon ahead like a Viking warrior in search of new lands to plunder. So exhilarated was he by the dipping motion of the vessel that he began to quote speeches extempore from his favourite plays, hurling iambic pentameters into the white foam with joyous prodigality. Owen Elias was also excited by his first sea voyage and talked volubly to James Ingram about the delights that lay ahead for them on the Continent.

While some were thrilled by the experience, others were simply relieved that it was not the ordeal they had feared. Edmund Hoode found a quiet corner in which he could meditate on the problem how *The Chaste Maid of Wapping* could arrive in Prague in Bohemian disguise. Barnaby Gill tucked himself against the bulwark and used his pomander to keep out the salty tang of the sea, inhaling dramatically through flared nostrils to attract what attention he could. Adrian Smallwood grew accustomed to the swell so quickly that he was even able to instruct Richard Honeydew, the youngest of the apprentices, in how to accompany himself on the lute.

Nicholas Bracewell was unable to enjoy the ambiguous pleasures of being at sea again. Anne Hendrik's report had been highly unsettling.

'Are you sure that is what you heard?' he asked.

'Yes, Nick.'

'There could be no mistake in the translation?'

'Jacob taught me well. My German is not perfect but it was more than adequate for this.'

'And the two men were looking at us?'

'They were studying you,' she said. 'They were keeping the whole company under surveillance.'

'I wish that you had kept *them* under surveillance a little longer, Anne, instead of running straight to me. You might have seen their faces and marked their apparel so that I was able to identify them. As it was, you only viewed them from behind, and that leaves me short of necessary detail.'

'I was frightened, Nick!'

'I know, I know,' he soothed.

'That man talked of murder,' she recalled with a shudder, 'with such evil pleasure in his voice. I could not bear to stand beside him a moment longer. That is why I rushed directly to you.'

He put a comforting arm around her. 'You did right and I am very grateful to you. What you chanced to overhear may save a life. Forewarned is forearmed. I will spread the word.' He heaved a sigh. 'But we take precautions against an invisible foe. You and I have been twice around the ship together to search high and low, but you did not recognise those men.'

'I thought I saw one of them, Nick. But I cannot be sure.'

'Remain vigilant.'

'I will, I will.'

'And stay close to me at all times.'

'You do not have to give me that advice,' she said with a smile. 'I will not let you out of my sight. That man terrified me. Why could anyone wish to harm a member of the company?'

'I do not know, Anne.'

'He was ready to *kill* someone.'

'He will have to get past me first.'

'What if you yourself are the victim?'

She buried her head in his chest and he held her tight. It was minutes before she was able to speak again. Controlling her fear, Anne looked up at him.

'I am ready to search the vessel again with you, if that would help,' she offered. 'They are aboard somewhere.'

'So are many other passengers, and those two men are concealed in the press.'

'We know that they are German. That gives us a start.'

'Perhaps, and perhaps not, Anne. You heard them speak in German, but that may not be their native tongue. It might simply have been used as a common language between men of different nationalities. We have Dutch, Danish, and Polish merchants aboard. I have also heard French spoken here.'

'There must be *some* way to find them.'

'There is, Anne. We wait until they come to us.'

'If only I had seen their faces!'

'You saw and heard enough.' Nicholas glanced around. 'But it is time to go below deck before the storm breaks.'

'What storm? I see no signs of it.'

'It is coming, believe me. Let us gather up the others.'

His prediction was remarkably accurate. The blue sky ahead was only a distraction from the dark clouds that crept up behind them. Westfield's Men were heedless victims of the sea's swift treachery. The wind stiffened, the waves became hostile, and the first drops of rain were carried on the air. A yell from the boatswain brought the crew running to get their orders. The *Peppercorn* was in for a buffeting.

Firethorn soon discovered that he did not have Viking blood in his veins and he abandoned his station in the prow as the first torrent of water washed over it. Elias and Ingram had their conversation terminated and Hoode's authorial musings were also interrupted. Gill's pomander was knocked out of his hand and the music lesson became impossible as the ship began to heave with more purpose. Nicholas tried to gather his fellows together to assist them below.

George Dart suffered the full impact of the sudden change in the weather. Scurrying to join the others, he tripped over a rope and fell headlong onto the deck. As he dragged himself painfully up, he was knocked off his feet again by a stray wooden bucket that slid across the wet timbers. When he finally got upright, the ship listed so sharply that he was flung against the bulwark and drenched by the biggest wave yet. With a mind full of terror and a mouth full of sea water, he crawled after his colleagues on all fours.

[56]

Nicholas assembled the company below deck so that he could both protect them and offer some assurance. Three years at sea with Drake on the circumnavigation of the globe had taken him through all kinds of tempests and he still had nightmares about the remorseless battering which the *Golden Hind* received on its way through the Straits of Magellan. To anyone who had endured such extremities of weather, the squall was no more than a trifling inconvenience, but Nicholas could see that it seemed like a typhoon to the others.

'We will all drown!' wailed Gill, green as his doublet.

'There is no chance of that,' said Nicholas calmly. 'The vessel is sound and the crew able.'

'No ship can stay afloat for long in a storm like this.'

'It can, Master Gill. Put your trust in the *Peppercorn.*'

'We are trying, Nick,' said a pallid Firethorn, 'but it is difficult to trust any craft which tosses us about so. We are like so many dice shaken in the pot before being thrown out on the table. Must we submit to this torture?'

'Try to forget the storm,' said Nicholas.

'Forget it! Can a man who is being hanged forget the rope? You are our sailor. Help us. Tell us what to do.'

'First, you must hold fast to known facts.'

'What do you mean?'

'The *Peppercorn* has sailed to and from the Netherlands many times. Take comfort from that. It has survived far worse squalls than this without loss of life or damage to the hull. I have spoken with some of the crew. We could not be in a more secure craft.'

'Secure!' gasped Firethorn.

'We are like corks in a waterfall,' said Elias, as he lurched a few feet to starboard. 'This storm hurls us where it wishes. Is there nothing we can do, Nick?'

'Stay below and sit it out.'

'Teach us how to escape from this ordeal.'

'Fill your mind with other thoughts, Owen.'

'I am more worried about emptying my belly,' groaned the Welshman, both hands on his stomach. 'I feel as if I am about to spew up a barrel of ale that I never had the pleasure of drinking. If this be voyaging, I'd as lief stay in London and take my chances against the plague.'

'What did *you* do in bad weather, Nick?' asked Anne.

'Do you really wish to know?'

'Yes!' chorused five sufferers.

'It may not work for you but it saved me.'

'Tell us your secret,' she said.

'I sang.'

'You what?'

'I opened my lungs and I sang,' he admitted. 'Most men cursed at a hurricane, as if foul words could keep it at bay. But I sang to keep my mind occupied.'

'They must have thought you were mad!' observed Gill.

'Nobody hears you in a howling gale.'

Firethorn was incredulous. 'You sang? In a condition such as we poor wretches are in, you had breath enough to *sing?*'

'I found that it helped.'

'I can barely speak,' croaked Hoode. 'This storm has robbed us of our voices. Which of us could even sing one line of a song?'

'I could,' said Adrian Smallwood bravely.

The whole company turned towards him. Feeling as queasy as any of them, Smallwood made a determined effort to overcome his seasickness and sang in a ringing baritone voice.

> *Now is the month of Maying,*
> *When merry lads are playing.*
> *Fa la la.'*

He looked around his fellows and tried to shake them out of their self-pity. Even though the vessel began to rock more violently, Smallwood persevered as a choirmaster.

'Come on!' he exhorted. 'Sing away this storm. We would never have beaten the Armada with sailors such as you. Show your spirit. Sing in defiance. Who'll join me?'

'I, for one,' volunteered Nicholas.

'And me,' said Elias. 'You will never find a Welshman shirking a chance to sing. Lead on, Adrian. We follow.'

Smallwood sang out with even more gusto this time.

> *Now is the month of Maying,*
> *When merry lads are playing.*

Fa la la.
Fa la la.
Each with his bonny lass,
Upon the greeny grass,
Fa la la.
Fa la la.'

Nicholas lent his support and the rich deep voice of Elias blended with those of his companions. Firethorn was the next to take up the song, then Ingram, then Richard Honeydew. Anne soon joined them, and others were caught up in the melody. Even the bilious Gill joined in while Hoode—unwilling to open his mouth again lest more than words gush out—tapped his foot in time to the rhythm of the piece.

Huddled below deck, the other passengers watched with blank amazement at the incongruous recital. Foreigners amongst them decided it was yet further evidence of the madness of the English and they responded with scorn, sympathy, or amusement. Led by Adrian Smallwood, the choir surged on regardless.

'The Spring, clad all in gladness,
Doth laugh at Winter's sadness.
Fa la la.
Fa la la.
And to the Bagpipes' sound,
The Nymphs tread out their ground.
Fa la la.
Fa la la.
Fie then, why sit we musing,
Youth's sweet delight refusing?'

And so it went on. A ragged band of players, frightened by the storm, shaken until they were about to vomit, wondering if they would ever see dry land again, slowly blended together in harmony to work their way through song after song. Adversity united them, and the man who had revived their spirits was Adrian Smallwood. It was very gratifying to Nicholas because he had recommended the actor for inclusion in the touring company.

The repertoire of songs did nothing to still the troubled waters of the

North Sea, and the vessel continued to roll alarmingly as it sailed on. Several of the actors peeled off at intervals to vomit into one of the wooden buckets provided for the purpose and their contribution towards the recital was thereafter muted. But the singing carried on until the company began to fall asleep, one by one, from sheer exhaustion. Adrian Smallwood ended as he began, with a solo performance.

It was a rough crossing. Inclement weather throughout the night blew the *Peppercorn* off course and added hours to their voyage. There was one small advantage for Westfield's Men. Gathered together in a corner below deck, they were easier to protect from the feared attack, and Nicholas shared the watch under the swinging lanterns with Firethorn, Elias and Smallwood. No threat came. Nicholas surmised that the assassin had either been disabled by the heaving motion of the ship or that Anne Hendrik had misheard him. She herself slept fitfully against the shoulder of her lodger and dear friend.

Dawn revealed billowing waves through a blanket of rain and few passengers ventured up on deck. The members of the company woke sporadically and were surprised to find themselves still alive and unharmed. When they had relieved themselves in one of the fetid privies, some were even able to rediscover their appetite. The worst was definitely over.

Time glided past and the bucking rhythm of the vessel seemed to ease. The yell from the look-out filtered down to them. Land had been sighted. When the weary travellers started to drift up on deck, they learned that the rain had ceased and that the sky was slowly clearing. The swirling wind still played havoc with the rigging and the choppy waves still climbed high enough to scour the deck occasionally, but the sight of their destination helped the passengers to accommodate these discomforts without any sense of panic.

Nicholas escorted Anne to the bulwark to take her first look at the little seaport of Flushing, situated at the mouth of the River Schelde and welcoming them to a harbour where many smaller vessels already bobbed and swayed. The welcome was illusory. When the *Peppercorn* tried to put in, its captain found the waves too strong and the wind too guileful, so he elected instead to sail on to Rammekins for surer anchorage.

Lawrence Firethorn was outraged by the change of destination. He took his protest across to his book-holder.

'Our passage was booked to Flushing!' he roared.

'We will not be too far away,' said Nicholas.

'Order the captain to deliver us to the town that is named on our passport. I will not endure such a hellish voyage and be put down on the wrong part of the Dutch coast.'

'The captain has no choice. He shows good seamanship. Would you rather stay aboard until the sea decides to calm? That might take a whole day.'

'Another day on this floating death-trap! Get me off!'

'Be patient,' counselled Nicholas, 'and you will soon have dry land beneath your feet again.'

'Thank heavens!'

Firethorn's relief was short-lived. When the company at last disembarked from the *Peppercorn*, the dry land had been turned to mud by a fortnight's steady rain. Disenchantment gnawed at the actor-manager. Having envisioned a triumphal arrival at Flushing, he was now limping ashore at Rammekins. Instead of being welcomed like a victorious admiral after a naval battle, he was a complete nonentity forced to lead a bedraggled company on foot across a squelching quagmire.

Supporting Anne by the arm, Nicholas again took the full force of his employer's ire. Firethorn was incandescent with righteous indignation.

'Could they not supply us with horses?' he demanded.

'We were not expected to land here.'

'This country is barbaric!'

'Other passengers must walk as well as us.'

'This mud almost reaches to my knees.'

'Flushing is only four miles away.'

'Four miles of this misery?'

'Anne fares worse than us,' noted Nicholas, breaking in on the other's self-absorption. 'If we had to struggle through this mire in a dress—as she does—we might have just reason to complain. Yet Anne bears it all with a brave smile. We should learn from her example.'

Firethorn accepted the rebuke with good grace and showered Anne with profuse apologies for the next mile. The rest of the company trudged along behind them in a mood of dejection. Not even the resilient Smallwood could manage a song now. The only person missing was George Dart. Nicholas had no qualms about leaving Dart behind to guard the wicker baskets containing their costumes and properties until a cart could be sent for him from Flushing. It was inconceivable that the diminutive assistant stagekeeper could be the intended victim of the death threat. The murderer—if he existed—would be stalking another member of the company.

Flushing was an English possession, a cherished bridgehead on the Continent which to some extent compensated for the disastrous loss of Calais on the eve of Queen Elizabeth's reign. Ceded by the Dutch in recognition of military support against the Spanish invaders, Flushing showed the influence of English occupation. It had an English church, English settlers, and a permanent garrison of English troops. When the weary, mud-covered travellers reached the town, they saw English faces and fashions at every turn.

But it was by no means a home from home. Dutch inhabitants were cold and hostile, feeling that the English had not merely taken their town away from them. They had changed its name as well. The busy little port of Vlissingen was now the military base of Flushing, full of soldiers on their way to battle or wounded men and corpses returning from it. Overcrowded and insanitary, the place was haunted by profiteers, adventurers, and others who could exploit the wartime situation. The town was inhospitable and there was a pervading sense of unease.

It was Gill's turn to have a fit of disillusionment. He gazed around with utter disgust and stamped a sodden foot.

'This whole escapade is a catastrophe!' he exclaimed.

'Give it time to unfold, Barnaby,' said Hoode.

'It has unfolded far enough, Edmund. I am imprisoned in the hold of a ship, subjected to a voyage of sheer terror, forced to ruin by best shoes and hose by wading through the mud, then confronted with this cesspit!' He folded his arms and turned away. 'I expect better, I deserve better, I am owed better!'

'We all share your disappointment.'

'It was cruel to inveigle me into this calamity.'

'You are a calamity in yourself!' sneered Firethorn.

'To come here, I turned down some highly tempting offers.'

'Why?' mocked the other. 'What did Clement Islip promise to do to you? Hold you between his thighs and play you like his viol? Be your own fair maid?'

'There is no point in bickering,' said Hoode, stepping between the two men. 'Our first task is to find somewhere to stay in this unfriendly town.'

'It is already arranged,' said Firethorn. 'That is what Lord Westfield gave me to understand. Nick?'

'Yes?' asked Nicholas, stepping forward.

'Be our pathfinder here. Where do we go?'

'We stay right here.'

'In the town square?' said Gill with disdain. 'We are renowned actors, not street beggars. We demand respect.'

'I believe that we are about to receive it, Master Gill.'

Nicholas had seen the horseman approaching them at a steady trot. He was a tall, slender young man in neat apparel and he was already composing his features into a polite smile of welcome. The horse came to a halt in front of them. The rider touched his hat deferentially.

'I am seeking Master Lawrence Firethorn,' he said.

'He stands before you,' announced the actor with a hand on his chest. 'Who may you be, sir?'

'Balthasar Davey, at your service. Secretary to Sir Robert Sidney, Lord Governor of Flushing. I am sent to welcome you to the town and to apologise for the gross inconvenience you have clearly suffered.' He dismounted from the saddle. 'Sir Robert sends his compliments and bids me conduct you to the inn where you and your company will lodge for the night.'

'Thank you, Master Davey,' said Firethorn, pleased by this new development. 'We drop from fatigue and need refreshment.'

'I will take you to it directly.' He turned to Anne and spoke with courtesy. 'But I see that you have a lady with you. We have only a short distance to walk but I will happily offer her the use of my horse for that journey.' He glanced at the soiled hem of her dress. 'You have already marched too far on foot, I think. Travel the rest of the way in some comfort.'

Anne acknowledged the kind offer with a smile and was about to refuse it but Nicholas took the decision for her.

'Thank you, sir,' he said, taking her by the waist and hoisting her up into the saddle in one fluent move. 'This is Mistress Hendrik, who has been our companion thus far from London. Her business takes her to Amsterdam and we seek advice as to how she can reach it in the safest and swiftest way.'

'Put the matter in my hands,' said Davey obligingly. 'If Mistress Hendrik will spend a night at the inn, I will ensure that she may set off for Amsterdam in the morning. Will that satisfy you?'

'It will,' said Anne with gratitude.

Balthasar Davey tugged on the reins and led his horse along the road. Restored by the promise of hospitality, the company followed eagerly. Nicholas fell in beside their guide and introduced himself.

'One thing more,' he said. 'Our baggage was too heavy to drag from Rammekins. A member of the company stayed behind to guard it. I would retrieve it and him as soon as possible.'

'Your wagons await you at the inn.'

'Good.'

'I will find someone to do this errand for you.'

'No,' said Nicholas firmly. 'It is my responsibility. I will drive the wagon myself without delay.'

'So be it.'

The inn was a long, rambling, ramshackle building with a steep roof whose thatch was in need of repair, but its defects were willingly overlooked by guests in need of rest and sustenance. English ale and wholesome food awaited them. With four walls around them at last, they were mollified. After an inauspicious beginning, their visit to the Continent might yet be redeemed. They were expected, after all.

Nicholas did not share in the repast. When he had shown Anne to the privacy of her bedchamber, he went out to the stables where an ostler was harnessing two of the horses between the shafts of a wagon. Nicholas was soon rumbling off in the direction of Rammekins to collect the abandoned George Dart. Curled up on a basket like a stray dog, Dart shivered in the grudging sunshine and scanned the road to Flushing with large and fearful eyes. When he saw Nicholas approaching with the wagon, he burst into tears of joy and fell on to the ground from his perch. He soon rallied when Nicholas praised him for discharging his duty so well and promised him a nourishing meal once they returned to the inn. After loading the baskets into the wagon, they set off on a creaking journey along the muddy track.

They had gone well over a mile before Nicholas realised that they were being followed. A sixth sense made him turn sharply and he caught a glimpse of a stocky man on a roan some fifty yards or more behind them. The lone horseman quickly dropped back and sought the cover of some trees. Nicholas said nothing to his companion. Flicking the reins, he coaxed a brisk trot out of the animals and they made light work of pulling the wagon along. When he next looked over his shoulder, Nicholas saw no evidence of any pursuit.

It was late afternoon when they trundled up to the inn. The sun had belatedly decided to grace the day with its full force and this drew some members of a Dutch militia company out onto the tufted lawn at the rear of the building for a game of skittles. Inside the hostelry, Westfield's Men had already made themselves at home and were carousing happily. George Dart was given such a rousing reception that he forgot all about the privations of the voyage and the agonies of being left alone in a foreign country to guard the company's baggage.

Nicholas saw immediately that Firethorn, Gill, and Hoode were missing. He raised a quizzical eyebrow. Owen Elias spoke over the top of a tankard of ale.

'They are at the Governor's house,' he explained. 'Sir Robert Sidney invited them to his table and that smooth-faced secretary of his escorted them thither. We have plainer fare here but it goes down well with this ale. Come and join us, Nick. You must be starving.'

'I will speak with Anne first.'

'She is resting in her chamber and left word that she will come down to you anon.' He nudged his friend and chuckled. 'Forget your office for once. Stop worrying about the needs of others and put Nick Bracewell first.'

'I will admit to being thirsty, Owen.'

'Hungry, too, I wager.'

'Very.'

'Then let us address the problem.'

With a loud yell, Elias banged the table until one of the servingmen came to see what he wanted. Food and drink were ordered for Nicholas and he set about both with relish. James Ingram and Adrian Smallwood were at the same table. All four men were soon chatting amiably but Nicholas remained alert. He remembered Anne's warning very clearly and wondered if it might have a connection with the horseman who had trailed him.

They were in a long bare room with a scattering of tables, benches and stools. Apart from the actors, there were groups of English soldiers taking their ease during a break from fighting, watched resentfully by a few Dutch militiamen. Taunting remarks were occasionally tossed between the nominal allies. The tensions of war were clearly taking their toll.

Elias was buoyant again. 'This tour of ours will be a triumphal march!' he affirmed. 'I feel it in my bones.'

'That may just be the ague,' joked Smallwood.

'Do not rush to judgement,' cautioned Ingram. 'We have a long way to go yet, Owen. And we will spend far more time travelling than strutting upon a stage.'

'We are pioneers!' insisted Elias. 'Other companies have brought their plays to the Continent, but none of our standing. I may well turn out to be the first Welshman to have acted before the Emperor Rudolph. Perhaps I should insert some lines in my native language for him.'

'He would not understand them, if you did,' said Nicholas as he put his dish aside. 'The Emperor may not speak English, Welsh or any other tongue that you may know. He was brought up in the Spanish Court.'

'Spanish!' echoed Elias with distaste. 'I'll not speak that foul language for the Archangel Gabriel, let alone for a mere Emperor.'

'You spoke it readily enough for Banbury's Men,' reminded Nicholas. 'When you played in *The Spanish Jew* for them, you even sang a ballad in Spanish.'

'Only in mockery of King Philip!' he protested. Contrition came at once. 'You are right to jog my memory, Nick. I rue the day when I was foolish enough to join our rivals. I paid dearly for that act of madness. My heart and hand belong to Westfield's Men now.' His chuckle resurfaced. 'What is the point of travel if we cannot pick up every language that may lie in our way? I am turned schoolboy again.'

'This venture will educate us all,' said Ingram.

'Yes,' agreed Smallwood. 'Including our apprentices. Dick Honeydew has already begun his lessons on the lute. He is an apt pupil. We take only one lutanist to Bohemia, but there will be two of us on the return journey.'

'Is the lad that quick to learn, Adrian?' asked Elias.

'He will be a finer musician than his teacher one day.'

Before Nicholas could comment, he saw Anne descending the oak staircase and rose quickly to beckon her across. She exchanged greetings with them all and joined them at their table. The three actors talked respectfully with her before breaking away, one by one, to join their noisier fellows and to give Nicholas time alone for her on the eve of her departure for Amsterdam. Anne let him order a glass of wine for her but would only eat a light refreshment.

'I will not sleep after a heavy meal,' she said, 'and I need all the rest I can get before I set off tomorrow.'

'What time do you leave?'

'At dawn.'

He was shaken. 'So early?'

'It is a long journey, Nick. Soldiers and supplies are moving to and fro every day. Master Davey tells me I may join some men who are heading north. It means that I will have a military escort.'

'That puts my mind at rest a little.'

'The anxiety will be all on my side.'

'Why?'

'I heard what that man said aboard the *Peppercorn*.'

'Some idle boast, that is all.'

'He was in earnest, Nick. I am bound to fear.'

'The danger is over,' he assured her.

Nicholas made no mention of the man who had followed him on horseback from Rammekins. There was no point in sending Anne off in a state of apprehension to the bedside of a dying man. She had worries enough of her own. He simply luxuriated in her company for a couple of hours while he still could, then escorted her upstairs when she chose to retire. Promising that he would see her off at dawn, he took a lingering farewell.

When he rejoined his fellows, Nicholas was in time to see Lawrence Firethorn burst into the room, with Barnaby Gill and Edmund Hoode at his heels. All three were palpably flushed with wine. Firethorn closed on his book-holder, but his news was addressed to the entire company.

'Nick, dear heart!' he said effusively. 'We have broken bread with Sir Robert Sidney himself. Our reputation has come before us. His brother, the late and much-lamented Sir Philip Sidney, was his predecessor here as Lord Governor of Flushing. He praised us to the skies. Sir Philip saw me play Hector at the Bel Savage Inn and witnessed some of our finest hours at the Queen's Head.'

'He also commended my genius to his brother,' said Gill.

'And one of my plays,' added Hoode modestly.

'In short,' continued Firethorn, 'Sir Robert is not content merely to lodge us here before sending us on our way. He has called for a play from

Westfield's Men.' There was a flurry of interest from the company. 'Our first engagement is to be before the Governor, his staff and our gallant English soldiers.'

There was a derisive snigger from one of the soldiers at the far end of the room, a big, scowling man with a sash across his chest and a rapier at his hip. The actor-manager sailed over the interruption without even hearing it.

'Our play chooses itself,' he announced.

'Does it?'

'*Hector of Troy!*'

'Over my dead body!' howled an irate Gill.

'Yes, Barnaby,' he said. 'I cut you down with my sword at the end of Act Five. A most deserved end for you.'

'It is a hideous choice.'

'I am bound to agree,' said Hoode. 'Anything but that.'

'Support me here, Nick,' said Firethorn, turning to the book-holder. 'Hector is the only man fit for this occasion.'

The whole room was now listening to the argument and it showed nobody in a good light. Nicholas turned a public dispute into a private conference by leading Firethorn to a settle in the corner. Seated beside him, he used quiet persuasion in place of hot words. The others in the room gradually picked up their own conversations and left the two men alone.

'Hector is one of your greatest roles,' began Nicholas. 'it is justly acclaimed. But this may not be the time and place for him.'

'What better time than during a war? What more appropriate place than in front of English soldiers?' He grabbed the other's arm. 'Hector is a military hero. My performance will inspire our army to similar feats of heroism in the field.'

'I fear that it will lower their spirits.'

Firethorn felt betrayed. 'My acting? Lower spirits?'

'I talk of the play and not your performance,' reasoned Nicholas. 'This war in the Netherlands is now in its seventh year, with no sign of resolution. Many English soldiers have already sacrificed their lives and others will surely do so.'

'How does this bar *Hector of Troy?*'

'The army is weary and disheartened. Soldiers need a play which takes them away from war, not one which reminds them of it. They want rest, amusement, distraction. In place of a stirring tragedy, offer them a harmless comedy. There is another consideration,' he argued softly. 'Where is the performance to take place?'

'That was not decided.'

'Is there anywhere suitable in the army's quarters?'

'They have no quarters, Nick,' said Firethorn with a shrug. 'The soldiers are dispersed around the town in lodgings. The Governor himself does not have a residence of his own. He rents a house. Flushing may be an English town but it is crawling with Dutch landlords.'

'Where, then, are we expected to play?'

'I was relying on you to find a place for us.'

Nicholas pondered. 'Leave it to me,' he said.

Adrian Smallwood demonstrated his true value to the company next morning. He was indefatigable. In default of anywhere more suitable, Nicholas selected the inn itself as their theatre and he found the landlord much more amenable than Alexander Marwood had ever been. Decisions had to be taken quickly and implemented at once. Since there was no enclosed yard like that at the Queen's Head, Nicholas elected to set the stage up in the angle between the main body of the inn and the stables. The afternoon sun would strike the acting area directly and warm the back of the spectators' heads.

Smallwood was in action at once, helping the ostlers to lead the horses out of the stables and tethering them a distance away. Aided by George Dart, he rolled barrels into place, then lifted boards onto them to create a springy but quite serviceable stage. Nicholas screened the wall of the inn with a makeshift curtain so that one room could be pressed into service as the tiring-house and its neighbour as a storeroom for costumes and properties. The stage nestled beneath the windows, making it possible for actors to step through each set of shutters to make separate entrances. When it was cleared out by Smallwood, a stable was incorporated into the play as the home of one of its characters.

It was Smallwood's idea to utilise the upper window as a gallery where he and the other actor-musicians could play their instruments to best effect. The chamber had been vacated by Anne Hendrik at dawn and the landlord obligingly reserved it for use by Westfield's Men. A hundred other jobs needed to be done and Nicholas shared them out evenly, but it was Adrian Smallwood who somehow ended up doing most of them with an infectious cheerfulness.

'How did you contrive the miracle, Nick?' he asked.

'Miracle?'

'You turned *Hector of Troy* into *Mirth and Madness*. Nobody else could have worked so subtly on Master Firethorn.'

'I have had some practice,' said Nicholas wryly.

'What is your secret?'

'Patience and fortitude.'

'Heavy demands must have been made on both.'

Nicholas grinned. 'I have lived to tell the tale.'

The rehearsal of *Mirth and Madness* was attended by all kinds of errors and delays, as the deficiencies of the stage forced several changes to the text as it was played at the Queen's Head. But there was no sense of desperation. It was stock play from their repertoire and they knew they could make it work as successfully as it always had done. To his credit, Firethorn led his company with admirable commitment. The loss of his beloved Hector was a blow that left no visible bruises. At the end of the rehearsal, he gave them his routine blast of criticism in order to concentrate their minds. He then retired without any qualms to take refreshment in the inn.

Smallwood remained behind to help Nicholas with last-minute refinements. The two wagons were placed end to end at the rear of the rows of benches to provide additional seating at a raised level. Because there was no charge for admission, it was unnecessary to screen off the open side of the improvised auditorium. Nicholas fully expected customers from the inn and townspeople to converge on them out of curiosity when the performance was under way. He took a final look around.

'We are all done, Adrian,' he decided.

'Thanks to your leadership.'

'Take your share of the credit. You have worked as hard as any of us and with far less complaint.'

Smallwood beamed. 'I love this life, Nick.'

'This tour may put that love under severe strain.'

'It will not be found wanting,' vowed the other.

They slipped away for a frugal meal and were soon back in the tiring-house with the rest of the company. Spectators began to pour in and the benches quickly filled. Firethorn felt the need to make an oration to his fellows. Dressed in his costume, he beckoned them close to hear his urgent whisper.

'Lads,' he declared, 'this is a test of your mettle. We perform a trusty old play on a rickety stage in front of an untried audience. Anything may happen and we must be ready to respond to it. The good name of Westfield's Men must be preserved at all costs. See this afternoon as a chance to try our art on foreign eyes and ears. English soldiers will form the main part of our audience but there may be Dutch, Danish and German spectators out there as well. Include them at all times. Raise your voices. Broaden your gestures. Leave them shaking with mirth at the divine madness of Westfield's Men.'

They were ready. With no silken flag to hoist above their little playhouse, they used a trumpet fanfare to indicate the start of the play. Lawrence Firethorn stepped out in person to deliver the Prologue and set the tone. His words rang out effortlessly across a hundred yards or so.

> *'Mirth and madness are our themes today,*
> *So darker minds must seek another play*
> *To feed their gloom. All's froth and folly here,*
> *And Comedy itself will oft appear*
> *To grace this Flushing stage and mend a tear*
> *With laughter and with song. And have no fear*
> *That tragedy will come by stealth to turn*
> *Your joy to sighs. Our clownish antics spurn*
> *Life's miseries and with a Sidney's skill*
> *Govern your happiness.'*

The first laugh was led by Sir Robert Sidney himself, delighted at the way that his name had been worked into the verse. Seated on cushions in one of the wagons, he was accompanied by the erect figure of Balthasar Davey, immaculate as ever and trembling with controlled amusement. A ragged cheer went up from the English soldiers. Firethorn was saddened to see how many of them were wounded but it did not show in his voice. It continued to pound out the lines with exquisite timing until even those who did not understand a word of English were soon laughing.

He quit the stage to applause and passed the book-holder.

'You were right, Nick.'

'Thank you.'

'The ideal play.'

Nicholas had no time to savour the compliment. *Mirth and Madness* demanded all his attention. It was a rumbustious comedy with many changes of scene and some striking dramatic effects. Deft stage management was required to keep it moving at the requisite pace. Shorn of his usual complement of assistants behind the scenes, he had to take even more responsibility on his own shoulders. George Dart shared the increased burden, but he was taking a series of minor roles in the play and was thus of limited help.

Mirth and Madness was indeed an ideal choice. It was a visual delight from start to finish. Its plot was easy to follow, its comedy rich and varied, its characters engaging companions with whom to spend a sunny afternoon. Jaded soldiers were transported from the cruelties of a war to a world of helpless laughter. Dutch spectators marvelled at the quality of acting, which made their own indigenous travelling players look like floundering amateurs.

Nobody appreciated the performance more than Sir Robert Sidney. Vexed by the cares of office, he had appealed to Queen Elizabeth to relieve him of his duties in Flushing so that he could escape from a conflict which had already robbed him of his revered elder brother. There was a sublime Englishness about the play which allowed the Governor to spend two glorious hours in his own beloved country. Poised and handsome in his high eminence on the wagon, Sir Robert quickly surrendered to the general hilarity.

His approval did not go unnoticed by the members of the cast. Owen Elias came hurtling offstage after another riotous scene and paused beside Nicholas.

'Sir Robert is laughing his noble head off at us.'

'He is not the only one, Owen.'

'I had no idea that he was so young,' said Elias. 'He cannot have reached thirty yet. Why has he been deemed worthy of the Governorship at such an age?'

'His wife is Welsh,' said Nicholas with a teasing smile. 'That must have counted mightily in his favour.'

'Lady Sidney is Welsh? I knew he was a man of taste.'

Invigorated by the news, Elias went out for his next scene with even greater zest. The play was carried along by its own breath-taking momentum now. Lawrence Firethorn plundered his whole armoury of comic effects and gave endless pleasure with his extraordinary facial expressions, Barnaby Gill's hilarious songs and dances brought even more guffaws, and Edmund Hoode supplied some gentler humour as a parish priest who falls hopelessly in love with an unattainable young milkmaid.

Yet it was Adrian Smallwood who impressed Nicholas the most. The three leading sharers had taken their respective roles many times and had been able to refine their portrayals. Smallwood, by contrast, was making his first appearances in *Mirth and Madness*. Having mastered his supporting role at short notice, he also accompanied five songs on his lute, took part in three dances and still managed to lend a willing hand to Nicholas behind the scenes. In a selfish profession, Smallwood was a rare example of readiness to serve others.

When the play reached its giddy climax, the audience burst into frenzied applause. Westfield's Men had given them a priceless entertainment and rescued them from the harsher concerns of resisting Spanish aggression. As Firethorn led out the company to take their bow, the spectators surged forward to congratulate, embrace and cheer them.

Nicholas Bracewell was alone behind the scenes. When a hand closed on his arm, it belonged to no grateful spectator. Instead, he found himself looking up into the anxious face of the landlord. The man gibbered with embarrassment and motioned for Nicholas to follow. They went swiftly upstairs to the chamber which the book-holder shared with Owen Elias, Edmund Hoode and Adrian Smallwood. It had been ransacked. Baggage had been slit open and all their belongings scattered across the floor.

'Who found it like this?' asked Nicholas.

'A servant,' said the landlord in halting English.

'When?'

'During the play. She came up here with fresh linen and found all the rooms like this.'

'All of them?'

'Every chamber set aside for your company.'

Nicholas went to each of the rooms in turn to see for himself. Someone had searched them in great haste and left chaos in his wake. The landlord was deeply upset. Westfield's Men had brought a large audience to his inn and he had made a tidy profit selling food and drink to them. He mumbled his apologies and spoke of compensation for the outrage that had taken place under his roof. Nicholas paid no heed. His mind was racing with the implications of what had happened.

Hurrying back downstairs, he found that the actors had now withdrawn from the milling crowd into the privacy of the tiring-house. Inebriated with success, they were talking and laughing together. Nicholas saw at a glance that someone was missing. He pushed to the centre of the room.

'Where is Adrian?' he asked.

'He must be still onstage,' said Elias, looking around.

'No,' said Richard Honeydew. 'He went into the stable to fetch his lute. It was left in there after my last song.'

'That is right,' confirmed Hoode. 'I was waiting in the stable for my next entrance. Adrian quit the stage as a lutanist but rushed back on as a cuckolded husband with a foil in his hand. He'll be here in a moment.'

Nicholas did not wait. Stepping through the window, he brushed aside the curtain and went onstage. Spectators were still standing about in groups, enthused by the wonderful performance they had seen. There was no sign of Smallwood. Nicholas ran to the stable which had been utilised during the play to great effect. Its door was shut tight. He wrenched it open and stepped quickly inside.

Adrian Smallwood lay face-down on the floor, his head smashed violently open. His buff jerkin had been ripped from his back and a long-handled knife plunged deep between his shoulder-blades. The lute floated lazily in a pool of blood.

[CHAPTER FIVE]

It was a paradox. Over three hundred people had come to watch a play, yet not one of them had witnessed the real drama which had occurred at the inn. Watching a delightful romp, they missed the foul murder which took place under their noses. The killer had searched their rooms while everyone was distracted by *Mirth and Madness,* then used the swirling crowd as his cover when he struck down Adrian Smallwood. Or so it appeared to Nicholas Bracewell. He was convinced that the two crimes were linked but uncertain about the motives which inspired them.

When he raised the alarm, everyone was shocked to learn that one of the actors had been bludgeoned and stabbed only a short distance from where they stood. The goodwill engendered by the performance evaporated at once. While the audience was stunned, Westfield's Men were in despair. At the very moment when they were celebrating the first success of their Continental tour, one of their number was brutally killed. All of a sudden, the English possession of Flushing seemed alarmingly foreign. They were adrift in an alien land.

Nicholas was deeply shaken. Smallwood was both a friend and an invaluable member of the company. To lose him at all was a bitter blow, but to have it happen in this way was shattering. Without understanding why, Nicholas felt an obscure sense of guilt, as if it had been his duty to protect the actor. The guilt merged with his surging anger and prompted a vow to bring the killer to justice at whatever cost. Unfortunately, the vow was easier to make than to keep. Obstacles lay in his path. It was Balthasar Davey who pointed them out to him.

'You attempt the impossible, I fear,' he said.

'But I am involved in this to the hilt.'

'I understand that.'

'Adrian Smallwood was my fellow.'

'If he had been a complete stranger, he would not have deserved the hideous fate which he met. I am as anxious as you to see the murderer caught and hanged, but finding him is a task for the proper authorities.'

'I may have information that they do not, Master Davey.'

'Then it is your duty to pass it on.'

'I have already given a statement about how I found the body,' said Nicholas. 'My sole concern now is to track down the man who left it there.'

'What chance have you of catching him?'

'We shall see.'

'None, sir,' said the other politely. 'An assassin who can work so cunningly will not be reckless enough to remain in Flushing while you and others conduct a search for him. He will be several miles away by now.'

'Then I will pursue him!'

'How?'

There was a calm practicality about Balthasar Davey that made him formidable in argument. The Governor's secretary was keen to help in any way that he could, but he felt bound to oppose the course of action Nicholas wished to take. It was some hours after the play had ended. An official investigation into the murder had been set in motion and the corpse had been taken off by cart to the morgue in the English church. While the rest of Westfield's Men were drowning their sorrows in the inn, Balthasar Davey and Nicholas were in a private room at the rear of the premises. The secretary was acquainting the book-holder with the reality of his situation.

'Take my advice,' he said with a sad smile. 'Leave the town tomorrow and put this whole matter behind you.'

'We cannot desert our fellow. That would be cruel.'

'It is a cruelty which masks a greater kindness.'

'Kindness!' Nicholas blinked in disbelief. 'Abandoning a friend at a moment like this? You call that kindness?'

'I do. It would be a kindness to you because it would spare you untold pain and vexation. And it would be a kindness to your fellows to take them away from this unseemly business as soon as you may. I have heard actors are superstitious by nature. Keep them here to brood on the murder and that superstition will turn into morbid fear. Your company will suffer greatly.'

'There may be a grain of truth in that,' conceded Nicholas. 'But we will still not forsake Adrian.'

'Do you have any other choice?' asked Davey. 'You can hardly take his body with you. Pray for his soul and ride away from the scene of his murder. Tomorrow.'

'We will at least stay for the funeral.'

'That may not be for some days.'

'Why not?'

'Casualties of war,' said the other. 'We suffer heavy losses here. Wounded or dying men come in every day. Many others are already waiting for burial and their turn must come before Adrian Smallwood.'

'But he was a victim of murder.'

'That gives him no prior claims.'

'It should,' protested Nicholas. 'What sort of an uncaring place is this? Have you no human decency here?'

'We have as much as the war allows us.'

Nicholas boiled with resentment but it was not directed at Balthasar Davey. The Governor's secretary was not obstructing his wishes deliberately. He was very distressed at the murder, especially as it had occurred at the inn which he had chosen for the company. But living in the shadow of a long and expensive war had forced him to accept unpalatable facts. Emotion gave way to expediency. One man's death—however gruesome— had to be set against countless others on the battlefield. In the long catalogue of slaughter, the name of Adrian Smallwood was of no particular significance.

Nicholas was still agonising over the decision.

'I cannot bring myself to leave him here,' he said.

'You must.'

'He deserves to lie in his own parish churchyard, not in some nameless grave hundreds of miles away from his home.'

'He will not lack for English companions.'

'What of his friends, his family?'

'Write to them with these dread tidings,' said Davey. 'I will see that the letters are speedily dispatched. We are all too accustomed to sending bad news back to England.' He saw the doubt in the other's face. 'Sir Robert has asked me to give you his assurance that every effort will be made to find the villain who committed this heinous crime. And I give you my promise that your unlucky friend will have a Christian burial here in Flushing.'

Nicholas studied the secretary for a moment. Balthasar Davey was an elegant young man with an intelligent face which had been schooled to hide his true feelings. He had been gracious with Anne Hendrik and unfailingly helpful to Westfield's Men, yet there was something about him which troubled Nicholas. The secretary was holding something back. It was time to find out what it was.

'Why did you lodge us here?' asked Nicholas.

'It seemed the best choice. They serve imported ale here. I thought that a thirsty troupe of players would prefer to drink English ale out of pewter tankards rather than quaff Dutch beer out of ceramic mugs.'

'You misunderstand me. I wondered why you took such trouble on our behalf when you must have far more important things to do. Why did you not leave us to fend for ourselves?'

'That would have been ungentlemanly.'

'How did you even know that we were coming?'

'We are well-informed about any notable visitors.'

'We are a humble theatre company, passing through the town. Yet someone pays for our lodging and three of our sharers are invited to the Governor's table.'

'Sir Robert is fond of the theatre.'

'Did he order you to look after us?'

'Acting on a request from someone else.'

'And who might that be?'

'Lord Westfield,' said Davey easily. 'Who else?'

'I was hoping that you might tell me that.'

There was a long pause. Nicholas searched his face but it remained impassive. One thing was clear. Balthasar Davey was not responding to any request from Lord Westfield. Their patron's wishes carried no weight in Flushing. Inside his jerkin, Nicholas still had the pouch which had been entrusted to him. He suspected that his companion might have some idea what it contained.

'You will enjoy your time in Bohemia,' said Davey, trying to inject a note of optimism. 'I am sure that Westfield's Men will be a resounding success at the Imperial Court.'

'Have you been to Prague?'

'Indeed, I have. Some years ago, with Sir Robert. We both have fond memories of Bohemia. You will be well-received there. All the more reason why you should not linger here. It will be a very long journey.'

'We are braced against that,' said Nicholas. 'And this is by no means our first tour. We are used to travelling along endless roads in England.'

'You will find this expedition far more taxing,' warned Davey. 'And you will stop to give performances on the way. Even with sturdy horses pulling the wagons, it will take you weeks to reach Bohemia.'

'We are very grateful to you for providing such good transport. Why have you done so?'

'It was requested.'

'By Lord Westfield?'

'Who else?' said the other without a trace of irony.

Nicholas glanced towards the taproom. 'I talked with some of the English soldiers in there last night. They were very bitter about this war.'

'Not without cause, alas.'

'Their main complaint was a shortage of food and money. They also railed against a lack of munitions. They were hired to join the garrison here but arrived to find no quarters. My question is this, Master Davey. If the situation here is so desperate, how can you find the money to furnish us with a comfortable lodging before sending us on our way with wagons and horses that could be more profitably engaged in moving supplies?'

The secretary weighed his words carefully before replying.

'You are a perceptive man, Nicholas Bracewell.'

'We are not entirely ignorant of what has been going on here. Word trickles back to England. London hears all the rumours.'

'That's all most of them are. Rumours. False reports.'

'You have not answered my question.'

'Westfield's Men answered it for you this afternoon.'

'Did they?'

'You heard those same soldiers,' recalled Davey. 'They had real pleasure for the first time in months. Your play was a feast of entertainment which helped them to forget the war completely for a couple of hours.'

'That was our intention when we chose *Mirth and Madness.*'

'You are not the first to offer such distraction.'

'The first?'

'I served in the household of the Earl of Leicester for a time,' said Davey wistfully. 'It was an honour that I will always treasure. That is how I first came to Flushing. When the Earl arrived here to lead the army, I was part of a train which included lawyers, secretaries, chaplains, musicians, and acrobats. Yes, and players, too. Will Kempe among them.'

'Kempe?' said Nicholas in surprise.

'You know his pedigree.'

'All of London is aware of it.'

'Kempe is the equal of your own Barnaby Gill. A born jester who could raise laughter on a battlefield, if need be, with one of his jigs. He played his part in this war.'

'So did we, Master Davey, and we were proud to do so. But we were only briefly your guests. No host has ever spent so much money and care on us as you have done. I ask again. Why?'

'I was obeying a request.'

'Still from Lord Westfield?'

'Who else?'

Nicholas gave up. The secretary was too elusive for him. Balthasar Davey could play games with words all day long and he would always best Nicholas. The visitor rose to leave.

'I will return early tomorrow to bid you farewell.'

'How do you know that we will go?' asked Nicholas.

'Because you know the folly of staying. I will bring a map with me. It will be very crude because I am no artist, but it will show you the route you must take.'

'Thank you.'

Davey offered his hand and Nicholas stood up to shake it. There was a hint of genuine regret in the former's eye.

'I am sorry this had to happen,' he said.

'We held Adrian Smallwood in high regard.'

'Mourn him accordingly.'

'We will.'

Davey regarded the other shrewdly. 'It is a pity that you have to depart from the town, Nicholas Bracewell,' he said. 'I should like to have known you better.' He moved away but a sudden thought detained him at the door. 'Your chambers here were searched during the performance.'

'That is so.'

'Was anything taken?'

'Nothing.'

'So the thief searched for something he could not find.'

'Apparently.'

'It is still in your possession, therefore?'

'What are you talking about, Master Davey?'

'You are the ablest man in the company. It must be you. One more reason for you to ride out of Flushing tomorrow.'

'One more reason?'

'To save your life,' said Davey softly. 'I believe that the villain made a mistake. He did not intend to kill Adrian Smallwood at all. Your friend died because of his unfortunate resemblance to someone else. The murderer was really stalking Nicholas Bracewell.'

Westfield's Men sat around a table strewn with pitchers of ale and traded maudlin reminiscences of their dead colleague. Adrian Smallwood had been snatched away from them just as they were coming to appreciate his qualities as a member of the company. Notwithstanding his egoism, Lawrence Firethorn did notice the performances around him on stage and he was ready to pay generous tribute where he felt it was deserved.

'Adrian was a fine actor,' he said fondly. 'You could not fault his voice, his movement or his gestures. Even in minor roles, he had a real presence. Had he stayed with us, Adrian might have looked to become a sharer one day.'

'I will miss his companionship,' said Owen Elias. 'It is rare for a man to fall in so easily with his fellows. Adrian seemed to have been with Westfield's Men for years.'

'Would that he had!' sighed Edmund Hoode. 'It would have made my task as a playwright a trifle easier.'

'How so?' asked Firethorn.

'When I pick up my quill, I have to tailor the parts to suit the talents of the company. It would not have been so with Adrian. He could play anything—a lovesick shepherd, a scheming cardinal, a noble duke, a miserable beggar, a young gallant, an old greybeard, an Italian prince or a Flemish pieman; they were all grist to his mill.'

'I could play all those parts with equal skill,' boasted Barnaby Gill. 'And many more besides.'

'True, Barnaby. But even you could not have portrayed the sturdy woodcutter in *Double Deceit*. Adrian made that role his own. You do not have the height or build for the part.'

'I can act height. I can dissemble build.'

'We are not talking about you,' said Elias impatiently. 'Adrian was the more complete actor and that is that.'

'He was a mere hired man,' said Gill with a sniff.

'You are unjust to his memory,' chided James Ingram. 'Have you so soon forgot how he cheered us on the voyage by making us sing? He showed true leadership that day.'

'Which is more than you have ever shown, Barnaby,' added Firethorn. 'The poor fellow is dead. Brutally slain. Does not that mean anything to you?'

'Yes,' retorted Gill. 'It means that I will not sleep soundly in my bed as long as we are in this dreadful country. One of us has already been killed. Who is next? Supposing that the villain murdered me?'

'I would happily join in the applause.'

'That is a most callous remark, Lawrence.'

'Callous but honest. Show some respect to Adrian.'

'It was not my decision to bring him with us.'

'No, you were trying to force Clement Islip upon us.'

'Had Clement been here,' said Gill defensively, 'this would not have happened. He was more wary. Clement would never have turned his back to an armed assailant.'

'He would be too busy turning his back to *you*,' growled Firethorn. 'That is why you wanted to take that lisping milksop along with us. To face the same way as Clement in the bedchamber and satisfy your unnatural desires.'

'That is obscene!'

Gill leaped to his feet in a state of uncontrollable agitation and jabbered wildly, waving his arms, stamping his feet and rolling his eyes as if trying to dislodge them from their sockets. Firethorn goaded him on, Elias chuckled, Hoode tried to intervene, Ingram reminded everyone that they were there to mourn a friend and the other members of the company looked on with a mixture of amusement and sadness.

The argument was still at its height when Nicholas walked in. He stared at them with unfeigned disgust. Even the hysterical Gill was silenced by the book-holder's smouldering anger. Nicholas rarely lost his temper but he was clearly on the point of doing so now.

'Will you bicker like silly children?' he said. 'Adrian Smallwood lies dead on a stone slab not a few hundred yards away and you wrangle here regardless. Was he murdered in vain? Must you dishonour his memory in this shameful way? Can you not even raise a passing sigh for the loss of a good friend?'

Westfield's Men shifted uneasily in their seats.

'You are right to censure us, Nick,' said Firethorn at length. 'I must take the lion's share of the blame. It was I who provoked this quarrel.' He turned to Gill and took a deep breath before speaking. 'I owe you an apology, Barnaby.'

'I feel that I owe Adrian Smallwood an apology,' said the other pensively. 'He deserves our profoundest sympathy. He was indeed a competent actor. But I would still have brought Clement Islip in his stead.' He looked solemnly around the table. 'Gentlemen, I bid you good night.'

'Perhaps it is time for all of us to take to our beds,' suggested Elias as Gill walked away. 'We have drunk more than enough for one night. Let us grieve over Adrian in the morning with kinder hearts and clearer heads.'

The Welshman led the slow departure from the table. Only Firethorn remained. Seeing that Nicholas wished to talk to him alone, he motioned the latter to sit beside him.

'Forgive our behaviour, Nick. We do care about Adrian.'

'I know.'

'Do they have any notion who the killer may be?'

'None as yet.'

'What action has been taken to track him down?'

'Master Davey would not give me details.'

'Stabbed to death in broad daylight! And only minutes after he had helped to give such pleasure on the stage. It beggars belief! Who could do such a thing to Adrian? And why?'

'That is what I came to discuss.'

Nicholas looked around the room to make sure that nobody was within earshot. The place was fairly full but the other customers seemed to be locked into their own conversations. Taking no chances, Nicholas dropped his voice as a precaution.

'Do you recall the pouch you gave me for safekeeping?'

'Very well,' said Firethorn.

'That is what he was after.'

'Who?'

'The murderer. He first ransacked our chambers. When he could not find the pouch there, he followed Adrian into the stable and killed him.'

Firethorn was stunned. 'How do you know?'

'It is the only explanation that fits the facts.'

'But Adrian did not have the pouch.'

'The assassin thought that he did,' argued Nicholas. 'My guess is that he knocked Adrian senseless from behind, then tore off his jerkin to search it. Adrian was a strong young man. Even a savage blow like that would not keep him unconscious for long. He may have groaned for help, even tried to rise. The dagger was used to finish him off.'

'I am quite confused here, Nick.'

'The confusion was in the mind of the killer.'

'Why should he imagine that Adrian had the pouch?'

'He did not,' said Nicholas. 'He knew that it was in my possession. In some ways, Adrian and I might have been twins. In *Mirth and Madness,* he was wearing a buff jerkin much like this one of mine. The killer mistook him for me.'

'You were the intended victim?' gasped Firethorn.

'I believe so. Why should anyone stab a harmless young actor to death? There was no motive. Had I been cut down in that stable, the motive would have been all too clear.'

'Nick, dear heart!' exclaimed Firethorn, embracing him impulsively. 'We came that close to losing the very foundation of our company? Can this be true?'

'Unhappily, it can. The Governor's secretary confirmed it.'

'Balthasar Davey?'

'The idea had already crossed my mind but I chose to resist it at first. I had guilt enough over Adrian's murder. To know that he died in place of me is a chilling thought. I am overcome with remorse.'

'You mentioned the secretary.'

'Yes,' said Nicholas. 'Master Davey has an acute brain. He reached the same conclusion. Adrian Smallwood was killed by a man in search of the pouch I carry.'

'But the existence of that pouch is a secret,' said Firethorn in alarm. 'How does Master Davey know about it?'

'He knows far more than we.'

'It was entrusted to me and I gave it privily to you. Who told the willing secretary that it was in your charge?'

'You did, I fear.'

'I never breathed a word on the subject.'

'You did not need to,' soothed Nicholas. 'Master Davey made his own deductions. That was the reason you were invited to the Governor's house yesterday.'

'We were guests of honour. Sir Robert praised my work.'

'Deservedly so. But while the Governor was enjoying your company, his secretary was no doubt watching you carefully to decide if the pouch you had been given was somewhere about your person. He realised it was not.'

Firethorn gave a hollow laugh. 'Am I so easy to read?' he said. 'Can I fool a thousand spectators with a performance and yet be found out by Balthasar Davey? Alas, I can. I was an open book. He saw me in my cups. One more vain actor, crowing upon the dunghill of his achievements. Far too irresponsible to look after secret documents by himself. My behaviour told him all that he needed to know. The pouch was in your capable hands.'

'That intelligence came later,' suggested Nicholas. 'He surmised that you had given the pouch to someone else in the company. Master Davey's conjecture fell on me.'

'What of the killer?'

'He, too, came around to the same name.'

'Nicholas Bracewell.'

'He followed us from England on the *Peppercorn* and bided his time. Anne overheard his murderous intent but not the identity of his victim. It is probably just as well. Had she known that I was in such danger, she would have been sorely vexed on her journey to Amsterdam.'

'What is in that damnable pouch?' wondered Firethorn.

'Something of great value, it seems.'

'It has already cost us one life, Nick. I'll not let it rob us off another. My book-holder is far more precious to me than any secret documents.' He held out his hand. 'Give me the pouch. I'll take it straight to Sir Robert

Sidney and ask him to send it to Prague by official messenger.'

'That is the last thing you must do.'

'Why?'

'We have been entrusted with an important duty. If the documents could have been sent by any other means, they would have been. Westfield's Men were considered to be the safest couriers.'

'Safest! It has made us anything but safe, Nick.'

'We must still deliver the pouch to Doctor Talbot Royden.'

'We are more likely to deliver another dead body to a hole in the ground. And the chances are that it may be yours. I will not take that risk.'

'I will,' said Nicholas firmly.

'Why?'

'Because it is the only way to find Adrian's killer.'

'Will you invite destruction?'

'I must. I want him.'

Bowing to expediency, Westfield's Men decided to leave on the following morning. They wanted to stay for the funeral, but loyalty to Adrian Smallwood had to be weighed in the balance against practicalities. Bohemia was their final destination and they had been asked to arrive in Prague by a specific date. A delay of some days in Flushing would make it difficult for them to comply with that request, and they did not wish to linger in a town that was so redolent of the horrors of war.

The English presence was reluctantly tolerated by the local burghers and openly resented by ordinary townspeople. Younger members of the community expressed their animosity in a more obvious way. While the company was loading its two wagons outside the inn, a group of children came to spit at them and make obscene gestures. The mirth and madness of the previous day had been supplanted by a more usual rancour.

The well-bred James Ingram was shocked by the display.

'Why do they hate us?' he asked in dismay. 'We are fighting in this war on their side.'

'And occupying their town,' Elias pointed out.

'An army must have a garrison.'

'These children are too young to understand that, James. All they see is an invasion by uncouth soldiers, who strut about their streets and lust after their mothers and sisters. In their eyes, we are just another set of filthy interlopers.' He looked across at the jeering gang. 'I have a lot of sympathy for them.'

'Sympathy?' Ingram was astonished. 'With that behaviour?'

'It is no worse than some of the things I did at their age. You forget that I was born in a country that has seen more than its share of English soldiers. Wales did not seek the Act of Union any more than these lads sought to hand over their town to foreigners.' He clapped his friend on the shoulder. 'Ignore them, James. Every actor must endure a hostile audience from time to time.'

They continued to help with the loading. Both men wore a sword and dagger, as did most of the company. The death of their colleague had put them all on guard. Nicholas Bracewell and Lawrence Firethorn were the only ones with an awareness of the likely motive behind the murder and they resolved to keep it that way. If the others realised that they were carrying documents which made them vulnerable to further attack, they would be sent into a communal panic.

When the company were ready for departure, Balthasar Davey rode up with two soldiers in attendance. He reined in his horse beside Nicholas and Firethorn.

'I am glad to see that you took my advice,' said Davey.

Nicholas sighed. 'It was not an easy decision.'

'But it has been taken,' said Firethorn briskly. 'There is nothing to keep us here now. We are keen to ride out of such an unfriendly town.'

'I am sorry that our welcome turned sour,' said Davey with an apologetic shrug. 'We tried to make your visit here as pleasant as was possible in the circumstances. You certainly lifted our hearts with your play and for that we are truly grateful.' He indicated his companions. 'I have brought you some guides to escort you a few miles out of the town and set you on the right road. Beyond that point, you will be on your own, but this may be useful to you.' He took a folded sheet of parchment from his belt and handed it to Nicholas. 'It is the map I promised. With the names of towns or wayside inns where you may conveniently break your journey.'

'Thank you, Master Davey.'

'You have been a kindly host,' said Firethorn with a hint of irony, 'but we well understand why you wish to speed our departure. Farewell, sir.'

'Adieu!' replied Davey, quite unruffled. 'Sir Robert sends his compliments and wishes you a safe journey. Do not fret over Adrian Smallwood.

I will make sure that he is buried with honour and you may pay your respects at his grave when you return to Flushing.'

'We are ever in your debt,' said Nicholas.

He climbed into the first of the wagons and took up the reins. James Ingram was beside him while Edmund Hoode sat among the baggage with George Dart and the apprentices. The rest of the company were travelling in the second wagon. Owen Elias was its appointed driver, with Firethorn at his side. It was not a happy departure. Westfield's Men had fond memories of their fallen comrade and those memories would be ignited when the little cavalcade went past the church where Adrian Smallwood lay on a cold and lonely slab.

Balthasar Davey watched them set off. Led by their two guides, and accompanied by the cruel gibes of the Dutch children running after them, the wagons rolled forward on the first stage of their onerous journey to Bohemia.

Thanks to the ease of their task, the horses kept up a steady pace without effort. They were accustomed to dragging carts that were crammed with men and munitions. Hearts were heavy in the wagons, but the loads were comparatively light for the two powerful animals between each set of shafts. It was not long before the two soldiers wheeled off the road and gestured for the travellers to continue. Westfield's Men rumbled on into open country. They were on their own now.

Nicholas kept glancing over his shoulder to make sure that they were not being followed, but there was no shadowing horseman behind the second wagon. He felt a sense of relief. There was safety in numbers and he would not be in danger while he was surrounded by his fellows. At the same time, he sensed that the murderer was too determined a man to give up the search he had undertaken. Sooner or later, he would be back.

What Nicholas did see were the gloomy expressions on the faces of his passengers. Edmund Hoode was so laden with sadness that he might have been meditating on his latest doomed love affair, and the four boisterous apprentices, who chatted incessantly on most days, were strangely silent on this one. Three of them were managing to hold back tears but Richard Honeydew was weeping enough for the whole quartet. His cherubic face was glistening, his mouth agape with despair. Nicholas handed the reins to Ingram and beckoned the boy to come to him. Richard Honeydew was lifted bodily and placed between the two men.

'Take heart, Dick,' said Nicholas, an arm around him.

'I miss Adrian.'

'So do we all. Dreadfully.'

'He was kind to me,' bleated the boy. 'Like you. He took an interest in me. Adrian was teaching me to play the lute. He was such a gifted musician. Truly, I had so much pleasure from that instrument.'

'You will do so again, Dick.'

'How can I? My tutor is dead.'

He succumbed to a fresh burst of tears and Nicholas held him tight for a few minutes. The book-holder then reached into the back of the wagon. He lifted up an object which he had wrapped carefully in soft material. Nicholas set it down in the boy's lap.

'Here, lad. Take this to give you some small cheer.'

'What is it?'

'See for yourself.'

Honeydew began to remove the material and soon realised what he was holding in his hands. He was overjoyed.

'Adrian's lute!'

'He would have wanted you to have it.'

'But it is far too costly for me to buy.'

'It is an heirloom. It carries no price.'

'And is it really mine?'

'Only if you promise to practice on it diligently.'

'Every day!'

'That is what Adrian would have expected of you.'

The boy was completely overwhelmed by the gift. He held it with the tender care of a mother holding a baby. When he plucked at the strings, he gave a sudden laugh of disbelief. Adrian Smallwood had gone but he would at least have something by which to remember him. His tears began to dry in the sun.

Nicholas was pleased to be able to offer him some solace. A murder which had shaken the hardiest of them had devastated the apprentice. Richard Honeydew was habitually teased by the other three boys because they envied his superior talent. In Smallwood, he had found someone who rescued him from their mockery. Nicholas tried to keep a paternal eye on the lad, but his duties as book-holder consumed much of his time and attention. The lute was a tiny recompense for the loss of its owner but it brought Honeydew unexpected delight. Nicholas made no mention of the blood he had washed off the instrument.

James Ingram was glad to surrender the reins to Nicholas again. Keeping the two horses trotting along at a comfortable pace was not as easy as his friend made it look. The animals took advantage of an inexperienced driver and the wagon swayed all over the road. Nicholas soon imposed his control on them. The landscape was flat and fertile, allowing them to see for miles in all directions. The road was no more than a rutted track but it was dry and hard beneath their wheels.

Richard Honeydew slowly recovered his curiosity.

'Are we in Germany yet?' he asked, nursing the lute.

'No,' said Nicholas. 'Nor shall we be by nightfall. We will not reach the border until well into tomorrow and there may still be days before we arrive in Cologne.'

'Will they let us perform there?'

'We hope so, Dick.'

'I am afeard they will not like us.'

'Remember the dictum of Master Firethorn,' said Ingram. 'It is the duty of an actor to *make* an audience like him. As we did in Flushing.'

Honeydew tensed. 'The audience may have liked us but the townspeople did not. Those Dutch boys hated us. Will it be any different in Cologne?'

'So we are led to believe,' said Nicholas. 'The Emperor himself urged us to visit the city and promised to warn them in advance of our coming. It is not some crowded little seaport like Flushing. Cologne is one of the largest cities in the Empire, famed for its beauty. Is that not true, James?'

Ingram nodded. 'So I have heard tell.'

'But we are *English*,' observed the boy.

'That is part of our appeal. Foreigners arouse curiosity.'

'It goes deeper than that, James,' said Nicholas. 'A few English companies have been here before us and made a very favourable impression. Theatre is a serious profession in London. It is not so in Cologne or Frankfurt or any of the other places we visit. The quality of our plays and players sets us well above anything else they may have seen. Only companies from Spain or Italy could compete with us and they do not have an Edmund Hoode to devise wonderful dramas. Nor do they have actors as accomplished as Lawrence Firethorn, Barnaby Gill, Owen Elias or James Ingram here.'

'You over-praise me, Nick,' said Ingram modestly.

'Your time will come, James.'

'My fear was of another kind,' explained Honeydew.

'Fear?'

'Yes. We are English, they are German. We speak one language, they speak another. We follow one religion, they hold to a different faith. Will not all this drive us apart?'

'Who knows?' said Nicholas. 'We must take our hosts as we find them and trust that they will overlook our faults. From what I hear—and that is not much—there has been a great upheaval in Germany over the question of religion. The Pope still rules firmly in some areas, but others have been yielded to the Lutherans, the Calvinists, and sects whose names and creeds I do not even know. It behoves us to tread warily.'

A sound like the report of a musket startled them. Lawrence Firethorn had given a full-throated yell. Bored with the leisurely pace at which they were moving, he seized the reins from Owen Elias and cracked the whip of his voice at the two bay mares pulling his wagon. The vehicle lurched straight into life, swung crazily out to one side of the road and went thundering past its companion. Firethorn roared with laughter and challenged the other wagon to catch him. With a sharp flick of the reins, Nicholas goaded his own horses into a canter and the race was on.

Passengers in both wagons were happy to trade discomfort for exhilaration. Each time a wheel hit one of the frequent potholes, they were violently bounced and shaken, yet they still urged their respective drivers on. Firethorn was in his element, crackling with vitality, laughing madly and handling his horses with the reckless bravery of a Roman charioteer. Nicholas was a more skillful but cautious driver, who was content to keep his wagon within easy reach of his rival's without endangering his passengers by a foolish attempt to overtake at such speed.

When they saw the two vehicles hurtling towards them, other travellers quickly got out of the way. Three carts were driven off the road, horsemen were scattered, and a group of ambling peasants dived into some bushes for cover. The race continued for well over a mile, until a ford provided a natural finishing post. As his horses splashed through the water, it acted as a brake on the wagon and Firethorn did not need to heave too hard in the reins to bring his animals to a halt on the bank. Nicholas was soon drawing up beside him.

'We needed to wake ourselves up, Nick,' said Firethorn, hopping to the ground. 'The weight of gloom was slowing us down and I sought to cast some of it off.'

'We proved one thing,' said Nicholas. 'Our horses are sound in wind and limb. They enjoyed the race as much as us. I think they deserve a rest.'

'So do we.'

While the horses were watered, the company jumped out of the wagons to stretch their legs, compare bruises, satisfy the wants of nature and eat some of the fruit which they had brought with them. Richard Honeydew sat with his back against a tree and practised for the first time on his own lute. Two of the other apprentices had a playful fight. Owen Elias went upstream to see if his quick hand could catch a fish or two. Dusting off his doublet and hose, Barnaby Gill wished that he had stayed in London with a certain young musician. James Ingram's thoughts were still with their murdered colleague.

When it was time to move on, Firethorn first called them together so that he could impart his vision.

'Gentlemen,' he said soulfully, 'we have suffered pain and sadness thus far. We have lost a cherished friend and were forced to leave him behind to be buried in foreign soil. You all know his virtues. Adrian Smallwood will never be forgotten by any of us. But he was first and foremost an actor, and he would not wish his death to leave a lasting grief. Adrian was proud of Westfield's Men. Let us resolve to justify that pride by giving of our best in the true tradition of this company.' He struck his Hector of Troy pose. 'Do not look back. Forward lies our road. Destination is all. Remember where and why we are bound. Westfield's Men are to be honoured guests at the Court of Emperor Rudolph. Let that inspire you. Do not trudge there with spirits low and heads hung down. March into Prague like conquerors. The city is there for the taking!' He smiled inwardly. And so, he thought to himself, is the fair maid of Bohemia. She is mine!

When they slipped across the German border on the following day, Firethorn's speech still echoed in their ears and they were excited by the thought that they had just entered the Holy Roman Empire. Most of them took the grandiose name at face value and had no conception of the chaos that lay behind it. It would be some time before they learned that Germany was a bewildering mass of electorates, principalities, duchies and prince-bishoprics, owing their allegiance less to the Emperor than to various religious and political factions. Westfield's Men were innocent children in an enchanted forest filled with invisible wolves.

Days took on a fixed pattern. They would set out at dawn and vary their speed until noon. After rest and refreshment, they would press on until early evening before taking another break. A final push before nightfall took them to one of the capacious German inns, where food was served in huge quantities and where local inhabitants were often in a state of permanent drunkenness. They slept in large rooms that contained several beds or mattresses, grouped around a central stove of such size and significance that they were grateful they were not there during the winter. Germany in the snow was evidently a traveller's ordeal.

In the summer, it was a constant delight, with verdant meadows, rolling hills, rich woodland, sparkling streams and sunlit vineyards to catch the eye. Towns and villages were picturesque but solidly built, a compromise between romance and reality that reflected something of the German character. To the gaping visitors, who had never been outside England before, it was enthralling. To Nicholas Bracewell, who had voyaged around the whole world, it was still fascinating.

Firethorn did not waste their time on the road. While he savoured with the others the pleasures of the traveller, he kept their mission firmly before their gaze. Every journey was a rehearsal of a play, every wayside stop an opportunity to practice dances or to stage fights. Westfield's Men worked hard to keep their repertoire in a state of good repair because they knew it would be put under the closest scrutiny.

While rehearsals shaped each day, it was something else which gave them direction. The Rhine was a revelation to the newcomers, a majestic waterway which rose in the Swiss Alps and wended its way for over eight hundred miles until it fed into the North Sea. Like the Thames, it was a main thoroughfare, with sailing ships, barges, ferries, hoys, fishing-smacks and rowing-boats riding on it in profusion. There was a slow, unhurried, timeless quality about the Rhine. Along both banks, at points of scenic beauty or strategic importance, it had a succession of charming little towns and quaint villages. Nicholas felt a pang of regret that Anne Hendrik was not there to share such sights with him.

The river was their guide. Whether looping capriciously or running straight for miles, it eventually took them to their destination. When they got their first sight of the city, they brought the wagons to a halt and stood to marvel at what lay ahead. Nothing had prepared them for the glory that was Cologne. It was dazzling. Built on a graceful curve in the Rhine, it was an ancient city which had once been the largest in Germany and one of the wealthiest in Christendom. Much of its grandeur still clung to it like robes of tissued gold.

London might be bigger, especially now that it was pushing out into ever-widening suburbs, but they only ever saw the capital from the inside. They had absorbed its impact and taken its wonders for granted. Cologne was different. It was a dignified city of high towers, soaring steeples, fine houses and stately civic buildings, standing respectfully in the shadow of a mighty cathedral whose Gothic extravagance made Saint Paul's look plain and homely and whose spire rose to a height which dwarfed its London counterpart. Westfield's Men were struck dumb when they saw how much time, energy, money, love and sublime artistry had been dedicated to the service of God. Cologne Cathedral was a monument to centuries of belief.

It was still the centre of a vigorous Christianity and they could hear dozens of bells chiming even at that distance.

'Cologne is a Roman Catholic city,' warned Nicholas. 'We must be very careful what we say and how we behave.'

'We are here to entertain them,' stressed Firethorn, 'and not to convert them. Nor should we let them convert us to their Popish practices.'

'It is magnificent!' sighed Hoode, still wide-eyed.

'Ha!' snorted Gill.' All that I see is a crumbling mausoleum of the Old Religion. And are we to debase ourselves by offering them our plays? It is an insult to my faith.'

'The only Superior Being in your life is yourself,' said Firethorn sharply. 'When we perform at the Queen's Head, we share our bounty among Anglicans, Roman Catholics, Huguenots, Calvinists, Jews, Anabaptists, Atheists and creeping Puritans who come to sneer at our work. Theatre serves all religions. Even the God-forsaken will not be turned away by us.'

With Gill silenced, the wagons rolled on once more and they were able to take a closer inventory of Cologne. The city was fronted by several wharves and there were so many craft at anchor that it was almost possible to use them as stepping-stones to the opposite bank. Originally built on the western bank, the capital of the Rhineland had long since outgrown its fortified walls and spread out in an easterly direction. The river both divided the two parts of the city and joined them closely together.

Driving the first wagon, Nicholas led the way through the crowded streets in search of the inn recommended by Balthasar Davey. The secretary's advice had been trustworthy so far. His choice of the White Cross had to be respected. While the book-holder was concerned with finding a place to stay, the actor-manager wanted to let the whole city know that they had arrived. Standing in his flamboyant apparel in the rear of the second wagon, he declaimed a martial speech to the tallest spires. A drum was beaten, a trumpet blared, the actors went into an elaborate mime and everyone knew that the players had come to Cologne.

The stocky man in the garb of a merchant did not need to be told that they were coming. He was lounging outside the White Cross as the two wagons rumbled around the corner. His presence went completely unnoticed by the newcomers. Nicholas Bracewell had glanced over his shoulder many times during the journey but he never thought to look in front of him.

Someone was waiting for them.

[CHAPTER SIX]

Fortune favoured them at last. After suffering the rigours of the voyage, the cruel loss of one of their number and the cumulative fatigue of long days on the road, they found some warm consolation awaiting them in Cologne. It was Nicholas Bracewell who made the discovery. Lawrence Firethorn sent him off to the Burgomaster to seek permission for Westfield's Men to play in the city. Nicholas could not have had a more positive response.

A big, fleshy man with a rubicund face, the Burgomaster wore a resplendent mayoral chain of solid gold which rested on his expansive paunch. Whenever he laughed, the chain bobbed merrily up and down. He oozed wealth and well-being. His command of English was uncertain and his accent guttural but he made himself understood.

'Willkommen, Herr Bracewell!' he said, pumping Nicholas's hand. 'The English comedians always we like to see in Köln. Lovely city, ja? How long you stay?'

'Only for a few days, I fear.'

'Is all?'

'We have to ride on.'

'Where you go?'

'Frankfurt am Main,' explained Nicholas. 'After a short stay there, we go on to Eisenach, Weimar and Prague. That is our main destination. Westfield's Men have been invited to play for two weeks at the Imperial Court.'

'Wunderbar!' said the other, chortling with approval and making his chain rattle. 'Is big honour. You play the comedy for our Emperor, ja? Good.'

'Did you not know of our visit?'

'Nein.'

'In his letter, the Emperor said that he would write to tell you that we were coming here.'

'Emperor Rudolph,' said the other with a philosophical shrug, 'he forgot. Many things he promise, he not remembers. On the fringe of the Empire, Köln is. Prague, long way, ja?' His chuckle returned to set his chain in motion again. 'No matter. We pleased here to see Wizzfeld's Men.'

'Westfield's,' corrected Nicholas politely. 'Lord Westfield is our patron and he secured our passport to travel abroad and play where we could find an audience.'

'Here, an audience you have.'

'We are very grateful.'

'Köln thanks you. Wizzfeld's Men is famous. The Emperor invite them. We must see them also, ja?'

'We are at your disposal,' said Nicholas deferentially.

'Natürlich!'

The genial Burgomaster went off into a peal of laughter and his chain bobbed once more. They were in the Council Chamber at the imposing Rathaus, the town hall where civic business was conducted. It was a spacious room with a vast table in it. The Burgomaster was built on the right scale for such a place. A smaller man would have been dwarfed to insignificance. Nicholas was delighted with the cordial reception he had been given. It was a good omen. His host was friendly and willing to help in any way. Nicholas took the opportunity to find out as much as he could about Cologne and its relation to the Empire. The Burgomaster talked fondly about the former but more guardedly about the latter. Nicholas garnered invaluable information.

When the discussion was over, he hastened back through the streets to the White Cross. It was early evening and most of Westfield's Men were washing down a large meal with mugs of German beer. Owen Elias was making his companions laugh wildly at his anecdotes. Nicholas was pleased to step into a happier atmosphere. They had not forgotten Adrian Smallwood but they had managed to put the horror of his murder behind them. Lawrence Firethorn beckoned his book-holder across to the table he shared with Barnaby Gill. Both men were anxious to hear the tidings.

'Well?' prompted Firethorn. 'What happened?'

'Westfield's Men are welcome in Cologne.'

'Did you mention my name, Nick?'

'Several times,' lied the other.

'And mine, I trust?' asked Gill.

'Of course. We are to give two performances here.'

'Where?' said Firethorn.

'The first will be in a public place and the Burgomaster himself will be there with the entire Council and their wives. The audience could be of considerable size.'

'Was payment mentioned?'

'We are allowed to charge admission.'

'This is excellent news!'

'The second performance will be at the palace,' said Nicholas. 'The Duke of Bavaria and other important guests are visiting Cologne, so we will have distinguished spectators. It pleased the Burgomaster that we gave him first call on the services of Westfield's Men.'

'Why?' asked Gill.

'Cologne is ruled by the Archbishop. He is also the Elector and thus wields temporal as well as spiritual power. The Burgomaster feels that he and his Council are the true government. There is great rivalry between the citizens and the Archbishop. The spirit of Hermann Grein lives on.'

'Who?'

'Hermann Grein,' repeated Nicholas. 'He lived hundreds of years ago but the Burgomaster talked about him as if he were still alive. When he was himself Burgomaster, this Hermann Grein won a victory over one Archbishop Engelbert here in Cologne. The Archbishop wanted revenge. Burgomaster Grein was invited to the monastery for a conference. The monks kept various wild animals there, including a lion. Two canons trapped the Burgomaster in a courtyard with the lion. If the man had not been wearing his sword, he would have been torn to pieces. He fought bravely enough to kill the animal but was savagely mauled and nearly died.'

'Did the poor wretch survive?' said Firethorn.

'By the grace of God, he did. The citizens of Cologne rescued him. Growing suspicious, they forced their way into the monastery and recovered their Burgomaster in time. The two canons involved in the plot were hanged at the monastery gate and Hermann Grein was slowly nursed back to health.'

'An amusing-enough story,' said Gill with a yawn, 'but what bearing does it have on us?'

'A fair amount,' replied Nicholas levelly. 'It helps to dictate our choice of play. The rivalry between the citizens and the Archbishop may not be as deadly as in the days of Burgomaster Grein, but it is still there. We would be foolish to stage a play which sets Church against Commonalty, and there are two or three in our repertoire.'

'A timely warning, Nick,' said Firethorn gratefully. 'We do not wish to fan the flames of any dispute in the city. 'Tis a pity we lack the actors to play *The Knights of Malta*. That would delight both citizens and Archbishop.'

'Bore them, rather,' said Gill contemptuously. 'Your Grand Master would send the whole of Cologne to sleep.'

'I will send you to sleep in a moment,' retorted the other, fingering his dagger. 'For all eternity.'

'*The Knights of Malta* will not serve here,' argued Nicholas quietly. 'A play about the Turkish menace would not be the wisest choice. It is too close to the truth. The Turks are attacking the eastern border of the Empire even though they have signed a peace treaty. The people of Cologne may not wish to be reminded of that distant threat. Comedy is in request yet again, I think.'

'And so do I,' added Gill. '*Cupid's Folly*, it must be.'

'That would be folly indeed!' sneered Firethorn.

'They want laughter, song, dance. They want *me*.'

'Even drunken Germans cannot be that misguided!'

The familiar bickering began again and Nicholas left them to it. Stealing away from the table, he walked towards the figure he had noticed on his own in the far corner. It was Edmund Hoode, crouched over a sheet of parchment with a quill in his hand. The pen was hovering indecisively.

'How now, Edmund?' said his friend, lowering himself onto the stool opposite. 'Is your teeming brain at work on *The Fair Maid of Bohemia*?'

'If only it were, Nick!' sighed the other.

'What is amiss?'

'My Muse has deserted me.'

'You always say that.'

'This time, it is true. My mind is empty. The storehouse of my imagination is bare. The mice scamper around in there, unable to find even the tiniest crumbs.'

'You are tired, that is all,' reassured Nicholas. 'The journey has taxed each one of us. A good night's sleep will soon revive you and fill that storehouse until it bursts apart with fresh ideas.'

'No, Nick. I have written my last play.'

'Those words, too, have often been on your lips.'

'Never with more conviction.' He lifted both hands up in a gesture of despair. 'I have nothing new to say.'

'Novelty is not expected. All you have to do is to take an old play by Edmund Hoode and dress it in a clever disguise. You have fashioned such costumes a hundred times.'

'I have lost my needle and thread. Look,' he said, lifting the sheet of parchment in front of him, 'this is the fruit of two hours' work. All I have contrived to write is the title and the name of its misbegotten author. The chaste maid refuses to leave Wapping. She'll have none of Bohemia!'

He tossed the sheet over his shoulder with disgust and buried his face in his hands. Nicholas consoled him gently. It was a service he had often rendered and his touch was delicate. Hoode was slowly weaned away from his crippling melancholy. Nicholas waited until he had coaxed the first faint smile out of his friend before he made his offer.

'Let me help you,' he suggested.

'How?'

'Not as your co-author, that would be far too great a presumption on my part. I only wish to be a servant, who fetches and carries things for my master. I bring the bones of ideas, you put flesh upon them.'

'You do not know *The Chaste Maid of Wapping* well enough.'

'I know it as well as its author,' said Nicholas. 'Better than he at this moment. You forget how often I have seen it rehearsed and played. The first scene, for instance, could be transported to Bohemia with one simple device.'

'One?'

'If you are bold enough to use it.'

'What is it?' asked Hoode, interested at last.

'Pick up your pen and I will tell you.'

The drooping playwright took up his quill and dipped it into the inkwell before him. Once he began to write, his hand never paused for a second as a stream of ideas, images and daring concepts poured from Nicholas. Though not an author in his own right, he had a grasp of narrative and of theatrical effect that was the equal of any. Hoode's enthusiasm was brought quickly back to life again. Instead of simply listing his friend's comments about the play, he started to challenge, to criticise, to amend, to refine.

It was only a matter of time before his own creative juices flowed freely again. When he replaced the first page with a second, it was his imagination which made the pen dance across it. Nicholas was no longer needed. Hoode was talking to himself and hearing nobody else. The book-holder retrieved the discarded sheet of parchment from the floor and gazed around the room. Firethorn and Gill were still squabbling cheerfully, Elias was still carousing with the others, George Dart was slumbering over his beer again and the resident poet with Westfield's Men had been rescued from a pit of misery and filled with brimming confidence. It was once more the company he knew and loved. Nicholas was content.

When the actors eventually tumbled into their beds, they needed no lullaby to ease them asleep. They had spent several hours celebrating their arrival in Cologne and collapsed instantly beneath the joyous weight of their over-indulgence. As he lay awake in the darkness, Nicholas heard their individual snores merging into a general drone. While his companions sank into oblivion, he had too much to keep him awake.

Adrian Smallwood remained at the forefront of his mind. He had not only lost a staunch friend, he had seen a highly talented actor cut down in his prime. The sense of waste was overpowering. Nicholas was also distressed by his inability to do anything by way of recompense. Back in England, he could at least attempt to trace Smallwood's family in York and pass on the sad tidings, but it might be months before he was home in London again. Finding the killer was the only thing which would assuage his feelings of guilt and helplessness. That would take time, patience and a degree of sheer luck.

Anne Hendrik was another source of anxiety. She was an able woman with a good working knowledge of Dutch, but she was still a foreigner in a land not wholly amicable towards the English. Nicholas was certain that she would be welcomed in Amsterdam by the family into which she had been married, but how and with whom would she return to Flushing?

What sort of return voyage would she have? Was she missing him as painfully as he was now missing her? Where *was* she?

Nicholas was still asking that question when his eyelids finally closed for the night. He dozed peacefully but lightly. Sharing a bedchamber with seven of his fellows did not make him feel totally secure. Smallwood had been murdered while scores of people were at hand. The same killer would not be deterred by the presence of two apprentices and five snoring actors. Nicholas kept the dagger in his hand throughout the night. But it was not needed.

He awoke at dawn to the sound of carts and wagons rattling past in the street on their way to market. Cologne was a noisy city. Bells were soon ringing, voices were raised, dogs were barking and yelping. His companions slept untroubled through the morning's pandemonium but Nicholas was wide awake. He grappled with his concerns over the death of Adrian Smallwood and the safety of Anne Hendrik until a third person glided gently into his thoughts.

Doctor John Mordrake had entrusted him with a curious commission. Nicholas was employed to deliver a small wooden box to the very man to whom the secret documents were being sent. What connection did Mordrake have with the mysterious Talbot Royden? Why was he prepared to pay so handsomely to have his gift put into the latter's hands in Prague? Nicholas sat up with a start as a new consideration arose. He believed that Smallwood had been murdered in error by a man in search of the documents that he himself was carrying. Balthasar Davey shared that belief.

Supposing that they were both wrong? What if the killer was really after the wooden box? Mordrake's gift was also a form of secret document. Would someone commit a murder in order to seize it? Nicholas reached into his purse for the object and examined it in the half-dark. It looked so small and innocuous. Did it really have the power to kill one man and put the life of another in danger? Were its contents so lethal? The box suddenly felt like a lead weight in his palm. He put it quickly away.

With a performance due that afternoon, there was an immense amount of work for the book-holder to do. Fair weather was a crucial factor in an outdoor performance. Light was poking its fingers in through the cracks in the shutters, but that told him little about their chances of a fine day. Taking care not to disturb the others, he dressed in silence and crept out of the chamber. When he stepped into the stableyard, he saw that they had been blessed with dry weather. The sky was clear and only a faint breeze was trying to brush the wisps of straw across the ground.

Before he could go back into the inn, Nicholas experienced the sensation he had felt on the drive from Rammekins. He was being watched. He sensed that it was a hostile gaze. Instead of swinging around sharply to catch a glimpse of the man, he pretended to have noticed nothing untoward. He sauntered across to the pump in the middle of the yard and worked its arm to fill a bucket with water. Then he casually removed his jerkin to hang it on the corner of a wagon. With his back to the wagon, he dipped both hands into the cold water to sluice his face and beard. He made sure that he took longer than usual over his ablutions. After drying himself on a piece of sacking, he retrieved his jerkin and ambled into the building.

The stocky figure dodged the market traders in the street outside and hurried across to the Cardinal's Hat, a commodious inn chosen for its proximity to the White Cross. As he went upstairs, he congratulated himself on his opportunism. It had taken only a second to remove the document from the pocket which had been sewn inside the jerkin. His objective had been achieved without the need for more bloodshed.

Once inside his chamber, he locked the door and crossed to the window to get the best of the light. He tore the ribbon from the parchment and unfolded it eagerly. As he read the words on the paper, he reached into his pocket for the little notebook which he always carried with him. It listed a wide range of codes and ciphers. He was confident that he could soon unveil the secret message that lay behind the scrawled words. Then he read the document again and blenched.

THE FAIR MAID OF BOHEMIA

a comedy in five acts

by Edmund Hoode

Newly amended, corrected and enlarged from the tale of Nell Drayton, a chaste maid from Wrapping, stolen from her cradle at birth and forced into a life of drudgery until reunited with her noble family, thus showing the triumph of true love over setback and adversity.

Beneath the title of the play was a failed attempt to write a Prologue for it. The author was so dismayed with the poverty of his verse that he had slashed through every line with a vengeful quill. No secret message could be unlocked because it did not exist. What the man was holding was the sheet of paper which Edmund Hoode had discarded in a fit of self-disgust at the White Cross.

The fair maid now took even fouler punishment. Tearing the parchment to pieces, the man flung them to the floor and ground them beneath his heel as if killing some loathsome insects. His rage was short-lived. Realisation froze him to the spot. He had been duped. Nicholas Bracewell had deliberately allowed him to steal the document in order to draw him out of cover. The man was left empty-handed while the book-holder had gained two valuable pieces of information. He now knew for certain that he was being followed and that his shadow was after one thing.

The man smiled, then chuckled, then laughed at his own folly. He had been completely taken in by the ruse. Nicholas won a new respect from him. In the resourceful book-holder, the man had a worthy adversary. It would add more spice to his assignment. Westfield's Men would need to be trailed in a very different way from now on. Nicholas would be more wary than ever and the rest of the company would be alerted.

As he thought about the sturdy figure who had washed himself in the stableyard, the man's laughter took on a darker note. Instead of jeering at his own folly, he was savouring the pleasure of a duel with an able opponent. There would be no swift dagger-work in an empty stable this time. He wanted the utmost enjoyment from the death of Nicholas Bracewell.

The play which was set before the citizens of Cologne that afternoon was *Love and Fortune*. It was a compromise. Lawrence Firethorn was desperate to portray one of his gallery of tragic heroes and Barnaby Gill argued vehemently for *Cupid's Folly* because he took the leading role of Rigormortis in that pastoral comedy. Nicholas imposed a truce on the warring actors and guided them towards common ground. *Love and Fortune* gave Firethorn a part in which he could unleash both his thunder and his comic brilliance while Gill was appeased by his generous haul of songs and dances. As it was another staple drama of Westfield's Men, it needed no exhaustive rehearsal. They donned it like familiar apparel.

A stage was erected against the building which stood at right angles to the town hall. Curtains hung from horizontal poles along the other two sides to screen off the rectangle. Chairs and benches were laid out in rows at the front, with standing room behind them for the bulk of the audience. Seats were also placed in the upper windows of the town hall so that the Burgomaster, his Council and their wives could view the entertainment from a privileged position.

As in Flushing, curtains at the rear of the stage hid the tiring-house from view. It was in the hallway of the building. A stout wooden box below the stage enabled actors to mount it with ease before bursting between the curtains to make an entrance. When not doubling as characters in the play, the musicians could make use of an upper room as their minstrels' gallery. Nicholas had been diligent in his preparations. Since Nathan Curtis, their master carpenter, had been left behind in London, it was the book-holder who devised and built the cunning trapdoor through which a number of surprise appearances would be made.

The beaming Burgomaster had been as good as his word. He had provided Nicholas with four able-bodied servants, who took some of the massive load from the inadequate shoulders of George Dart, and he persuaded every citizen of distinction to attend the performance. Market-day had swelled the numbers in the city, and many from the surrounding areas decided to avail themselves of the rare treat to see a performance by an English theatrical troupe.

Nicholas converted his German assistants to gatherers and placed them at strategic points to collect money for admission. Four albus was an attractively low price to pay. Westfield's Men had an audience three times the size of that in Flushing. It flattered their vanity and stimulated their desire to give of their best.

Owen Elias could not resist peering through the curtains.

'The whole city is out there!' he said.

'Let them see you during the play,' advised Nicholas at his shoulder, 'and not before. The time to appraise the spectators is when you stand before them.'

'I know, Nick. But my curiosity was whetted.'

'About what?'

'I had to see if they were in the audience.'

'They?'

'Some of those eleven thousand virgins.' Nicholas's smile threw the Welshman on the defensive. 'They do exist,' he claimed. 'We drank with a German watchmaker last night. His English sounded more like double Dutch, but one thing he did make clear was that there are eleven thousand virgins in Cologne. The city is famous for them.' He grinned with frank lechery. 'There'll be a few less in number by the time I quit this place.'

'You are centuries too late,' said Nicholas, taking the curtain from his hand to close it again. 'Your watchmaker forgot to tell you that the eleven thousand virgins existed in Cologne a long time ago. They accompanied Princess Ursula on a pilgrimage to Rome. When Ursula was martyred by Attila the Hun, she was made into the patron saint of Cologne.'

Elias was deflated. 'How do you know all this?'

'The Burgomaster gave me a history of the city.'

'There are *no* virgins here?'

'Not in the numbers you hope for, Owen.'

'I have been cruelly misled.'

'Only by the heat of your desire.'

'You speak true, Nick,' admitted the other with a wry grin. 'We Celts are too goatish. When I first heard about those virgins, I thought my codpiece would burst asunder.'

'Save your strength for the play.'

He led the disappointed actor back to the tiring-house. Spirits were high among the rest of the cast. A substantial audience was awaiting them in a state of anticipatory delight. This was no routine assignment in their calendar. Westfield's Men were making their debut before German spectators and were not quite sure how their work would be received. They needed an unqualified success in order to purge the sad memories of their last presentation. *Love and Fortune* would be a shroud to lay over the corpse of Adrian Smallwood.

Nicholas juggled his many responsibilities with the composure that was typical of him. His outward calm concealed his deep anxiety. He was being stalked by a man who would have no compunction about killing him in order to lay hands on the documents he was carrying. Nicholas had told Firethorn of his discovery and they had decided to take Owen Elias and James Ingram into their confidence. Four of them were now on guard against possible attack, but it was not enough. As long as his identity was unknown, the advantage would always lie with an assassin who could choose when and where to strike.

'Stand by!' Nicholas called, marshalling the company.

'Speak up and follow me!' ordered Firethorn. 'And spare a thought for dear Adrian. This performance is for him.'

Music played, then Elias went out to deliver the Prologue. The ovation he collected raised the general excitement even higher. Firethorn and Gill virtually ran onto the stage to play the first scene together. They struck sparks off each other which ignited the whole cast. *Love and Fortune* had never been played with more attack and commitment.

Cologne adored it. Whether laughing at the wild antics or sighing with the forlorn lovers, they were in their element. They understood only half of the plot and less than a quarter of the dialogue, but that did not dim their appreciation one bit. Movement and gesture were eloquent interpreters. Songs and dances were self-explanatory. And Firethorn's storming performance in the central role was stunning. Gill's clown was the perfect foil for him. Whenever the two of them came together, the play took on an extra bite and richness.

What kept them enthralled was the overall quality of the company. Westfield's Men were undoubted professionals. With Nicholas at the helm behind the scenes, the play was like a seamless web that grew larger and more ornate with each minute. The spectators thought of their own strolling players and winced. The performance of *Love and Fortune* made their homespun actors look like raw beginners. Two hours flew past in two magical minutes, then applause came in an irresistible avalanche.

It was led by the Burgomaster, standing in a window with his wife and family, cheering loudly and laughing until tears of joy trickled down his cheeks. The cast were kept onstage for ten minutes or more before the acclaim began to show signs of abating. When he led his troupe back into the tiring-house, Firethorn embraced each one of them with gratitude. Even Gill got a spontaneous hug of thanks.

'That performance had everything!' declared Firethorn. 'We were at the height of our powers and the audience worshipped us. What more could we want?'

'A few of those eleven thousand virgins,' said Elias.

'The city is ours. Tomorrow, we storm the Palace.'

'Not with *Love and Fortune*,' warned Nicholas.

'It is our greatest weapon, Nick. You saw its power.'

'Over the good citizens of Cologne, yes. But there will be a very different audience at the Palace. You play in front of prelates and nobles. The Archbishop may prefer something less full of noise and bawdy humour.

Meat for the commonalty may stick in the throat of the Church.'

Barnaby Gill agreed and pushed forward the claims of *Cupid's Folly* yet again. Firethorn countered angrily with *Hector of Troy*. They wielded the two plays like broadswords and the others backed out of range. The issue was still undecided when the Burgomaster sailed into the tiring-house. His eyes were glistening, his mouth was locked in a permanent grin and his cheeks were like two giant red apples left out in the rain.

'Wunderbar!' he announced. 'Wizzfeld's Men! Wunderbar!'

'We thank you, sir,' said Firethorn, giving his most obsequious bow. 'We are humble players whose only wish is to serve our masters. It has been an honour, Herr Burgomaster.'

'Magnificent, you are, Lurrence Feuertorn.'

'Firethorn,' enunciated the other. 'Lawrence Firethorn.'

'You please us. I help.'

His hand went towards his midriff and Firethorn hoped that he was about to open his purse. Instead, the Burgomaster plucked a letter from his belt and proffered it.

'To Frankfurt, you go. Ja?'

'We do, sir.'

'You take.'

'Thank you,' said Firethorn, taking the letter but handing it straight to Nicholas with a bitter aside. 'Is that what he calls help? Turning us into his couriers'?

'You read. Ja?' urged the Burgomaster. 'In German, I write, and that letter sent to Frankfurt. Emperor Rudolph, he forgets. Frankfurt not been told you come, maybe. Now they know. My letter tell them. Written by Wizzfeld's Men.'

'But we wrote no letter,' protested Firethorn.

'I do for you, to help,' said the Burgomaster with a gleeful chuckle. He turned to Nicholas. 'Read. For all.'

When he unfolded the letter, Nicholas realised that what he held was an English translation. The Burgomaster had taken great pains on their behalf. His application for permission to play in Frankfurt was couched in the language of deference. Nicholas read it out to the whole company in a firm voice.

'High Honourable, Respectable, Praiseworthy, Highly Learned Lords, Herr Burgomaster and the Council. Particularly Praise-

worthy, Gracious and Ruling Lords, our company of players has
stayed briefly in Cologne, where we were well-received, and we
set out now towards Prague, where, by grace of the Most High
Emperor, we are to display our talents at the Imperial Court.
As our journey takes us close to your illustrious city, we did not
wish to neglect to visit such a famous and praiseworthy place,
and to present our plays to the High Council, according to its
will. This is why we submit this most humble request to the
Council, and ask it for the great honour of graciously allowing
us to play in Frankfurt for a short time: for we are experienced
players, trained as actors from our youth, commended for our
performances before Her Gracious Majesty, Elizabeth, Queen
of England, and renowned for our plays, wherein we present
no vices or condemnable tricks, only things appropriate to decency and decorum, in addition to charming English music
and excellent dances, which will the better increase the pleasure
of the spectators and the listeners. Accordingly, we hope that
the High Council will not refuse our humble request but will
most kindly permit us to engage in theatrical performances for
the entertainment of your justly celebrated city. Forever grateful. Your humble servants.'

There was dead silence. Annoyed to learn that a letter had been sent
on their behalf without his knowledge, Firethorn speedily adapted to the
idea. His problem was to contain his mirth at the cringing humility of the
missive's tone. As he glanced around, he saw that the rest of the company
felt the same way. They were struggling to hold in their amusement.

The Burgomaster beamed. 'Is good. Ja?'

'Very good,' said Firethorn.

Then the dam burst. Laughter poured out of him in a torrent and it set
of a dozen minor tributaries. The whole company was soon rocking help-
lessly. A Burgomaster in Cologne would know how a Burgomaster in
Frankfurt wished to be addressed and his letter would no doubt win them
a favourable hearing, but that took nothing away from its submissive crawling and its essential ridiculousness. As the laughter built to a crescendo,
Nicholas was afraid that the Burgomaster would be offended by such a reaction to his help but the latter readily joined in the wild cachinnation. It
never occurred to their affable host that they were laughing at him.

'Is good. Ja?' he shouted.

The whole company gave its reply in unison.

'Is very good. Ja! Ja! Ja!'

Hours later, some of them were still draining the dregs of the joke. As they sat around a table at the White Cross, they revelled in their triumph and giggled at the memory of the Burgomaster's letter.

'Did you ever hear such stuff?' howled Elias with a mug of beer in his hand. 'That letter did everything but get down on its knees to lick the arse of the Burgomaster of Frankfurt.'

'Do you speak of the Particularly Praiseworthy, Gracious and Ruling Herr Burgomaster?' teased Ingram.

'I do, James. Most humbly and cravenly.' said Elias.

'And do you really believe that our plays are free from all vices and condemnable tricks?'

'No, I do not.'

'They are full to the brim with both,' said Firethorn.

'Thank heaven!' added Elias.

And the table roared again. Nicholas gave only a token smile. His amusement at the wording of the letter had soon faded and he was struck by the extraordinary benevolence that lay behind it. On the strength of his long interview with Nicholas—and before he had seen Westfield's Men perform *Love and Fortune*—the Burgomaster had taken it upon himself to smooth their passage across Germany by writing to his counterpart in Frankfurt. He would no doubt have sent a covering letter of his own to reinforce the request to be allowed to play in the city.

Firethorn read the mind of his book-holder and moved him aside.

'Do not blame them, Nick. They needed this laughter.'

'I know.'

'Besides,' said the actor-manager, 'that letter may not have sounded quite so obnoxious in German. Then again, it may have been far worse.' He gave a chuckle, then lowered his voice to a whisper. 'You are missing Anne, I think.'

'Yes,' admitted Nicholas. 'Very much. I fear for her.'

'There is no need.'

'She is alone in a foreign country.'

'Anne is a capable woman. She will survive.'

'Adrian was a capable man. He did not.'

'That was different, Nick.'

'I know, and it is wrong of me to fret. She will have arrived safely in Amsterdam by now, where she will be looked after by the entire Hendrik family. They will be delighted that she has put herself to such trouble and expense in order to see her father-in-law once more.' He took a meditative sip of his beer. 'But I do miss her.'

'The pain of separation!' said Firethorn, stroking his beard. 'I know it full well. I miss Margery and the children as I would miss limbs that have been hacked off. While I enjoy the hospitality of Cologne, they live in the shadow of the plague. I lie awake at night thinking of them. Especially Margery,' he said with a nostalgic twinkle in his eye. 'She is a rare creature indeed.'

'I can vouch for that.'

'Owen may lust after his eleven thousand virgins, but Margery is worth all of them together. She is the perfection of womanhood—and I pine for her.'

'Write and tell her so,' suggested Nicholas.

'I will, I will.'

'The friendly Burgomaster will tell us how to send letters back to England.'

'Yes,' said Firethorn. 'He is so obliging that he will probably saddle his horse and ride off to deliver the letter for me in person. Is good? Ja?'

Firethorn emptied his own mug with one long swig, then set it down on the table. It was instantly refilled from a jug by a buxom tavern wench. He grinned lasciviously at her and forgot all about his long-suffering wife. As the girl bent over the next table to pour some more beer, he admired the generous proportions of her body with a practised eye. His thoughts flew swiftly to a much finer example of female beauty.

'Sophia Magdalena,' he sighed.

'Edmund is working zealously on the play.'

'I trust that he will enhance the importance of my role in it. I must dominate the stage as the tormented Earl who searches in vain for his lost child.'

'The Earl has been changed to an Archduke of Austria.'

'O happy transition!'

'And your daughter is brought up by simple shepherds.'

'My sweet, little, fair maid of Bohemia!'

'Dick Honeydew will shine in the role.'

'A pox on the role!' said Firethorn dismissively. 'The only person who shines in it is Sophia herself. She is radiant. Her beams are warmer than those of the sun. At the Queen's Head, she lit up the whole innyard with her presence. That is where I sensed my kinship with her. Sophia Magdalena of Bohemia. My own fair maid. So eager to see me again that she prevailed upon the Emperor to invite us to Prague.'

'That may not be quite what happened,' said Nicholas.

'What other explanation is there? She fell in love with the Grand Master and I lost my heart to her. That is why I will happily ride half-way across the Continent at her behest. She waits in Bohemia for her faithful knight to arrive.'

Nicholas forbore to point out that the knight's fidelity had been pledged to his wife only minutes earlier. In talking with such fondness and consideration about Margery, the actor-manager had looked back wistfully to London. His gaze was now fixed on Prague and nothing would deflect him. The wayward knight now rode solely under the banner of Sophia Magdalena.

'Onward!' said Firethorn, holding an imaginary sword in the air. 'In the east, my pleasure lies. Onward to Bohemia!'

'The journey will be a difficult one.'

'I will swim lakes to reach her. I will hew down whole forests. I will climb the mountains as Hannibal once did in search of conquest. Sophia is distraught without me.'

'She is not the only person we seek in Prague,' reminded Nicholas. 'There are others.'

'Not for me. Sophia Magdalena is enough. She is Prague.'

'Emperor Rudolph is our host.'

'Only because of her.'

'That may well be, but we must pay due homage to him.' He felt the pouch inside his jerkin. 'And we have to deliver the documents to Doctor Talbot Royden.'

'He has gone right out of my mind.'

'Bring him back,' urged Nicholas. 'Keep his name in your thoughts. These documents have already cost Westfield's Men dearly. As long as they are in our possession, the company remains in danger.'

'From whom, Nick? That is what I want to know.'

'We can but guess.'

'The worst enemy is one who will not show himself.'

'I brought him out of hiding this morning.'

'But you did not see the villain. He remains a phantom.'

'That is why we must exercise the greatest care,' stressed Nicholas. 'You have a burning desire to reach Prague. Let us be sure that the whole company reaches it with you.'

'I will be Vigilance personified.'

'We will all need to take that role.'

Firethorn quaffed his beer and leaned closer to him.

'Who is this Talbot Royden?' he wondered.

'What did Lord Westfield tell you about him?'

'Nothing beyond the fact that he was a doctor of repute. Our patron simply pressed that pouch into my hands and urged me to deliver it to this fellow.'

'How did he speak the man's name?'

'His name?'

'With pleasure?' asked Nicholas. 'With distaste? With familiarity? Can you remember?'

Firethorn was reflective. 'It seems a long time ago, Nick. I was so thrilled at the idea of travelling to Bohemia that I paid scant attention to this trivial service we were asked to perform.'

'Because of that trivial service, Adrian Smallwood died.'

'Secrecy,' recalled Firethorn. 'That is what Lord Westfield sought to impress upon me. Above all else, the documents were to be kept secret. As they have been.'

'Not from the murderer.'

'How did he know of their existence?'

'We will find that out in due course. But you have not answered my question. How did our patron say the name of Talbot Royden?'

'As if he had never laid eyes on the man.'

'Then all we know about the good doctor is what we may deduce,' mused Nicholas. 'If he is employed at the Imperial Court, he must have a high standing in his profession. But in what branch of medicine or science is he most learned? Is he a personal physician to Emperor Rudolph himself? Or does he have some other function? How did he get to Bohemia in the first place?' He felt the wooden box in his purse. 'And what links does he maintain with England?'

'Doctor Talbot Royden is an enigma,' said Firethorn.

'Not entirely. He enjoys the favour of the Holy Roman Emperor and he would only do that by dint of some remarkable skills. Of one thing we can be certain.'

'What is that, Nick?'

'Talbot Royden is a species of genius.'

The laboratory was situated in what had once been the largest apartment at the castle. It was a long, low, narrow room whose ceiling was supported by a series of arches which divided the place into bays. Tallow candles burned with such abundance that the laboratory had the feeling of a chapel, but it was dedicated to a stranger religion than Christianity. Chemical odours of competing pungency mingled with the abiding smell of damp. Spiders flourished in dark corners. Mice and beetles traversed the wooden floor in search of food. A lazy black cat spent most of its time asleep on a wooden stool.

Tables were laden with jars of weird liquids and coloured powders. All kinds of scientific equipment was scattered about. A surgeon's chest—complete with a gruesome collection of knives, pincers and scissors—stood open on an oak chest. Beside it lay the saw that was used for amputations, its teeth blunted by recent use. Leather-bound tomes, written in many languages, were stacked everywhere. Learning lay cheek-by-jowl with instruments for letting blood.

The two men stood in front of the furnace at the far end of the room. Even with its iron door closed, it gave off a fierce heat.

'Open it,' ordered Talbot Royden.

'Has it had time enough?'

'Do as I tell you, Casper.'

'Yes, Master.'

'Open the door slowly.'

Royden took a precautionary step backwards. He was an ugly man in his thirties with a bulbous nose and porcine eyes. His compact body was hidden by a long red gown decorated with the signs of the zodiac. His hat covered his ears, the back of his neck and most of his forehead. He was sweating profusely.

His young assistant wore a leather apron over his shirt and breeches. He put on thick gloves before he reached out to open the door of the furnace. As it swung on its hinges, there was a dramatic surge of heat and light. The whole room seemed to be on fire. Caspar's intelligent face registered both hope and fear. With a pair of large tongs, he reached into the furnace to pull something out with great tenderness before setting it down on the block of stone beside the furnace.

Both men watched carefully as the small cauldron hissed and glowed. When it began to give off a succession of sparks and peculiar noises, Doctor Talbot Royden clicked his tongue in irritation. It was speaking to him in a language that he understood.

'It is not yet ready,' he admitted.

'We were too hasty,' said Caspar respectfully. 'It was my fault, Master. Perhaps I extracted it too quickly from the furnace. Or did not bring the fire to the requisite heat.'

'No, Caspar. It is my judgement that is awry.'

'What must we do?'

'What else?' said Royden wearily. 'We try again.'

But they were not allowed to repeat their experiment. Before the assistant could use his tongs again, the door of the laboratory was flung open and four armed soldiers marched in. They surrounded Royden and looked suspiciously down at the sizzling cauldron.

'Is it a success?' grunted one of them.

'Not yet,' conceded the alchemist.

'Arrest him.'

'Stop!' protested Royden as he was seized by two of the soldiers. 'I am in the middle of an important experiment.'

'A failed experiment.'

'The augmentation process is very tricky.'

'Take him away!'

'You will regret this!' yelled Royden as he was dragged unceremoniously away. 'I will report you to the Emperor.'

'We are acting on his orders.'

Caspar was horrified at the sudden change in their fortunes. Years of patient work had been halted in a matter of seconds. It left him utterly bewildered. He turned to the soldier who had barked the orders.

'Doctor Talbot Royden is a brilliant man,' he argued.

'He was.'

'You cannot treat him in this vile way.'

'We just did.'

'He is a scientific genius. His work must go on.'

'Not at the Emperor's expense.'

'Why not?'

'Ask him.'

'But we were almost *there*,' insisted Caspar.

'Almost is not good enough.'

'Doctor Royden simply needs time.'

'He will have plenty of that now.'

'Why?' asked the other. 'Where have they taken him?'

'To his new home.'

'Home?'

The man gave a callous grin before strutting off.

'Where is this home?' called Caspar.

'The castle dungeon.'

[CHAPTER SEVEN]

A persistent drizzle greeted them next morning but it could neither soil memories of their triumph on the previous day nor dampen their enthusiasm for the performance that lay ahead. Rain, sleet or snow would have no effect at all on them. Westfield's Men were due to play at Court, and that made them impervious to bad weather. When they actually went into the banqueting hall at the palace, their spirits rose even higher. It was the ideal place in which to stage a play.

The hall was long but quite broad and its high ceiling gave an impression of more space than really existed. The floor was polished oak and the walls were covered with a series of portraits in gilt frames. Tall windows allowed light to flood in from both sides. If need be, curtains could be drawn and candelabra used to illumine the stage. All the benefits of an indoor performance were at their beck and call.

There was even a dais at one end of the hall for the regular music recitals that were held there. Nicholas Bracewell had merely to increase its size to accommodate the swirling action of a five-act drama. Doors on both sides of the stage gave access to an ante-chamber which was immediately designated as their tiring-house. The rehearsal was virtually painless and Firethorn only had to upbraid them once. Even George Dart got everything right. Voices and instruments carried beautifully. Everything pointed to another theatrical victory.

But it was not to be. The problems began with the choice of play. After being forced to stage two comedies that would be more accessible to foreign audiences, Lawrence Firethorn asserted his authority and demanded the right to exhibit his talent in a more serious drama. *The Corrupt Bargain* caused a faint tremor when its selection was first announced.

It was a fine play but the company remembered its last performance only too well. Incapacitated by a raging toothache, Firethorn had been unable to take the leading role. His deputy, Ben Skeat, an old and trusted actor, had suffered a heart attack in the middle of the play and died onstage. Though the company had somehow struggled on without their protagonist, it was an experience which had scarred their souls. Superstition clung tenaciously.

The excellent rehearsal stilled most of their doubts. Even in its attenuated state, Firethorn's portrayal of the exiled Duke Alonso of Genoa quickened the pulse of all who saw it. He brought a subtle power and a deep pathos that Ben Skeat could never have matched, and the latter's tragic departure from the text soon faded from memory. Every part he touched, Firethorn made his own, and Duke Alonso was no exception. With such a striking performance at its heart, *The Corrupt Bargain* became a far more interesting and exciting play. Its author, Edmund Hoode, dared to hope that it could be redeemed from the obscurity into which it had been cast.

Mishaps were only minor at first. James Ingram tore a sleeve as he was putting on his costume, George Dart cut his hand while testing the edge of the executioner's axe and Richard Honeydew broke a string while practising on the lute. Such normal accidents were taken in their stride, as was Barnaby Gill's last-minute outburst of pique at the way his preference for *Cupid's Folly* had been brutally ignored. By the time of the performance, Nicholas had everything and everyone in the tiring-house completely under control once more.

Unfortunately, his supervision did not extend to the audience. From the sounds which they heard seeping through to them, they knew that they were graced by a large and august assembly. There would be no standees here, no common folk straining their necks to catch a glimpse of the action over the heads of the crowd in front of them. Everyone was seated. The usual hubbub of the Queen's Head was now a subdued murmur. *The Corrupt Bargain* would be watched with close attention and reverence.

That, at least, was their conviction as they launched the piece on the placid waters of the Archbishop's Palace. It floated smoothly at first.

Owen Elias earned muted applause for the Prologue and Edmund Hoode impressed as a kindly Provost. Honeydew's first song drew sighs of contentment from the ladies while their husbands wondered if they really were looking at a boy in female attire and studied his anatomy and movement with fascination. Colorful costumes and clever scenic devices gave the drama an added lift. Understandably nervous at first, the company soon found its rhythm.

Then Firethorn made his entrance and there was a gasp of astonishment. The actor put this down to his extraordinary presence on a stage and he hurled himself into his first speech with gusto. Disguised as a friar, the exiled Duke had returned to Genoa to regain power from his duplicitous younger brother, Don Pedro. Firethorn was busily explaining his plan in rhyming couplets when his eye fell on the noble figures seated in the front row. He had no difficulty in identifying the Archbishop of Cologne in his sacerdotal robes, nor could he fail to notice the splendour of the Duke of Bavaria. It was the man who sat between them who caused him to falter.

Not only was the guest wearing a habit identical to that of Firethorn's, his swarthy complexion and Mediterranean cast of features marked him as an Italian. Bernado of Savona was the Abbot of the Monastery of Saint Peter. Though he spoke no English, he heard his native Genoa mentioned time and again. It persuaded him that Duke Alonso was less of a noble hero than a comic figure who was there primarily to mock him. As the Abbot's discomfiture grew, consternation spread throughout the audience. The corrupt bargain which they saw was a theatre company in league with the Protestants to subvert the monastic traditions of the Roman Catholic Church.

Once the notion had a hold on the audience, it was very hard to dispel. Firethorn, the putative hero, began to attract glares and hisses. The rest of the company struggled on manfully but the frown remained on the face of Bernado of Savona. Only the inspired clowning of Barnaby Gill brought any relief. His songs amused them and his jigs diverted them, but even he fell foul of a staid gathering when obscene gestures which always won guffaws elsewhere were now met with stony silence. The tiring-house was a place of mourning.

'They hate us,' wailed Gill. 'It is the wrong play.'

'No!' insisted Firethorn. 'It is the right play. We happen to have offered it to the wrong audience.'

'You have estranged them, Lawrence.'

'They need a little wooing, that is all.'

'We are deep into Act Three,' complained Hoode, 'and they are still hostile. Clearly, they despise my play.'

'The Archbishop wrinkled his nose at me,' said Elias.

'The Duke of Bavaria yawned during my last song,' said Gill in a tone of outrage. 'I blame Lawrence for this.'

'There is no point in blaming anyone,' said Nicholas, swiftly interceding. 'The play must run its course and there is still time to win them over.'

'Not while my double sits glowering in the front row,' said Firethorn. 'He could teach Marwood how to pull faces.'

'Your appearance offends him.'

'It has been offending me for years,' sneered Gill.

'What can I do, Nick?' asked Firethorn, ignoring the gibe. 'Were I the villain, I could understand their dislike of me. But I am the hero, garbed like a holy friar. I am a symbol of all that is good and wholesome. Wherein lies my sin?'

'Your disguise,' said Nicholas.

'It is the only way that Alonso may return to Genoa.'

'Discard it in the next scene.'

'But I only reveal myself in the last act.'

'Do so earlier.'

'That would ruin my play!' protested Hoode.

'No, Edmund,' said the book-holder. 'It may rescue it.'

Firethorn was baffled. 'How do I maintain my disguise?'

'Wear a hat and a cloak. Hug the corners of the stage. Turn your face away from people who might recognise you. As long as you pose as a friar, *The Corrupt Bargain* is doomed. Abandon the cowl and show them who you really are.'

'Madness!' opined Gill.

'A betrayal of my work!' exclaimed Hoode.

'It may well be both,' said Firethorn, frantically weighing the implications. 'But it may also be our only salvation. What is more important? The fate of one paltry drama or the standing of Westfield's Men?'

'It is not a paltry drama, Lawrence!'

'Perform it as written and we sink into further ignominy. Amend the play and we may hang on to our reputation.' He heard the music which introduced his next scene. 'It is decided. I am sorry, Edmund. We must all make sacrifices for our art.'

Leaving Hoode in tears, he charged back onstage, to be met by the same wall of antagonism. The Archbishop of Cologne was glaring at him, the Duke of Bavaria was curling his lip and Abbot Bernado looked as if he was about to excommunicate the actor. Firethorn took them all by surprise. Striding to the very edge of the dais, he tore off his cowl to reveal his ducal attire and stood before the audience in his true character. The measured voice of a friar now became the mighty roar of a dispossessed ruler. In the space of one glorious minute, he transformed a room full of grumbling enemies into an appreciative audience. At the end of his speech, it was the Italian Abbot who first put his tentative palms together to applaud.

Not all of the damage could be repaired, and vestigial doubts remained in the minds of the spectators. But the emergence of Duke Alonso into the light of day helped to salvage a great deal. The plot was now clarified, the hero identified and the embattled heroine—the winsome Richard Honeydew—able to reap her full harvest of sympathy as she was confronted with a stark choice between yielding her body to the tyrant or watching her brother die. *The Corrupt Bargain* was at last allowed to work its spell upon the audience.

Behind the scenes, its author was quite inconsolable.

'This play has a curse upon it, Nick!' he moaned.

'That curse has just been lifted,' said Nicholas as another round of applause rang out in the hall. 'Listen to them, Edmund. They are hailing your work.'

'What they are clapping is a travesty of my play. When Lawrence flung off his disguise, he altered the whole direction of the piece. We have had to improvise in every scene.'

'With great success.'

'But at a hideous cost.'

'Be comforted,' said Nicholas. 'It remains a fine play.'

'Not when it is savaged like this,' retorted Hoode. 'I do not know which is worse. Ben Skeat dying in the middle of *The Corrupt Bargain* or Lawrence Firethorn coming to life as the Duke of Alonso two acts before he is due to do so. The play is bewitched.'

'So—at last—is our noble audience.'

[121]

'Not by my art. They watch dribbling idiocy out there.'

Nicholas felt sorry for his friend, but the book-holder's main concern was to keep the action moving. He signalled to George Dart to carry a bench onstage, then waved Owen Elias and James Ingram into position for the next scene. Actors who had been coming into the tiring-house with sad faces now showed a smiling eagerness to go back onstage. They knew that the tide of disapproval had at last been turned.

Success was modified by the earlier failure of the play. There was still a lingering suspicion in some minds that Roman Catholicism had been ridiculed. When they came out to take their bows, the actors were given pleasant smiles and polite applause. After their sustained ovation on the previous day, this was a decidedly tepid response, but at least they had won their audience over. Their cherished reputation had been partially vindicated.

Disappointment ensued. Expecting to be presented to the dignitaries, Firethorn and his company were dismayed to find themselves paid off and ushered out of the Palace. Instead of being treated as distinguished players, they were summarily dismissed like unwanted servants. As they made their disgrunted way to the inn, Firethorn sat in the first wagon beside Nicholas. The actor-manager was seething.

'That was shameful!' he railed. 'We gave our all and they turned their aristocratic backs on us.'

'Only to avoid embarrassment,' suggested Nicholas.

'Embarrassment?'

'We caused unwitting offence with our play.'

'How was I to know that my twin would be sitting in the front row? And from Genoa! What greater misfortune could we have faced? My performance must have seemed like a personal attack on him.'

'You retrieved the situation superbly.'

'Only at your instigation, Nick. If I'd kept that damnable cowl on until the final scene, I'd probably have been hanged from the rafters by now! Did they not recognise great acting when it was offered to them?'

'They were overcome by it,' said Nicholas tactfully. 'You were too convincing in the habit of a friar. That is why your portrayal had such an effect on them.'

'I never thought of it that way,' said Firethorn, his ire cooling somewhat. 'You may be right. I was the victim of my own brilliance in the role. That is some recompense. And there is more in that purse they gave us. What did it hold?'

'Several florins.'

'Money is the best kind of applause.'

While Firethorn slowly rallied, the rest of the company was still morose and Hoode was almost suicidal. For the second time in succession, his play had been hacked to pieces in the name of expediency. It was a dispirited troupe which trickled back into the White Cross. A familiar face awaited them.

The Burgomaster swooped with a beaming smile.

'Wizzfeld's Men!' he gushed. 'Danke! Danke vielmals!'

'What is he saying?' asked Firethorn.

'He is thanking us,' explained Nicholas.

'For what?'

'Visit to the Palace,' said the Burgomaster. 'The play, they no like very much. I hear, I have friends in Palace. Our play, we love. You give the city the best. Thank you, my good friends. This I give to Wizzfeld's Men.'

And he pressed a bag of coins into Firethorn's hand.

'What have we done to earn this?' said the actor.

'Put the city of Köln first. We love you. Danke.'

He embraced Firethorn, kissed him on both cheeks, gave a cheery wave to the rest of the company, then went out, chuckling happily. The Burgomaster was delighted with their setback at the Palace. He believed that the company had deliberately chosen its finest play to offer to the city while reserving an inferior one for the Archbishop and his guests. Firethorn used the unexpected bounty in the most practical way.

'Order a feast!' he said, tossing the money to Elias. 'We will spend our last night here in revelry. And do not be downhearted,' he told his company. 'We have only been rebuffed by an Archbishop, a Duke, and a mere Abbot today. They are of no significance to a company which will soon be winning plaudits from an Emperor.'

Rudolph II, Holy Roman Emperor and King of Bohemia, sat on his throne in full regalia. His vestments were embroidered with gold thread and his heavy crown resembled a bishop's mitre which had been turned sideways to reveal a band of gold surmounted by a tiny cross. Held in his left hand, the massive sword of state rested on its point. The sceptre of office was held in his other hand and rested on his shoulder. He exuded a sense of quiet power and majesty. In outward appearance, he was an archetypal Defender of the Faith. All that Rudolph needed to do was to decide exactly which faith he was defending.

The distinctive Hapsburg face was devoid of expression. Large, protruding eyes gazed unseeing into the distance. The nose was like the beak of a bird, the undershot chin was the family signature. The drooping lower lip moved imperceptibly as he talked to himself. Rudolph was now in his fortieth year, but the weight of his melancholia made him seem older. His attitude suggested a man who was rueful about the years which had passed and fearful about those to come.

Studying him intently, the Milanese artist was undeterred by his subject's mood of dejection. He saw what he wished to see and his brush transposed his vision to the canvas. Short, fat and amiable, he offered a complete contrast to the sad, motionless figure on the throne. The artist was bristling with nervous energy and constantly shifted his feet or shrugged his expressive shoulders. They were alone in the Presence Chamber at the castle. The portrait was slowly taking shape.

A staff rapped on the door, then it swung open to admit the tall, spare figure of the Chamberlain. He padded across the marble floor to take up a position at the Emperor's right ear. Rudolph gave no indication that he was aware of his visitor. The arrival of the Chamberlain in no way distracted the artist. His brush worked away at the same busy pace as before.

Clearing his throat noisily, the newcomer spoke in German with a mixture of deference and irritation. It was difficult to hold a conversation with a man who had absented himself from the world and its immediate responsibilities.

'The Papal Nuncio is here,' he announced.

'Why?' mumbled Rudolph.

'He has an appointment to see you.'

'Cancel it.'

'You have already cancelled two appointments with him,' said the Chamberlain. 'He comes on important business.'

'From the Pope?'

'Of course, Your Imperial Highness.'

'Then we know what he is going to say.'

[124]

'It would be a kindness to hear him say it.'

'I will. In time.'

'When? Later today? Tomorrow? The day after?'

'When I feel able to face him.'

'The Papal Nuncio grows impatient.'

'That is his privilege.'

'You cannot go on refusing to see visitors.'

'Why not?'

'It is not politic, Your Imperial Highness.'

'I am not a political animal.'

Rudolph set the sword and sceptre aside before lifting the crown from his head and setting it on his lap. He turned his wondering eyes on the Chamberlain.

'What else have you come to tell me?'

'You have several other appointments today.'

'Cancel them.'

'We must not keep doing that.'

'Postpone them instead. I am not ready for them.'

'When will you be ready?'

'You will be told.'

The Chamberlain pursed his lips in annoyance but made no comment. He was about to move away when he remembered something else he had to report.

'Doctor Talbot Royden has been arrested.'

Rudolph blinked. 'On whose orders?'

'Yours.'

'Why did I have him arrested?'

'He has failed yet again.'

'But he promised me that he would succeed this time.'

'He did not.'

'This is intolerable!' said Rudolph, rising to his feet. 'I need men around me who can keep their word. I want a Court that is the envy of the civilised world. I demand success and achievement in every branch of the sciences and the arts. Has Doctor Talbot Royden been told that?'

'Many times.'

'Send him to the dungeons.'

'He is already under lock and key.'

'What further punishment should I inflict upon him?'

'That is up to you, your Imperial Highness.'

Rudolph sat down on his throne to consider the question. His anger slowly ebbed and it gave way to a sudden outburst of manic laughter. The Chamberlain edged away from him. Rudolph clapped his hands together with glee.

'I know what I will do for the good doctor!' he said.

'What is that?'

'Send him a basket of fruit.'

The Chamberlain was mystified. 'Fruit? A basket of fruit?'

'The perfect gift,' insisted the other before turning to the artist and translating his edict into fluent Italian. 'I am sending my prisoner a basket of fruit.'

'Fruit?' said the other with a giggle.

'From the Emperor!'

As the two of them went off into another peal of wild and inexplicable laughter, the Chamberlain made a dignified exit.

The journey to Frankfurt took two days longer than they had anticipated. When they left the Rhine Valley and headed east, they came up against topographical problems of all kinds. Hills, mountains, woodland and waterways slowed them down, and the appalling condition of the roads was another delaying factor. One of the wagons lost a wheel when it hit a boulder at speed and precious hours were taken up by the repair.

Westfield's Men soldiered on bravely and Firethorn kept up their spirits by leading rehearsals of plays from their repertoire. By common consent, *The Corrupt Bargain* had been eliminated from the list they would offer to their audiences. Robbed of one of his plays, Edmund Hoode was determined to make amends with another. He worked conscientiously on *The Fair Maid of Bohemia*, sitting beside Nicholas Bracewell so that he could profit from the book-holder's advice. It was not the first time a play had been written on the hoof. During a tour to the West Country, the two friends had collaborated on ideas which eventually grew into *The Merchant of Calais*. Hoode was keen to revive that fertile partnership.

'Barnaby is calling for an extra song,' he said.

'He already has enough,' argued Nicholas. 'The play can carry two more songs but they should be given to Owen and to Dick Honeydew.'

'That was my feeling as well.'

'It will lend more variety to the singing.'

'That was the joy of Adrian's voice,' observed Hoode sadly. 'It was such a welcome contrast. This play cries out for an actor like Adrian Smallwood.'

'I know. But you have made good progress, Edmund.'

'Thanks to you.'

'All that I have done is to make a few suggestions.'

'You fired my imagination, Nick. Whenever I faltered, I took fresh inspiration from her.'

'Her?'

'Sophia Magdalena. The fair maid who arranged for us to be invited to Bohemia. The least I can offer her by way of thanks is a play in her honour. It is an expression of my deep and lasting devotion to her.'

'But you only saw her that once.'

'It was enough.'

'She struck a chord with the whole company.'

'You, too, will fall in love with her, Nick.'

'I am already spoken for,' said the other softly. 'You pursue your fair maid of Bohemia and I will hold fast to my fine lady of Bankside.'

'It may be a long while before you are together again.'

'We are resigned to that.'

'Absence serves to whet the appetite.'

'True.' He flicked the reins to goad the horses into a trot. 'Tell me more about the play. What other changes have you made to it?'

Hoode needed no more encouragement. He talked at length and with enthusiasm about the heroine's translation from Wapping to Bohemia. Nicholas was pleased to hear that some of his own ideas had been incorporated and developed. It was evident that, by the time they reached Prague, the revisions would be complete and the play fit for rehearsal. After the harrowing experience at the Palace in Cologne, the playwright was in sore need of a triumph to restore his morale.

Absorbed by what he heard, Nicholas did not lose sight of caution. He knew that they were being followed. Ever since they left Cologne, he sensed that they were being trailed even though he never laid eyes on the man in their wake. When he saw a copse ahead, he decided to take a more positive step. Handing the reins to Hoode, he waited until the wagon merged with the overhanging branches, then jumped to the ground. The others assumed that he was going to relieve himself and a few good-natured jeers followed him behind a tree.

Secure in his hiding-place, Nicholas waited for ten minutes or so but no following horseman came by. When he stepped out into the road, all that he could see behind them were a few peasants travelling on foot. The wagons had halted on the other side of the copse for him. As Nicholas hurried after them, he decided that the man was either too clever to be caught in the trap or had somehow got ahead of them again. They could not afford to lower their guard for a second.

He was still there.

The Taunus offered a stern challenge and slowed them down even more. Wrapped in thick forests, it rose to a greater height than any of the other Rhineland Schist Massifs, and they had to struggle up mountain tracks and through narrow passes. At one point, the road was so steep that the passengers had to leap off the wagons and help to push them from behind. They were grateful when they met the downward gradient. Their efforts were eventually rewarded with a first sighting of their next destination.

Frankfurt was another beautiful city, steeped in tradition and occupying a strategic point on a major river. For over seven centuries, Germany had elected its rulers there and emperors were now crowned in its majestic cathedral before being honoured at a coronation banquet in the palatial Kaisersaal. Frankfurt had developed into one of the most thriving commercial centres in Europe. So closely interwoven had its past been with the great events in German history that it could lay claim to being an unofficial capital.

Impressed by the size and the location of the city, the visitors could see from a distance the soaring cathedral tower, ornamented in the Gothic style and topped by a dome and lantern-tower. It reached up to heaven with a multitude of churches and tall buildings scrabbling after it. Westfield's Men were by no means the only travellers on the road. The closer they got to Frankfurt, the thicker became the traffic. They were soon part of sizeable crowd converging on the city.

When they entered through the gates, they were carried along by the stream of heavily laden carts and riders towing pack-horses. Over the general clamour, they could hear music being played ahead of them. Sporadic applause and laughter broke out. It was only when they reached the main square and saw it awash with stalls that they realised how timely their arrival was. Frankfurt was holding one of its bi-annual fairs. Merchants had poured in from all parts of Europe to buy, sell or borrow from the city's banks. Acrobats, jugglers, musicians and other itinerant entertainers were offering their wares.

Lawrence Firethorn took one look at the seething mass of people and responded in the true spirit of an actor. Arms outstretched, he stood up in the wagon and shouted with joy.

'An audience!'

The huge influx of visitors meant that accommodation was difficult to find. The inn recommended by Balthasar Davey was already full and they had to trawl through the city for an hour before they finally found somewhere to lay their heads. As soon as the company was safely bestowed at the Golden Lion, its book-holder was sent off to the city hall to see if their written request for permission to perform in Frankfurt had been accepted by the Burgomaster and his Council. Since a long walk through crowded streets exposed him to possible danger, Nicholas asked Owen Elias to act as a trailing bodyguard. The Welshman kept ten or fifteen yards behind him but his strong arm was not needed in his friend's defence.

The city hall was another tall, arresting building of Gothic proportions and extravagance. Leaving Elias to keep watch at the doorway, Nicholas went in alone. Everyone had mocked the obsequious letter from the Burgomaster of Cologne, but at least it had prepared their way. Westfield's Men would not arrive in Frankfurt as unexpected strangers. Nicholas had every reason to expect a courteous welcome from the city. As he stepped into the hallway, he got something infinitely better.

'Nick!'

Anne Hendrik leaped up from the bench and ran to fling herself into his arms. His amazement gave way to delight and he hugged her to him.

'What are you doing here?' he asked.

'Waiting for you.'

'Why?'

'Why do you think?'

She kissed him on the cheek, then led him across to the bench. Holding her hands, he sank down beside her. They were so excited at seeing each other again that they gabbled simultaneously. Nicholas held up a palm to silence her, then took a deep breath before speaking.

'I thought that you were in Amsterdam,' he said.

'I was, Nick.'

'How did you find your father-in-law?'

'I arrived too late,' she said with a rueful shake of her head. 'He died a week earlier. I missed the funeral by a few days. But it was not a wasted journey,' she continued with a brave smile. 'The family were very pleased to see me and I was able to pay my respects beside his grave. Jacob could have expected no more of me. I loved his father as my own.'

'It must have been a grievous shock to you.'

'It was, Nick. To go all that way and find him gone. I was desolate. The thought of a long, lonely journey back home was too much for me. So I gave way to impulse and came here.'

'Why to Frankfurt?'

'Because you told me that Westfield's Men would visit the city after you had been to Cologne. I hoped that I might get here in time to meet up with you. I have been sitting on this bench for two whole days.'

'Why come to the city hall?'

'I knew that it was the first place you would visit on your arrival. The company cannot perform without a licence from the Burgomaster and his Council.' She squeezed his hands and gave a smile. 'So here I am, Nick.'

'I could not be more delighted to see you,' he said with a grin of disbelief. 'But how did you get to Frankfurt? How did you travel all the way here from Amsterdam?'

'The Hendrik family knew some Dutch merchants who were coming to the fair here to sell their goods. They agreed to take me along as their passenger.'

'How was the journey?'

'Long and uncomfortable.'

He was touched. 'You endured all that just to see me?'

'To *be* with you.'

'In what way?'

'I did not come here to exchange a brief greeting,' she explained. 'When I fell to thinking about it, I decided that you needed me. A group of English actors, roaming a country whose language they do not speak, is in want of an interpreter. I flatter myself that I might fill that office.'

'You mean that you will stay with us for a while?' he said in surprise. 'Lodge with us here in Frankfurt?'

'And ride on to Bohemia.'

'Bohemia!'

'If you will have me.'

'Nothing would please me more, Anne. This is manna from heaven. I never dared to expect such a miracle.'

'Would the company accept my help?'

'They will be overjoyed by your offer.'

'Good. It is settled.'

'But what about England? What about your business?'

'What about them?'

'How will Preben fare while you are away?'

'Exceeding well,' she said. 'He will fill my place with ease. I sent a letter from Amsterdam to explain that I might be out of the country longer than I planned. Preben will understand. I have no worries on that score.' She ran a hand through his beard. 'The truth is, I could not bear to be parted from you for that length of time.'

'Nor I from you.'

'Then you approve of my idea?'

'I revel in it. You have lifted a burden from my heart.'

'You are not the only person I wanted to see,' she teased. 'I missed Lawrence Firethorn as well. And Barnaby. And dear Edmund, of course. James Ingram, too. The other person I am eager to meet again is Adrian Smallwood. I have not forgotten how he piloted us through that terrible storm.' She saw his face darken. 'What is wrong, Nick?'

'We suffered a dreadful loss in Flushing,' he said.

'Adrian?'

'He is no longer with us, Anne.'

'I cannot believe that he left the company.'

'It was not of his own free will.'

'What happened?'

'He was murdered.'

Anne's jaw dropped and she gave an involuntary shiver. He put a steadying arm around her as she tried to assimilate the horror of what she had just been told.

'Adrian murdered?' she whispered. 'By whom?'

'That remains a mystery,' he confessed. 'But let me give you the full details. It is only fair that you should know how we stand. When you do, you may have second thoughts about travelling with a company that is under such severe threat.'

. . .

Westfield's Men were not merely welcomed in Frankfurt, they were feted. Their request to play in the city—sent on their behalf by the obliging Burgomaster of Cologne—was unanimously approved by the Council, one of whom, a wealthy mercer, had visited England the previous summer and actually seen the company perform at the Queen's Head. When his colleagues heard him singing the praises of Westfield's Men, they wanted the actors to stay for ten days, but that was not possible if they were to reach Prague by the stipulated date. It was agreed that they would give performances on three successive afternoons before continuing on their way.

Anne Hendrik's appearance on the scene was viewed as a boon by most of the company. However, not every voice was raised in her favour. Barnaby Gill made sure that Nicholas was out of earshot before he gave vent to his complaint.

'We do not want her meddling in our affairs,' he said.

'Anne is not a meddler,' asserted Firethorn.

'She is a woman. That says all.'

'She is a lady, Barnaby. Though I do not expect you to know the difference. A gracious lady whom we all respect.'

'That is so,' agreed Hoode.

'Anne speaks German like a native of the country, and that is more than any of us can boast. She is a godsend to us.'

'Speak for yourself, Lawrence,' said Gill.

'I speak for my whole company.'

It was the morning after their arrival and the three sharers were watching the makeshift stage being erected in a corner of the square under the supervision of Nicholas Bracewell. Trestles had been provided by order of the Council, along with the poles and material necessary for screening off the temporary theatre. Accustomed to public performance in the open air, the actors were not troubled by the constant din all around them. If they could out-shout the multiple bells of London, they could cope with the tumult of the Frankfurt fair. Anne Hendrik was also surveying the preparations. Gill let his jaundiced eye fall on her.

'There is no place in the theatre for a woman,' he said.

'A lady,' corrected Firethorn. 'A lady.'

'Woman, lady, widow or maid. They are all anathema.'

'Not to any man with red blood in his veins.'

'I came into the profession to escape womankind.'

'You came in search of Clement Islip and his kind,' said Firethorn scornfully. 'Pretty boys with a pair of bewitching buttocks. That is all a theatre company means to you.'

Gill fumed. 'I came to exercise my art,' he said.

'Corrupting innocent youths.'

'Mistress Hendrik will hinder our work!'

'That is not true, Barnaby,' said Hoode reasonably. 'Anne's presence will curb some of the bawdier talk and that is all to the good. Obscenities are too readily exchanged when drink is taken. I am with Lawrence here. Anne will be a great benefit to us in a number of ways.'

'Name me one,' challenged Gill.

'Dignity. She will lend us some dignity.'

'There is no gainsaying that,' added Firethorn.

A full rehearsal of *Love and Fortune* was not deemed necessary. It was fresh in their minds from Cologne and was a proven success in front of a German audience. Firethorn contented himself with making the company walk through the piece in order to get used to the feel of the stage and to assess the conditions in which they would perform. A large booth had been commandeered for use as the tiring-house. Beside it was a smaller tent in which scenic devices and properties could be kept.

Nicholas suggested an improvement which Firethorn readily embraced. Music was to be played between each of the five acts of the play to enable costumes and scenery to be changed, and to allow the audience time to absorb what they had just seen. The action of the play would be slowed but this was outweighed by the gains. Even without Adrian Smallwood, the company had four actor-musicians, and the quartet were pleased to be featured much more in the revival of *Love and Fortune*.

Chairs and benches were set out on raised platforms down at the rear of the auditorium. Complimentary seats were offered to the Burgomaster and his Council, but others paid four albus to watch the play from a sitting position. Standees were charged half that price. The day's takings would be subject to a ten per-cent city tax but that did not alarm Westfield's Men. When they saw the best part of a thousand people crowding into their theatre, they knew that they would make a tidy profit out of two hours' strutting on a stage.

Minutes before the performance was due to begin, Firethorn spoke to his company like a general addressing his troops on the eve of a decisive battle.

'Gentlemen,' he declared, 'it is time to show a German audience the true worth of English actors. We delighted with this play in Cologne but we must go beyond delight today. We must woo, we must ensnare, we must excite, we must captivate. Frankfurt has never seen players of our quality before. Let us scorch vivid memories in their minds and leave them gasping in astonishment. Remember, friends,' he said, wagging a finger, 'that we have two more performances to give here. If we distinguish ourselves today, we shall have even more people coming to see us tomorrow and the day after. Think of England, think of reputation.' His eyes glinted. 'Think of money!'

He had them straining to get out on the stage.

Anne Hendrik sat near the back and watched it all with fascination. She had seen the play more than once at the Queen's Head, but this version was very different. It was played at a more measured pace and included additional songs and dances. Most of the wit and word-play was lost on the audience but they were entranced by the visual aspects of the production. Musical interludes allowed them time to discuss the plot before new twists were introduced to it. Moments of crude farce sent them into hysterics. Anne found herself studying the audience more closely than the play.

Frankfurt cheered the performance to the echo and all but drowned out the rival hullabaloo of the fair. The Burgomaster was thrilled by what he had seen and insisted on meeting the entire company. Since he spoke no English at all, Anne came into her own as an interpreter. Enthusiastic in his praise of everyone, the Burgomaster was especially taken by Barnaby Gill's brilliant mimes. He talked excitedly to the clown for five minutes.

'What on earth is the fool saying?' asked Gill.

'He says that you were splendid,' translated Anne. 'He and his wife have never laughed so much in their life.'

'Oh!' said Gill, basking in the commendation. 'It is good to know that the city is run by a man of such discernment. What else did he say about me? I want to hear every word.'

Anne paraphrased freely and he lapped up the flattery. Nicholas looked on with amusement. She was already proving her value to the company.

Even Gill was coming to appreciate that. Firethorn could not resist a gibe at the clown.

'Who said that a lady had no place in the theatre?'

'I did,' affirmed Gill. 'And I hold to that view.'

'After all that Anne has just done for us?'

'Drama is the domain of men.'

'Translate that into German.'

Gill conceded a unique smile of self-deprecation.

'Even I have my limitations,' he said.

Three days in Frankfurt helped to erase ugly memories of Flushing and uneasy recollections of *The Corrupt Bargain* in Cologne. Westfield's Men could do no wrong. *Marriage and Mischief* won them countless new friends at their second performance and *Cupid's Folly* extended their fame even further on the final afternoon. As they returned to the Golden Lion to celebrate their achievements, they were in a buoyant mood.

'I begin to love this country,' said Owen Elias.

'It is growing on me as well,' agreed James Ingram.

'I still do not like the beer,' said George Dart timidly. 'It is too strong for my stomach.' His face brightened. 'But I like the sausages. They are wonderful. Wunderbar!'

'You are not the only person to like them, George,' said Elias. 'Do you know what a German's idea of happiness is?'

'No, Owen.'

'Lange Würste, Kurz Predigen.'

'What does it mean?'

'Long sausages, short sermons.'

'Food before faith,' observed Ingram. 'They're a practical people, the Germans.'

'Their women have a similar motto,' said Elias.

'Do they?'

'A long sausage, twice a night.'

Dart was puzzled. 'The women eat sausages at night?'

'If their menfolk are lucky!'

The jest produced ribald laughter from some of the others but its meaning was way beyond Dart. He turned his attention to the monster sausage before him. As he popped the end into his mouth, his fellows gave him a mocking cheer. None the wiser, he chewed away contentedly.

Nicholas was at a table with Firethorn, Hoode and Anne Hendrik. While the actors were toasting their success on the stage, the book-holder was reflecting on the financial benefits of their visit. Part of his job was to collect, count and look after all the money paid for admission to the performances. In addition to what the gatherers had taken, there was a generous donation from the City Council. Three days in Frankfurt had brought in as much as three weeks at the Queen's Head. It made Firethorn think fondly of home once more.

'Margery must share in this good fortune,' he said. 'I must find a way to send money back to her in Shoreditch.'

'She will surely be grateful,' said Anne.

'There will be others of the same mind,' added Nicholas. 'They have wives and families as well.'

'So much money in such a short time!' said Firethorn, rubbing his palms together. 'Germany has enriched us.'

'And ennobled us,' Hoode pointed out. 'We came here as threadbare players and they treat us like minor aristocrats. In England, we are reviled as shiftless actors. Here, we are gentlemen of a company.'

'It is no more than we deserve, Edmund. Wait until we get to Bohemia. The Emperor will probably give us knighthoods.'

Evening soon merged with night and the atmosphere at the inn grew steadily rowdier. Westfield's Men were not the only roisterers. Other travellers were staying there and the Golden Lion also had its regular customers from the locality. It was only a matter of time before the drinking songs began in lusty German. Anne decided that it was time to retire to bed. They were leaving at dawn next morning and she needed her sleep. Nicholas escorted her away from the revelry before it took on an even more boisterous note. After taking a fond farewell outside her bedchamber, he urged her to lock her door and open it to nobody. Anne gave a wan smile.

'I would feel safer if you were with me,' she said.

'It is where I would love to be, Anne, but . . .' He glanced downstairs. 'It is awkward. I have other duties.'

'I understand.'

'They are envious enough of me, as it is.'

She nodded. What they could easily do in the privacy of her house became trickier when he was with the whole company. Nicholas did not want to expose Anne to lewd gossip or himself to the knowing looks of his colleagues. Discretion was the first priority.

'There will be time,' he promised. 'One day.'

'I will wait.'

She blew him another kiss and retreated behind the door. When he heard the bolt being slipped home, he went downstairs to the taproom. Firethorn and Hoode had moved to the main table to be with the rest of the company. Nicholas saw that a stranger had joined them.

'Come and sit here, Nick,' said Firethorn, making room on the bench. 'Meet our new friend. I'll call him plain Hugo because my tongue cannot get round his other name.'

'Usselincx,' said the stranger. 'Hugo Usselincx.'

'This is Nick Bracewell. The mainstay of the company.'

Nicholas exchanged greetings with the newcomer and sat opposite him. Usselincx was a well-built man of short stature, but his shoulders were so rounded and his manner so diffident that he seemed even smaller than he was. He was soberly dressed in the Dutch fashion with a cap that was pulled down over his forehead. A nervous smile hung around the wide mouth. His English was good but overlaid with a Dutch accent.

'I came to congratulate you,' he said softly.

'You saw the performance this afternoon?'

'Hugo saw all three performances, Nick,' said Firethorn with a hearty chuckle. 'He is a stauncher patron than Lord Westfield.'

'I only found out this evening where the company was staying,' explained Usselincx. 'I would not normally have come. I am very shy. But I had to make the effort this time.'

'That is very gratifying, Master Usselincx,' said Nicholas.

'Please. Call me Hugo. It is easier.'

Nicholas was trying to weigh up the man. Frankfurt was full of merchants—many from Holland—but Hugo Usselincx was not one of them. He had none of the assertiveness of a man who lives to haggle. The dark attire suggested a religious affiliation of some kind. Having been appraised himself, the Dutchman was carrying out his own shrewd scrutiny of Nicholas.

'Master Firethorn was right to call you the mainstay.'

'Why?'

'Because you kept the company together,' said Usselincx. 'You are the book-holder, are you not?'

'How did you know that?'

'Because you do not look like an actor and you are the only member of the company who did not appear onstage. You were behind the scenes, Nicholas Bracewell. Working hard to make the play flow from scene to scene. The book-holder is an important man. Especially in a company like yours.'

'You have seen English players before?'

'Many times. I lived in London for a while.'

'Oh?'

'I saw you wondering if I was in holy orders,' said the other with a smile. 'You were close. I am an organist. I have worked in churches and cathedrals all over Europe. Earlier this year, I was in London. I heard much about Westfield's Men and saw you perform *Black Antonio* at the Queen's Head.'

'I hope you enjoyed it, Hugo,' said Nicholas, warming to him. 'What brings you to Frankfurt?'

'I am on my way to Prague to take up a post there. The Týn Church. It is very famous.' He looked around the actors. 'I could not believe my luck when I discovered that Westfield's Men were here. I should have left two days ago but I stayed on so that I did not miss a single performance.'

'We are bound for Prague ourselves.'

'So Master Firethorn was telling me.'

'We are to be guests of honour at the Imperial Court,' said Firethorn. 'By personal invitation of the Emperor.'

'No honour could be higher.' He peered at Nicholas. 'I hope that our paths may cross again. If there is some way that I may watch you play in Prague, I will find it.'

'You will be most welcome, Hugo,' said Firethorn. 'But if you go by the same route, why not travel in company with us?'

'That would be an imposition. Besides, I am days behind now. I must ride hard to make up lost time.' He rose to his feet and offered his hand to Firethorn. 'Farewell—and thank you for this pleasure.'

'We are always pleased to see a friendly face, Hugo.'

'Yes,' said Nicholas. 'We wish you Godspeed!'

Usselincx took his hand between both palms and shook it. As he backed away, the Dutchman plucked a small purse from his belt and tossed it to Firethorn.

'Spend that for me in celebration of your triumph.'

When Firethorn shook out the coins, he was surprised at the man's generosity. Before he could thank him, however, Hugo Usselincx had given a simpering smile and disappeared.

'Frankfurt is a city of wonders!' said Firethorn. 'Money drops out of the sky.'

'We would do well to save it against harsher times,' suggested Nicholas. 'Shall I take charge of it?'

'No, Nick. It is ours to spend and that is what we will do with it. We'll drink the health of Hugo Usselincx.' He put an arm around his friend. 'Do not look so disapproving. This money may be spent, but plenty more will fall into our laps. We may find that it grows on trees in Bohemia.'

'I doubt that.'

'So will I when I am sober again. But tonight I will get as gloriously drunk as a lord. Then I will fall into my bed and dream sweetly of Sophia Magdalena. The fair maid herself.' He smacked his friend between the shoulder-blades. 'Come, Nick. Be honest. You long to see her again yourself.'

'I do,' admitted Nicholas, 'but my first task will be to seek out someone else in Prague.'

'And who is that?'

'Doctor Talbot Royden.'

H̲e was still not used to the noisome stench of the dungeon or to its chilling coldness. Talbot Royden sat in the straw in a corner, huddled over the single candle they had allowed him. Since he had been thrown in there, he had been given no food or drink. Were they intent on starving him to death? His head was still spinning at the speed of what had happened. Instead of being the respected Doctor Royden, he was one more miserable prisoner in the castle dungeons. Why had Rudolph turned against him so suddenly and unaccountably?

Distant footsteps raised a faint glimmer of hope and he scrambled to the door. A guard came down the steps, lighting the way with a flaming torch that gave off an acrid smell. Peering through the bars, Royden rallied when he saw that his assistant was following the guard. Caspar was carrying a large basket that was covered with a cloth. His assistant was as confused as his master by what had happened, but at least he had retained his freedom. He was Royden's one link with the outside world.

'Caspar!' he called. 'What is going on? Why have they done this to me? Have you been to the Emperor to protest?'

'Yes, Master,' said the other quietly.

'Well?'

'He said that I was to give you this.'

'What is it?'

'You will see, Master.'

The guard unlocked the door and Caspar stepped into the dungeon. He offered his cargo to Royden with obvious embarrassment, then indicated that he should remove the cloth. When Royden did so, he was stupefied. The gift from the Emperor made no sense at all. In his hands, the prisoner was holding a huge basket of fresh fruit.

[CHAPTER EIGHT]

The mood of elation in which they left Frankfurt lasted for only a few days. Westfield's Men were soon weary of the discomforts of travelling over bad roads in changeable weather. Complaints surfaced, bickering developed. On the fourth day, one of the wagons overturned while fording a river. Injuries were minor, but half of the company were soaked to the skin and the wagon itself was badly damaged. Repairs cost them precious time. Because they could not reach the next town by nightfall, they had to sleep under the stars. It was a thoroughly dispirited troupe which set off at dawn next morning.

As setbacks continued to mount, even the placid Edmund Hoode began to grumble. He was seated beside Nicholas Bracewell, who was driving the first wagon. Anne Hendrik was directly behind them, listening to the strains of the lute on which Richard Honeydew was practising. Hoode gazed at the mountains ahead of them.

'Do we have to climb over those, Nick?' he moaned.

'There may be a pass through them.'

'Not with our luck!'

'It is bound to change soon.'

'Yes—for the worse. We have been on the road for a week now and we still seem no closer to our destination. Will we ever get there?'

'No question but that we will,' assured Nicholas. 'And the journey has not been entirely an ordeal. Eisenach was a pretty town and Weimar even more so.'

[141]

'But we only stayed a night at each, Nick. Had we performed at both, I would look back on them with far more pleasure. As it was, they were mere breaks from the tedium of travelling.'

'There was no time to linger, Edmund.'

'More's the pity!'

'We have to press on as hard as we may,' said Nicholas. 'That is why we have altered our route. Master Davey urged us to go by way of Leipzig and Dresden, but that would take us in a wide loop. This road—poor as it is—should get us to Prague all the sooner.'

'I think we have been going around in circles.'

'Only in your mind.'

Hoode gave a hollow laugh. The horses were ambling along, the wagon was creaking and the passengers were jolted every time they encountered deep ruts or scattered stones. The playwright was irked by their lethargic progress.

'Do you know what Balthasar Davey told me?' he said.

'What?'

'It was over that delicious meal we were given at the Governor's house in Flushing. Sir Robert spoke movingly of his late brother. Master Davey was equally complimentary. He told us that Sir Philip Sidney had once ridden all the way from Vienna to Cracow in a mere fourteen days.'

'Did he tell you what distance was covered?'

'Over five hundred and fifty miles.'

'That is extraordinary,' said Nicholas admiringly. 'Sir Philip must have been in the saddle for some forty miles a day. That is horsemanship of a high order.'

'Would that we could emulate him!' sighed Hoode. 'At this pace, we will be lucky to manage four miles a day. Do you think that we will reach Prague in time for Christmas?'

'Be of good cheer, Edmund!'

'How?'

'We are closer than you think.'

'Only another thousand bruising miles to go!'

Nicholas diverted him from his misery by introducing the topic of *The Fair Maid of Bohemia*. Hoode had now completed all the major changes to the play and only small refinements were left. Discussing his work—and recalling the lovely creature to whom it was dedicated—slowly helped to lift him out of his despondency. The miles drifted past more painlessly.

The second wagon had dropped some distance behind. A malaise had settled on its passengers as well. Taking his turn at the reins, Lawrence Firethorn found that even his optimism was ragged around the edges. They had tried to stave off boredom by changing passengers between the wagons each day but it had not worked. Firethorn was now carrying Owen Elias, George Dart, James Ingram, Barnaby Gill and the other three apprentices. All but Gill were asleep in the rear of the vehicle. He sat beside the driver to groan incessantly about their folly in embarking on the enterprise in the first place. The name of Clement Islip had more than one wistful mention.

The attack came without warning. They were wending their way through a wood at the time. Firethorn was now some fifty yards behind the other wagon and lost sight of it around a sharp bend. The robbers chose their moment to strike. Six of them came charging out of the undergrowth on their horses and surrounded the second wagon. Their yells were indecipherable but the weapons they brandished conveyed a clear message. Dazed passengers awoke to learn that they were being ordered out of the wagon on pain of death.

A seventh member of the band was meanwhile making it impossible for those in the first wagon to render assistance. He came riding out of the trees with a loud whoop and lashed at the rumps of the horses with a whip. They bolted at once and Nicholas suddenly found himself in charge of a runaway wagon. He did not stay on it for long. Cries from behind him told him of the ambush and he reacted with great speed.

Thrusting the reins into Hoode's hands, he dived head first off the wagon and knocked the rider from his saddle. The fall jarred both of them but Nicholas was the first to recover, pinning the man to the ground and raining blows to his head until he was senseless. He deprived the robber of his sword, then looked after the wagon long enough to see that Hoode was somehow getting the animals under control. Nicholas ran to collect the stray horse and clamber into the saddle. As he kicked his mount into a gallop and went to the aid of his fellows, he could hear the commotion ahead of him.

The three apprentices had leaped out of the wagon in terror and Barnaby Gill was pleading for mercy on his knees. Firethorn, Ingram and Elias were putting up a fight and even Dart was waving a token dagger at the attackers. When a horse came around the bend, the robbers expected an accomplice who would help them overcome the resistance of the actors. Instead, they had to contend with Nicholas in full cry.

He hacked the sword from the hand of the first man he met, then sent a second sprawling to the ground with a blow from his forearm. Nicholas engaged a third in such a fierce duel that the man took fright and swung his horse away. Inspired by the help from their book-holder, the actors fought off their attackers with renewed aggression. The apprentices snatched up twigs and logs to hurl at the robbers. Even Gill found enough courage to draw his dagger and wave it in the air.

As Nicholas wounded another man in the arm, the robbers gave up. Their leader called a retreat. He scooped up the man who had been buffeted to the ground, then led the other horses off through the trees. Nicholas pursued them for a hundred yards, then doubled back to the wagon, gathering the second stray horse on his way. His colleagues were shaken but excited.

'Thank heaven you came, Nick!' said Firethorn gratefully.

'An accomplice made our horses bolt so that you would be isolated.' Nicholas looked at his dishevelled friends. 'They chose the second wagon because it seemed less well-defended. They will rue their mistake now. All they collected was a few cuts and bruises while we have gained two horses out of the ambush.'

With Hoode at the reins, the other wagon came rumbling around the bend towards them. The modest playwright was astounded at his own heroism, having mastered the runaway horses and saved his passengers from any injury. When Nicholas saw that Anne was quite safe, he looked up thankfully at the panting driver.

'Well done, Edmund!' he congratulated. 'But what of the man I unseated from his horse?'

'He has fled into the trees,' said Hoode. 'When we rode past, he was limping away with his hands to his head, groaning piteously. He will remember his encounter with Nicholas Bracewell.'

'*We* must remember to be more alert,' warned the other. 'If the wagons had been closer together, that attack might never have occurred. Our safety lies in staying together.'

'From now on, we will be inches behind you,' promised Gill. 'That was the most terrifying experience of my life. We might all have been killed.'

'They were after your wagon and your valuables,' said Nicholas. 'You protected both bravely.'

'Yes,' added Firethorn with heavy sarcasm. 'Barnaby distracted them so cunningly when he begged for mercy like that. His knees were every bit as effective as our swords.' He let out a cry of triumph. 'We beat them, lads! We gave them a taste of English steel and sent the rogues packing. Nick has spoken true. Together, we survive—apart, we perish! Let us go forth as a united band of brothers. Nobody will then break us asunder. We are gentlemen of a company and gallant soldiers of fortune.'

Bohemia was disappointing. Nourished by fantasies on their interminable trek through Germany, they expected to cross the border into Bohemia and be met by stunning vistas of that fabled country. Nothing seemed to change. The same landscape rolled out before them, the same cows and sheep grazed in the fields, the same herds of pigs and flocks of geese obstructed them in villages and hamlets. They even got the same curious stares from the peasants as they passed, though the occasional words they overheard were now in Czech rather than German. Disenchantment swept through both wagons.

When they finally had struggled all the way to Prague, they needed something truly phenomenal to restore their faith and at first they believed that they were seeing it.

'Look at it!'

'Remarkable!'

'Wonderful!'

'Astonishing.'

'Incredible!'

'Have you ever seen such a city?'

'It is better than Cologne!'

'Or Frankfurt!'

'Or even London!'

'This is no earthly city,' decided Firethorn, hungrily devouring every morsel of the joyous vision before him. 'We have been travelling on a highway to Heaven itself!'

Wagons which had halted in awe now set off with urgency as Westfield's Men sought to enter the sacred portals. Exhausted actors were now throbbing with life. Drooping spirits were lifted to soaring heights. Bohemia was at last yielding up its celestial heart to them. Prague was a paradise.

It was a huge, gold-embossed galleon riding upon the back of the mighty River Vltava as it surged irresistibly through the very heart of the city. Castle and cathedral dominated Prague from their lofty eminence on the western hill and gazed down at the Karlův Most, the Charles Bridge, which spanned the river with sixteen vast but graceful arches. Built almost two centuries earlier by Emperor Charles IV, the bridge was the lifeline between the two halves of the city. Westfield's Men had never seen anything so immense and so ornately decorated. London Bridge was one of the finest sights of their own city but it had nothing like the scale and statuary of this.

The nearer they got, the more entranced they became.

'It *is* heaven!' argued Firethorn. 'The only place fit for an angel like Sophia Magdalena.'

'Count those spires,' said Hoode in wonder. 'Every church in Bohemia must be encircled by the city walls.'

'It has been a grim journey,' said Nicholas, turning to Anne. 'Do you regret now that you came with us?'

'Not after seeing this, Nick,' she affirmed. 'It beggars all description. I would have come twice as far and endured much worse privations in order to view this Elysium.'

'It is beautiful.'

'Beyond compare.'

'Let us hope it lives up to its appearance.'

Paradise was not without its problems. They caught the first whiff of one of them when they were still a few hundred yards away. The pervading stench of Prague was carried on the wind. It was caused by the piles of filth and excrement in the narrow streets. Flies buzzed everywhere. Dogs scavenged and fought. As they plunged into the city, its stink and squalor reminded them hideously of London.

Prague was an optical illusion. Seen from afar, it was indeed a golden city. Closer inspection revealed it to have rows of decrepit timber-framed cottages alongside stone hovels that were scarcely bigger than huts. Emperor Rudolph might live in a sumptuous abode up on the hill, but many of his subjects eked out a wretched existence in houses that were little more than kennels. The juxtaposition of magnificence and misery was every bit as grotesque as in London.

The two wagons first made their way to the river to take stock of its angry power as it surged along like a gigantic serpent in pursuit of a distant prey. Craft of all kinds were riding on the water in the afternoon sun. Wharves were busy along both banks. The smell of fish gave an added pungency to the city's abiding reek. People were hurrying to and fro across the Charles Bridge. Prague was a city with a lot of work to do. They saw no sign of laziness or leisure.

Nicholas led the way to the nearest inn so that the thirsty company could refresh themselves and sit on something more comfortable than the heaving boards of a wagon. The Czech landlord gave them a grinning welcome. Anne's command of German once more came into its own. Leaving them ensconced at the inn, Nicholas made his way up to the castle with Firethorn. The latter was anxious to make direct contact with the Emperor at the earliest opportunity.

'He will see us at once,' he predicted.

'Do not rely on that.'

'We are honoured guests, Nick. The Emperor has promised us free board and lodging, and all the delights of his Court.'

'He also promised to send letters to Cologne and Frankfurt on our behalf,' noted Nicholas, 'but they never arrived. It might not be wise to expect too much.'

'I expect everything,' boomed Firethorn.

As they climbed the hill, Nicholas took stock of the fortifications. Impressive from a distance, they were full of deficiencies at close hand. Ramparts were in need of repair and additional defences were required at the western end of the bridge. The guards who patrolled the castle were few in number and slack in their duties. The two visitors presented themselves at the castle gate and were waved through without any real discussion of their purpose in coming there. When Nicholas produced the letter bearing the Imperial seal, it was enough to gain them admittance.

'We should have brought Anne with us,' said Firethorn.

'Why?'

'As our interpreter.'

'She has her hands full back at the inn,' said Nicholas. 'Besides, this invitation was written in English, so they must have a translator here. We will find artists and scientists from all over Europe at the Court. Many different languages will be spoken, English among them.'

'We cannot be certain of that, Nick.'

'We can. Doctor Talbot Royden resides here.'

'I was forgetting him.'

'I have not been allowed to forget him.'

Nicholas was glad that they had arrived unscathed at their destination. When the ambush took place, his first thought had been that it was set up by the man who stalked him. It was something of a relief to learn that they were simply the target of a band of robbers. Now that he was inside the castle where Royden lived, he felt that his mission was accomplished. The secret documents and the wooden box from Doctor Mordrake could be handed over. Nicholas would never part with anything quite so readily.

They went through the first courtyard and into a much larger one. Guards stood about chatting but showed little interest in the visitors. It was only when they stepped through into the third courtyard that someone finally paid any real attention to them.

'Well met, gentlemen! Welcome to Prague!'

Hugo Usselincx was standing outside the door of Saint Vitus Cathedral when he saw them. Shoulders hunched, he shuffled across to them and waved his hands nervously in the air.

'I am delighted to see you both again.'

'It is good to see you, Hugo,' responded Firethorn.

'How long have you been here?' asked Nicholas.

'A few days.'

'You must have ridden hard.'

'I had to make up for lost time.'

'We had the most devilish journey,' moaned Firethorn.

'But we arrived safely,' said Nicholas, cutting off his memoirs about the ambush. 'And we are much taken with this lovely city.'

'Where are you staying?'

'That is what we have come to find out.'

'And what will you perform while you are here?'

'The very best plays,' boasted Firethorn.

'I will climb over the castle walls to see them.'

'That may not be too difficult a thing to do,' observed Nicholas, glancing around. 'Is Prague not concerned about its defences?'

'The Emperor has other interests,' confided Usselincx. 'But the city may not be as open to attack as it might look. The jest they make here is that Prague is protected from invasion by its smell.'

'We had noticed it, Hugo,' said Firethorn with a grimace. 'We also noticed how many churches there are here. Some are built of wood, most of stone, with roofs of slate and spires that shine like silver. The only church I could not pick out was the one that is made of tin.'

'Tin?'

'That is where you are organist, is it not? The Tin Church. Or so I remember you telling us.'

'I did, I did,' said Usselincx, suppressing a giggle. 'But the Týn Church is not made of tin.'

'What else is it made of?'

'Solid stone, Master Firethorn. When I said "Týn," I should have spelled the word for you. T-ý-n. It means a courtyard or an enclosed area, much like the one we are standing in. The Týn Church is in a courtyard behind the main square. Its full name is the Church of Our Lady Before Týn. It is old and beautiful, like so much here. Does that help you to understand?'

'Yes,' said Nicholas.

'No,' contradicted Firethorn.

'I keep you from more important things,' said Usselincx as he backed away. 'Enjoy your welcome from the Emperor. I look to see you again before long.'

They exchanged farewells, then headed for the palace which was opposite the south door of the cathedral. Firethorn liked their Dutch friend immensely but Nicholas had reservations about the man. He found his manner a shade too unctuous.

When they entered the palace, Hugo Usselincx went right out of their minds. Armed guards confronted them and demanded to know who they were. Nicholas produced the letter with the Imperial seal but neither man could understand the language in which it was written. One of the guards disappeared down a corridor with the missive and the visitors were forced to wait for several minutes.

The man eventually returned with a servant in tow. It was the latter who now held the invitation and he used it to beckon them after him. Nicholas and Firethorn were led down a long corridor and into a gallery that was festooned with the work of the various Court artists. The servant paused to run a fond eye over the extraordinary collection of paintings. He was a middle-aged man with a striking face and a mischievous smile. Ushering them out of the gallery, he took them to an apartment on the west side of the palace and halted outside the door. He studied both men for a moment, then offered the letter to the actor-manager.

'Lawrence Firethorn?' he said in passable English.

'Yes,' replied the other, taking the invitation.

'And you?' The servant turned to Nicholas. 'Name, please.'

'Nicholas Bracewell.'

'Masters Firethorn and Master Bracewell. Excuse me.'

After tapping on the door, the servant went into the room for a brief moment. When he reappeared, he conducted the two men into a large and well-appointed apartment with an ornate desk at its centre. The servant bowed out and closed the door silently behind him.

The Chamberlain rose from his chair behind the desk and regarded his visitors with solemn curiosity. He knew enough English to negotiate his way through a conversation.

'You are welcome,' he said, manufacturing a smile. 'My name is Wolfgang von Rumpf and I am the Chamberlain. You are,' he said, pointing to each in turn, 'Lawrence Firethorn and Nicholas Bracewell. Correct?'

'That is so, sir,' confirmed Firethorn.

'Pray be seated.'

The Chamberlain indicated the chairs in front of the desk and all three men sat down. Anticipating a more gracious reception, Firethorn was somewhat put out by the man's aloofness. Whoever else had issued the invitation, it had certainly not been Wolfgang von Rumpf. The Chamberlain glanced down at a document in front of him.

'We expected you a few days ago,' he chided.

'Unforeseen delays on the road,' explained Nicholas. 'One of our wagons broke down and we were ambushed by robbers.'

'Was anyone hurt?'

'Not on our side,' said Firethorn, 'but we swinged them soundly. Nicholas fought off three of them himself.'

'I see,' said the Chamberlain. 'I am sorry to hear about this. The Emperor had intended to arrange an armed escort for you, but . . .' He paused to choose his words with care. 'He was led astray by other matters. You reached Prague. That is the main thing. We are deeply grateful to Westfield's Men.'

'It is an honour to be here, sir.'

'Where and when do we perform?' asked Nicholas politely.

'We will come to that in a moment,' said the Chamberlain. 'First, we must accommodate our guests. The palace itself is full at the moment, alas, so we have lodged you at an inn. I am told that the Black Eagle will meet your needs.'

'Thank you.'

'No cost will be incurred by you. We will settle any bills. Westfield's Men will want for nothing.'

'That is very heartening,' said Firethorn with a grin.

'In due course, I will get someone to show you the hall where you will perform. When you choose a play, I would like to know its subject before I give my approval. We are in a sensitive situation here. I cannot allow any drama that is critical of our government or discourteous to our religion.'

'We understand,' said Nicholas.

'Good.' He sat back and looked from one to the other. 'Now, gentlemen. Is there anything you wish to ask me?'

Nicholas had several questions but the main one was dictated by the bulge beneath his jerkin. Ever since the secret documents he carried had led to the murder of Adrian Smallwood, he had been anxious to deliver them to the man to whom they were sent. He put a hand to his cargo.

'I believe that a Doctor Talbot Royden is at Court.'

'He was,' said the Chamberlain levelly.

'He is not here any longer?'

'Oh, he is still at the castle, Master Bracewell. But he is no longer in the hallowed position he once held.'

'I do not follow.'

'Doctor Royden is an astrologer and an alchemist. He was retained to provide personal services to Emperor Rudolph.'

'Personal services?'

'It matters not what they were,' said the other coldly, 'because he is no longer free to offer them. Doctor Royden has been arrested and thrown into the castle dungeon.'

'Why?'

'That is of no concern to you.'

'But it is,' said Nicholas earnestly. 'I must speak with him in order to pass on a message from England.'

'Out of the question.'

'Is he not allowed visitors?'

'No,' came the crisp reply. 'He is in disgrace.'

'Can we at least know why?'

[151]

The Chamberlain was peremptory. 'That is the end of the matter. Doctor Royden is being held on the Emperor's orders.' He glanced at Firethorn. 'Did you have a question?'

'A number, sir,' replied the actor. 'The first concerns the lady whose interest in Westfield's Men brought us here. The Emperor sent the invitation but we know that she must have encouraged him to do so.'

'That is so, Master Firethorn. Sophia Magdalena watched your company in London and was overwhelmed. She insisted that you were brought here.'

'She has been our guiding star.'

'Lawrence Firethorn was mentioned many times.'

'She wanted me!'

'Sophia Magdalena says you are a wonderful actor.'

'Ecstasy!'

'She will be pleased that you got here in time.'

'Not as pleased as I am,' said Firethorn, leaning forward with a chuckle. 'When may I see the fair maid herself?'

'At the wedding. Naturally.'

Firethorn gulped. 'The wedding?'

'That is why you are here,' said the Chamberlain. 'In a few days' time, Sophia Magdalena of Jankau is to marry the son of the Duke of Brunswick. The marriage will take place in the cathedral. Banquets will be held for a week thereafter. Your plays will be part of the wedding celebrations. Did you not realise that?'

Nicholas adjusted to the news with ease but Firethorn was staggered. Libidinous desires which had sustained him through fatigue and adversity now crumbled into dust. Imagining that Sophia Magdalena had—like so many gorgeous young women before her—fallen hopelessly in love with him during one of his monumental performances, the actor had never paused to wonder if there might be another man in her life. He was at once incensed at the magnitude of his own folly and shaken by what he saw as her betrayal of him.

'Sophia Magdalena?' he said under his breath. 'Rather would I call her *Mary* Magdalena. The sinful creature!'

The Chamberlain gave a pale smile. 'We look to you to select plays which are suitable for such an occasion.'

'We will be happy to do so,' said Nicholas, covering his companion's evident exasperation. 'By way of a wedding gift, we have brought a new play for the bride.'

'Excellent! What is it called?'

The Whore of Prague!' mumbled Firethorn.

The Fair Maid of Bohemia,' said Nicholas quickly. 'Our playwright, Edmund Hoode, has fashioned it with care for this joyful event. He will also take part in the play.'

'We look forward to seeing its first performance.'

'It will also be its last!' said Firethorn.

'Oh?'

'What Master Firethorn means,' intervened Nicholas, 'is that the play is new-minted for Sophia Magdalena. It belongs solely to her and will not be offered elsewhere. Beyond the confines of Bohemia, it would not have the same value or inner meaning.' He shot the actor a reproving glance. 'Was not that the decision you reached?'

'Indeed, it was,' said Firethorn, regaining his composure and smothering his frustration beneath a fawning smile. 'Westfield's Men offer the bride a wedding gift which will sing sweetly in her memory forever.'

'Sophia Magdalena will be duly grateful,' said the Chamberlain brusquely. 'But you will no doubt wish to view the hall where this piece will be staged.' He reached for a bell. 'I will have someone conduct you there directly.'

'One moment,' said Firethorn, intent on propping up his sagging pride in some way. 'There is something else we wish to do before that. We are the guests of Emperor Rudolph. His letter of invitation expressly requested us to seek him out as soon as we reached Prague.' He sat up straight in the chair. 'Let him know that Lawrence Firethorn has arrived and is desirous of meeting the Emperor.'

Wolfgang von Rumpf spoke quietly through gritted teeth.

'You have already done so,' he said.

'I fear that you are mistaken, sir.'

'Believe me, I am not.'

'The only people we have met since we arrived have been a Dutch acquaintance of ours, Hugo Usselincx, and your good self. When are we supposed to have met Emperor Rudolph?'

'On your way to this apartment.'

Firethorn exchanged a look of amazement with Nicholas.

'The servant?'

'That was the Holy Roman Emperor and King of Bohemia.'

'An underling in his own palace?'

The Chamberlain winced. He spoke with the distaste of a parent who is forced to acknowledge an obstreperous child as his own. He nodded wearily.

'The Emperor is somewhat eccentric,' he said.

Dressed in the garb of a keeper and carrying a large hunk of fresh meat, Rudolph strolled past the cages in his menagerie and waved familiarly at their snarling denizens. He paused to watch two white doves, perched side by side in their little domed prison, nestling up to each other with cooing affection. Touched by the sight of love in a place of such roaring anger, he moved on until he came to one of the largest cages. Three wolves were padding restlessly around, checking the perimeter of their limited territory in an endless search for escape. They paid no heed to the curious onlooker.

The animals were a gift from Russia and had white-tufted fur. Their feline grace concealed a deep and vengeful rage. When Rudolph tossed the meat through the bars, they pounced on it as if it were the man who had stolen their freedom. As they fought noisily and viciously over the meat, a profound sadness descended on their keeper. He was no longer feeding his beloved animals. He was watching his empire being torn apart by wanton brutality. His hands rested forlornly on the bars.

'Catholic, Protestant, Hussite,' he sighed, nodding at each animal in turn. 'Which wolf will devour the biggest portion?'

The sight soon appalled him. Turning sharply away, he went off quickly to seek the solace of his botanical gardens.

The Black Eagle was situated in one of the labyrinthine streets of the Malá Strana, the Little Side of the river. Most of the inhabitants lived in the larger part of the city on the eastern bank and Westfield's Men had already walked across the bridge to acquaint themselves with its many wonders. However, they found the Malá Strana more to their taste. It had a secretiveness that appealed to them. None of them could read the Czech name on the inn sign, but the crudely painted black bird of prey left them in no doubt where they were.

The inn was small but comfortable and their hostess was the image of hospitality. A big, bosomy woman with a roguish eye, she was thrilled to have been chosen to look after a famous English theatre troupe. After a regular diet of sausages and bacon in Germany, the visitors were pleased to find more fish and poultry being served. The local beer was dark and strong. An hour in its congenial company soon won them over.

While his fellows caroused, Firethorn stared blankly at the table and mused on the fickleness of destiny. The others might be toasting their arrival in Prague but it had so far brought him nothing but heartache and rejection. Three imperatives had taken them to the palace. A doctor, a maid and an Emperor. They had not made meaningful contact with any of them. Doctor Talbot Royden was locked away in a dungeon. Sophia Magdalena would soon be incarcerated in a marriage. And Emperor Rudolph seemed to be trapped in some weird and childlike prison of the mind. Three totally inaccessible people. Firethorn emitted a low moan. Prague was failure writ large across his soul.

Something warm and tender touched his left shoulder. It was one of the ample breasts of the hostess, resting casually on him as she bent over to refill his mug from a pitcher of beer. When he looked up, he was met with a grin as wide and wilful as the Vltava. It was not a handsome face. She had the high cheekbones of the Slav race and a flattish nose, but Firethorn was uncritical. At that moment in time, she seemed accessible. It was enough to stir his manhood. As she moved away, she let her other breast caress the side of his face. He supped his beer with beaming relish.

Anne Hendrik sat alone with Nicholas Bracewell on the other side of the room. She had learned to mix well with an exclusively male group and had shown a motherly concern for the apprentices and for the waif-like George Dart. Her pleasant manner, and her refusal to expect any special favours for being a woman, made her popular with the actors. But her real purpose in being there was to spend time with Nicholas, and Westfield's Men understood this.

Anne sipped a cup of sweet wine and nodded approvingly.

'This is quite delicious.'

'Drink as much as you wish,' he said airily. 'The wine will be paid for by the Chamberlain.'

'My needs are moderate, Nick. A cup or two will suffice.'

'Free beer is too great a temptation for the others. They will be roistering here until they drop from drunkenness or exhaustion or a mixture of both.'

'They have earned it after that journey.'

'You suffered everything that they did.'

'I have my reward,' she said quietly.

Nicholas acknowledge the compliment with a smile. Unlike the rest of the company, he could not relax so easily into their new home. Unfinished business irked him. As long as the documents were still on his person, he felt vulnerable. Nobody had appeared to trail him from Frankfurt, but that did not mean the danger had passed. He remained watchful.

'What are you thinking?' she asked.

'How much more pleasant a place like this is with you here.'

'I am not in the way, then?'

'The company have taken you to their heart.'

'Do you grow jealous?'

'Yes,' he teased. 'But sorrowful, too. I am sad that you have to share me with Westfield's Men.'

'I am used to that, Nick.'

'They rely on me.'

'So do I.'

They chatted amiably about how her business would be faring during her absence. She had no qualms about her deputy. Anne had not wasted her time in Germany. She had made sketches of all the unfamiliar fashions in hats she saw and intended to collect inspiration from Bohemia as well. What she was also keen to do was to be of more practical use to the company.

'Make me your tireman, Nick.'

'We are in sore need of one,' he admitted.

'If you have torn costumes, or need them adapted to fit more snugly, I am skilled with needle and thread.'

'Thank you.'

'I do not wish to feel I am only here to speak German.'

'You are not, Anne. I can vouch for that.'

She answered his smile with one of her own and their voices dropped to a more intimate level. They were so engrossed in each other's company that they did not see the young man who came into the inn and went to the table where the actors were lolling and drinking. After making enquiry, he crossed over to the couple.

'Pray excuse me,' he said courteously. 'They tell me that you are Nicholas Bracewell.'

'That is so,' said the other, appraising him.

'My name is Caspar Hilliard. I crave a word with you, sir.'

'You may have it willingly.'

'It is a private matter,' said Caspar, with a glance at Anne. 'I would value a moment alone with you.'

'You may speak freely in front of Mistress Hendrik,' said Nicholas. 'She is a close and trusted friend. I'll hear nothing that requires her to quit my company.'

The young man weighed her up carefully before reaching his decision. He sat on the bench beside Nicholas and spoke in a whisper, his eyes flicking from the book-holder to Anne.

'I heard that you were asking after Doctor Royden.'

'Who told you that?'

'I reside at the castle. Word spreads.'

'Only the Chamberlain knew of my interest.'

'It is one that I share, sir,' explained Caspar. 'I am Doctor Royden's assistant. At least, I held that office until he was cruelly and unjustly taken away from his laboratory.'

'His assistant?' said Nicholas.

'I have worked for him this three and a half years. Ever since Doctor Mordrake left Prague. My father was English but my mother hailed from Koblenz, so I learned German from birth. It was one of the things which recommended me to Doctor Talbot Royden. That and my knowledge of science.'

'Science?'

'I studied medicine at Padua.'

'Indeed?'

Nicholas was quickly warming to him. Caspar Hilliard had a long, intelligent, open face and a smooth-shaven chin. His suit was neat but not costly and he bore himself with modesty. He was patently worried about the fate of his employer.

'Why did you wish to see Doctor Royden?' he asked.

'I have something to discuss with him,' said Nicholas.

'No visitors are allowed.'

'So we were told.'

'Save one.'

'Who is that?'

'Me. I am allowed to take his food to him.' Another cautionary glance at Anne. 'If you wish to get a message to my master, I will gladly carry it for you.'

'I need to see him myself, Master Hilliard.'

'That may prove impossible.'

'Why?' wondered Anne. 'For what reason is he imprisoned?'

'It is a cruel whim of the Emperor's,' said Caspar with a shake of his head. 'He is a capricious man and subject to such moods. The harsh treatment is certainly undeserved. Doctor Royden and I have been working twelve hours a day on the experiment.'

'What experiment?' asked Nicholas.

'I am not at liberty to discuss it, sir.'

'Some branch of alchemy, perhaps?'

'Doctor Royden is an astrologer as well as an alchemist,' conceded the other. 'And he is learned in other disciplines as well. It has been a labour of love to serve him.'

'You talked of an experiment.'

'It was nearing success,' insisted the other. 'Time was all that we needed. Time and understanding. Emperor Rudolph denied both to us. My master was summarily arrested and dragged off to the castle dungeon. It was disgraceful.'

'Does he have no means of appeal?'

'The Emperor will not hear him. Nor me. I have begged for an audience to plead my master's case but I have been turned away. The Emperor pays no attention to a humble assistant.'

Nicholas sympathised with the young man's dilemma. Caspar Hilliard was a loyal servant to a master who had apparently been treated very shabbily. If Royden's fate lay in the hands of the strange Emperor, then his assistant had good cause for alarm. Nicholas thought of the servant who had escorted them at the palace to the Chamberlain. Rudolph was clearly a man of disturbing idiosyncrasies.

'I am glad to have made your acquaintance,' said Caspar with a nod at each of them. 'May I at least tell Doctor Royden that you were asking after him?'

'Yes,' agreed Nicholas. 'And you may give him my best wishes for an early release.'

'No further message?'

'None.'

'I see.'

'You mentioned Doctor Mordrake earlier on.'

'That is so, sir.'

'What connection did he have with your master?'

'They worked in the laboratory together. Doctor Mordrake was one of the Court physicians for a while but his interests extended well beyond medicine. It was at his suggestion that my master was invited here.'

'Did they work well together?'

'Extremely well,' said Caspar. 'At first.'

'What happened then?'

'Professional differences. That is all I can tell you.'

'Have they kept in touch with each other?'

'From time to time. Doctor Royden was in England the best part of a year ago. I know that they met up again.'

'For what purpose?'

'To talk about old times.'

'Even though they had fallen out?'

'They still had some things in common.'

'What were they?' pressed Nicholas.

'I really cannot tell you,' said Caspar with a slight hint of embarrassment. 'My master does not confide everything in me. I am only his assistant and not his father-confessor. They met in London. They talked. That is all I can say.' He cocked a head to one side as he studied Nicholas. 'Why are you so interested in Doctor Mordrake?'

'I met him once. At his house in Knightrider Street.'

'Then you will know what a remarkable man he is.'

'That was self-evident.'

'My master is even more remarkable,' said the other with pride. 'He will be grateful to hear that he may have another friend in Prague apart from me.' He stood up. 'Thank you for giving me your time. I bid you both adieu!'

'Farewell!' said Nicholas. 'Thank you for coming.'

'My pleasure, sir.'

Anne watched him leave before turning to Nicholas again.

'Why did you not entrust him with the message?' she said.

'Because I had no proof that he was who he said he was.'

'He was plainly honest.'

'I needed more than honesty, Anne.'

'But this was your one chance of getting those documents to Doctor Royden and you refused to take it.'

'I want to deliver them in person,' he asserted. 'I have not brought them all this way to hand them over to a young assistant, however charming and helpful he may be. Remember that the documents robbed Adrian Smallwood of his life. I wish to know why.' His manner softened. 'Besides,' he added with a wry smile, 'after what we were told about Doctor Mordrake, I cannot wait to put something from him into the hands of his old colleague and mark his response. It should be very revealing.'

Westfield's Men were initially overcome by the opulence of the palace. They wandered in a daze past an unending series of fine paintings, arresting sculpture, ornate tapestries, ancient books, rare maps and assorted curiosities from every corner of the known world. The collection of jewellery and ornaments alone must have cost an immense fortune. Emperor Rudolph might have his personal eccentricities but his patronage of the arts was unrivalled in Europe. His whole palace was a monument to his long and generous commitment.

When they were shown into the hall where the plays were to be performed, the actors were cowed by its splendour. Frescoes adorned its walls, statuary stood in alcoves and the high ceiling was a work of art. While most of them were still awe-struck by the sumptuous surroundings, Nicholas was surveying the practicalities of the space. He chose the end of the room which afforded them entrances through two doors and which would give them the best of the afternoon light.

Performances of one kind or another were fairly frequent and the palace carpenters had constructed a series of small platforms which could be fitted together to form a stage. When servants carried them into the hall, Nicholas was relieved to see that the Emperor himself was not among them. The stage was large enough but too low. Nicholas called for a second tier of platforms to be laid upon the first, giving the players the height they needed to dominate the room and to project their voices to best effect. Curtains were hung at the rear of the stage. Steps were placed behind them to assist the cast up onto the raised platform.

By the time that the puffing George Dart had dragged the last scenic device into place—an oak tree, expertly made by Nathan Curtis from a much baser wood—they were eager to begin the rehearsal. *The Three Sisters of Mantua* would be their first offering in the short season of plays at the Imperial Court. It was a light comedy with a simple plot and a clear distinction between its shining heroes and its dark villains. It also afforded three of the apprentices an early opportunity to shine in the title roles. Experience had taught them the inestimable value of music, dance and mime to a foreign audience. *The Three Sisters of Mantua* was liberally stuffed with them.

The company made heavy weather of an undemanding play. Fatigue, nerves and a late night at the Black Eagle conspired to produce all kinds of serious errors and disastrous lapses of memory. Firethorn brought them to a halt after Act Three.

'Shame on you!' he cried, stamping a foot to make the whole stage shudder beneath them. 'Shame on you and shame on me! For I am as big a culprit as any here. This performance is not fit for an empty room, let alone for an Emperor. Wake up, sirs. Stir yourselves. Remember who we are and why we are here. First impressions are crucial. Fail today and we will lose much of the goodwill we have built up. We must sweep the audience off its feet with our vitality and not lull it to sleep with our plodding delivery. Gird your loins and fight like men!'

Nicholas added his own strictures in the tiring-house. Delivered quietly to individual actors, they had even more impact than Firethorn's public blast. The actors writhed under the joint chastisement, but it was well-deserved. They were now keyed up to exonerate themselves. The improvement was instant, and *The Three Sisters of Mantua* began to live and breathe on the stage. As the performance gathered momentum, a new spirit coursed through them. A clever play started to look like a comic masterpiece. As the Duke of Mantua, the now superb Firethorn brought the piece to a close with the epilogue.

> *'Thus ends our play and this the moral is,*
> *That nothing holds more danger than a kiss*
> *Upon the lips. Love's potion has a taste*
> *That brought three sisters in great haste*

From Mantua to seek their hearts' desire.
Remember how they burned with Cupid's fire.
Their youthful folly earned them sharp rebuke,
For each one loved the self-same Mantuan Duke,
And while his noble heart was strong and free,
He could not give it to all sisters three.
Choose one, hold fast and stay forever true
Unto your love. That is the only way you
Find real peace and happiness on this earth
And understand what love is truly worth.'

The Duke of Mantua doffed his hat and gave a low bow to the non-existent audience. There was a long pause. It was broken by the most unlikely sound. A single pair of hands began to clap earnestly from the other end of the hall. They looked up in surprise to see the dainty figure of Sophia Magdalena, clad in her finery, acclaiming their performance with ladylike enthusiasm. It was the best accolade they could have wished.

The whole company was lifted by her presence and by her approval of their art. But her eyes were fixed firmly on Lawrence Firethorn as she spoke the two words in English that she had mastered.

'Thank you,' she said sweetly. 'Thank you.'

It was enough. His feelings of betrayal melted away in a flash. Sophia Magdalena had come back to him at last. All was forgiven. As her delicate palms clapped on, Firethorn heard a choir of angels in his ears. He felt transfigured.

He was in love again.

[CHAPTER NINE]

Crouched in the corner of his cell, Doctor Talbot Royden munched disconsolately on an apple and listened to the rat snuffling in the clotted straw. There was a savage irony in his predicament. A famous scientist, who strove to push out the frontiers of knowledge, could not even tell whether it was night or day now. A celebrated alchemist, who basked in the glow of his furnace, had only one flickering candle between him and total darkness. An Emperor's favourite had suddenly become the butt of his cruel humour. Royden spat out a pip, then hurled the apple core angrily at the wall.

Another tedious hour limped past before he heard the noise from above. Two sets of footsteps were descending towards him. A rush of light came from a burning torch. Royden leaped up and peered hopefully through the bars, shielding his eyes from the glare of the flames. One of the gaolers was bringing a visitor down to the prisoner.

'Caspar!' shouted Royden. 'Am I to be released?'

'Not yet,' said his assistant.

'Have you not spoken with the Emperor?'

'He refuses to see me.'

'Does my name count for nothing in Prague?'

'Unhappily, it does not.'

'Help me!'

'I am doing my best, Master.'

The gaoler unlocked the door so that they could have a proper conversation but he stayed close to keep them under observation. Since the man spoke no English, they were able to talk freely. Royden grasped his assistant by the shoulders and gabbled questions at him.

'What is going on?' he demanded. 'Why have I been cast into this foul pit? Who has turned the Emperor against me? When will they let me out of here? Tell me what you have found out, Caspar. Is there any comfort at all for me? Can I dare to hope? Or will I be left here to rot in perpetuity?' He tightened his grip. 'What time of day is it?'

'Not long after noon, Master.'

'It is eternal night down here.'

'How do you fare?' asked the other considerately.

'I dwindle, Caspar. I dwindle and decay.'

'Bear up.'

'This is the vilest torture.'

'Such affliction cannot last forever.'

'It will break my spirit.'

He slumped to the floor and sat in the straw. Caspar knelt beside him and tried to offer consolation, but Royden was close to despair. His assistant could see the tears in his eyes.

'There is one tiny ray of hope, Master,' he said.

'What is it?' begged the other. 'Tell me. Please tell me.'

'They have not touched the laboratory.'

'My materials? My equipment?'

'All safe.'

'My books? My records of our experiments?'

'Untouched.'

'You still have the key?'

'Yes,' said Caspar, patting his purse. 'I keep the room locked at all times. Nobody else may enter the laboratory. I am looking after it until my master returns.'

'God bless you!'

'The Emperor must relent.'

'What chance is there of that?'

'He is often given to charitable impulse.'

'Bohemia has a madman upon its throne. I have seen so much evidence of his lunacy over the years. My loyalty to him was grossly misplaced. I should have quit Prague a long time ago.' He spread his palms in supplication. 'I have done him great service, Caspar. Why will he not even see me?'

'His mind is taken up with the preparations.'

'For what?'

'The wedding.'

'Ah, yes!' sighed Royden. 'The wedding.'

'That may have been our downfall,' said Caspar sadly. 'The Emperor was counting on us. We were to provide a wedding gift that was quite unique. And we did not.'

'Only because his guards stopped us.'

'Our time ran out, Master.'

'Alchemy will not conform to time.'

'When the wedding is over, he may take pity on you.'

'Will I still be living?'

'Assuredly. Think of your laboratory.'

'I think of nothing else down here.'

'If the Emperor had turned against you, he would have destroyed your work completely. But it has been left quite unmolested for you to resume one day.'

'When?'

'After the wedding. That preoccupies him now.'

'Will I have to languish here until then?'

'I fear so, Master.'

'Out of sight, out of mind.'

'Not out of *my* mind,' promised the other. 'Nor that of a stranger from England who has been asking after you.'

'A stranger?'

'Nicholas Bracewell. Does you know him?'

'I have never heard the name before.'

'He travels with Westfield's Men, a troupe of players from London. They are to play a comedy this afternoon before the whole Court.'

'A comedy!' Royden gave mirthless laugh. 'Send them down to my dungeon and they will see a tragedy being performed.' His eyes narrowed. 'What did this Nicholas Bracewell want?'

'To speak with you.'

'Why?'

'He would not say.'

'What manner of man was he?'

'A fine, upstanding fellow, from what I could judge. He is only the book-holder with the company, but he is highly respected by all. A solid man, one not likely to give way if trouble came. Honest and trustworthy.'

'How did he earn such a good opinion from you?'

'I talked to him,' said Caspar. 'He impressed me with his strength of purpose. When I offered to bring a message to you on his behalf, he insisted on delivering it himself.'

'What sort of message does he have for me?'

'I have no idea, Master.'

'From whom does it come?'

'Not from Nicholas Bracewell himself, I think.'

The gaoler grunted to signal that the visit was at an end.

'Let him stay longer!' implored Royden.

'He has his orders. And I will come again.'

'Soon, Caspar. Soon.'

'As soon as they will let me.'

'And find out more about this Nicholas Bracewell. What possible interest can a book-holder in a theatre company have in a man like me?'

'He mentioned Doctor Mordrake.'

'Mordrake!' hissed the other, cringing against the wall. 'If he is an emissary from John Mordrake, keep him away from me. I do not want any message from that doddering old fool.'

The gaoler stepped forward to tap Caspar on the shoulder. The latter rose to his feet and nodded. Helping Royden up, he embraced his master before turning swiftly away. The prisoner waited until the door had been locked and both men had vanished before he looked down at the gift which his assistant had pressed into his hand during the embrace. Royden was holding three candles. Battle against the creeping darkness could commence.

'Thank you, Caspar,' he said with deep gratitude.

Sinking to the floor, he hid the candles beneath the straw until they would be needed, then he reached out to take another apple from the basket. As he bit into it, he discovered that it had already been gnawed by a rat. He flung it away in sheer disgust.

'Rudolph,' he said grimly, 'My curse upon you!'

Arrayed once more in his coronation robes, the Emperor sat on his throne and played idly with a ring on his left hand. His crown felt heavier than ever as the crushing weight of religion pressed down on his skull.

He endured the pain until he could bear it no longer, then removed the crown and set it on the floor. But the headache grew even fiercer now. Religion could not be so easily put aside.

Rudolph stood up in distress and massaged his throbbing temples with his fingertips. The movement did not disturb the work of the Milanese artist. His portrait of the Emperor continued to take shape beneath his brush. When his subject began to wander distractedly around the room, the artist kept one eye fixed on the throne as if it were still occupied. The pain finally eased. Rudolph sighed with relief. Noticing his companion for the first time, he spoke to him in Italian.

'Do you ever have headaches, my friend?' he asked.

'Now and again.'

'What do you?'

'I send for my wife to caress the pain away.'

'And if your wife is not at home?'

'I send for my mistress.'

Rudolph brooded on the problem. He had no wife for whom he could send and his former mistresses evoked some unpleasant memories. No woman could caress away the agony that descended on him. Indeed, he reflected, the Virgin Mary was at least partly responsible for it. He was still meditating on the inadequacy of womankind when the Chamberlain knocked and entered. His long strides brought him across to Rudolph.

'They are ready,' he announced.

'Who are?'

'The players from England.'

'Have they arrived at last?'

'Yesterday, Your Imperial Highness.'

'Sophia Magdalena will be pleased.'

'You have met two of them,' reminded the Chamberlain.

'Did I?'

'You conducted them to my apartment.'

Rudolph smiled. 'Ah, yes! Westfield's Men. Now I remember. What do they intend to perform for us?'

'*The Three Sisters of Mantua.*'

'A comedy or a tragedy?'

'A comedy,' said the other briskly. 'I have looked into the nature of the piece and deem it suitable for performance.'

'Nothing about religious dissension, I hope?'

'Nothing whatsoever.'

'Good. Let us meet these three sisters forthwith.'

The Chamberlain gave a slight bow and followed the Emperor towards the door. The artist, meanwhile, stayed at his easel and painted on. Rudolph swept out into the corridor.

'One question,' he said.

'Yes, Your Imperial Highness?'

'Have my wolves been fed today?'

'I believe so.'

'Make certain,' he ordered.

'I will.'

'Raw meat keeps all three contented.'

The delay added to the already high tension in the tiring-house. From their position in the adjoining room, Westfield's Men could hear the hall fill up with spectators. Their last private performance had been in the palace at Cologne before a conservative and rather sombre audience. Prague had a more lively Court. The actors could hear the hubbub and sense the animation. It sharpened their desire to begin the play. But it could not start until Emperor Rudolph was present.

'Where is the fellow?' complained Lawrence Firethorn.

'I have never been kept waiting this long before,' said Barnaby Gill in in jester's costume. 'It is unforgivable.'

'Yes,' said Owen Elias, 'in the time that we have been kept dawdling here, he could have ridden to Mantua and back to visit the three sisters in person.'

'Why is he holding us up?' wondered Edmund Hoode.

'Because it is his privilege,' said Nicholas Bracewell, trying to calm the tetchy atmosphere. 'This is no random gathering of spectators in the yard of a London inn. We are playing at the Imperial Court and must abide by its rules. What does it matter if we wait another hour? Our audience waits with us. They will not go away.'

The book-holder's philosophical attitude soothed many frayed nerves but Firethorn remained on edge. He prowled the tiring-house until he noticed Stephen Judd, an apprentice, attired as one of the sisters in the play.

'No, no, you imbecile!' he admonished. 'Look to your bosom, boy. A woman's paps come in pairs. And side by side.' He grabbed the padding which had slipped down inside the lad's dress and yanked it back into position. 'Our play is about three sisters of Mantua. Not the one-titted witch of Whitechapel.'

The laughter helped to ease the tension. Blushing a deep crimson, Stephen Judd used both palms to adjust his bosom to a more seemly and convincing position. A scrape of chairs and a shuffling of feet told them that the spectators had risen out of respect as Emperor Rudolph had finally made his entrance. Accompanied by Sophia Magdalena and the Chamberlain, he strode to the centre of the front row and lowered himself into a high-backed chair with gilded arms. His companions took the padded chairs on either side of him and the spectators were able to resume their seats. The hubbub became an expectant murmur.

'At last!' said Firethorn. 'Are we all ready?'

'We have been for hours!' groaned Gill.

'Take us in hand, Nick. Guide us with care.'

The book-holder took charge. At his command, four musicians played behind the curtain at the rear of the stage and their courante silenced the audience and set the mood for the play. Elias came out in a black cloak and delivered the Prologue in a bold voice with the exaggerated gestures he had learned to use in Germany. The rippling applause which he gathered was an indication of what was to come. They loved the play.

The Three Sisters of Mantua was by no means one of the best dramas in their repertoire. Its verse was often banal, its characters lacking in depth and its story too moralistic, but these defects became advantages on this occasion. The verse was largely incomprehensible, the unsubtle characterisation made identification of the dramatis personae much easier and the undertones of a morality play gave it a neatness of shape and meaning. As in Frankfurt, music was used between each of the acts to facilitate changes of costume and scenery.

It was the visual comedy and the poignant moments of thwarted love which delighted the audience most. When they were not laughing uproariously, they were sighing with one of the three sisters as each in turn was rejected by the Duke of Mantua. Firethorn was at his most commanding, Gill at his most hilarious and they set the standard for the rest of the cast. Richard Honeydew, playing the lute in public for the first time, accompanied the plaintive song with which the three sisters took their farewell of the Duke. Many a sleeve among the spectators was used to dab at moist eyes.

Emperor Rudolph was transfixed. Nothing as smooth and apparently effortless had ever been played at Court before. Every detail of the performance intrigued him and he scrutinised it with the open-mouthed intensity of a child watching an ingenious clockwork toy. While they took note of his grandeur and his reaction, the company were once again caught up in their admiration for Sophia Magdalena, closer and even more beautiful to them this time, and drawing the best out of them simply by being there.

Firethorn wooed her shamelessly as the noble Duke and directed the Epilogue to her with moving conviction. When he bowed low to his fair maid of Bohemia, she was so thrilled that she stood up to lead the applause. The whole Court rose to its feet in approbation and the actors luxuriated in the ovation for several minutes. Rudolph remained seated but one palm beat against the arm of his chair in dignified salutation. The Emperor was pleased. Westfield's Men had been accepted.

Steps were brought so that Rudolph could be escorted up onto the stage to be introduced to the leading sharers. Gill fawned monstrously and Hoode became tongue-tied in the face of majesty. Neither of them enjoyed the treasured moment which fell to Firethorn. Luminescent with excitement, Sophia Magdalena followed her great-uncle up the steps and offered her hand to the actor-manager. The kiss which he placed upon it was both an act of homage and a promise. His lips tingled for minutes. It was the Emperor who had the last word. When he congratulated Firethorn on his performance as the Duke of Mantua, the latter beamed obsequiously and gave a bow.

'I am your obedient servant!' he said with humility.

'No, Master Firethorn,' countered a smirking Rudolph. 'It is I who was *your* obedient servant.'

He went off into such a peal of infectious laughter that everyone joined in and the whole room echoed with wild mirth, even though most of them had no idea what the source of amusement was. Only the Chamberlain and Sophia Magdalena were immune. They were too accustomed to Rudolph's eccentricities to find them quite so diverting anymore. Wolfgang von Rumpf remained aloof. Sophia Magdalena took quiet enjoyment from watching Firethorn's huge and uninhibited delight. Like everything else about him, his capacity for exultation was magnificently theatrical.

Nicholas Bracewell and George Dart were the last to leave. Everything had been cleared off the stage and stored in a room which had been put at their disposal. Nicholas surveyed the empty hall with quiet satisfaction.

'We acquitted ourselves well, George,' he remarked.

'I never dreamed that I would visit such a palace,' said Dart, looking around with veneration. 'It is the most wonderful theatre in which we could ever play.'

'That is not quite true.'

'What could possibly outshine this?'

'The Vladislav Hall,' said Nicholas, pointing in the direction of the door. 'Master Firethorn and I were shown it during our visit here yesterday. It is even bigger and more impressive than this hall.'

Dart gaped. 'Bigger?'

'Much bigger, George. It is used for coronation feasts and for assembles of Bohemian noblemen. Great matters of state are settled there. In bad weather, they have even held indoor jousting tournaments there, with the knights entering by means of the Riders' Staircase.' He smiled at Dart's expression of utter amazement. 'But you will see the Vladislav Hall for yourself when we play there.'

'I thought that all our work was to be staged here.'

'All but one of our plays. *The Fair Maid of Bohemia*.'

'We perform that in this bigger hall?'

'We do, George. That is where the wedding banquet will be served. Westfield's Men will be one part of an entertainment which will go on throughout the day in celebration of the happy event. We will play before a vast and distinguished audience.'

'My knees are trembling already.'

'They will be steady enough on the day.'

'I hope so,' said Dart, consumed by feelings of inadequacy. 'Have you finished with me now?'

'One last service.'

'What is it?'

'Some of our costumes were left at the Black Eagle for repair and alteration. There is a doublet that Adrian was to have worn in *Double Deceit*, for instance. It had to be tailored to fit the more slender frame of James Ingram.'

'I miss Adrian horribly,' confided the other.

'So do we all, George.'

'And will his murderer go scot-free?'

'Not if I have anything to do with it,' said Nicholas seriously. 'But let us concern ourselves with those costumes. Mistress Hendrik will have finished sewing them by now.'

'It is kind of her to take on that task.'

'She is anxious to contribute in some way to our success here, though she has already done that in no small measure.'

'I know that she has helped me and I could not be more thankful. She has been a second mother to me.'

'Go to her now and ask for the costumes.'

'What must I do with them?'

'Bring them back here and put them with the rest of the wardrobe, for we will use most of them tomorrow.' Dart nodded dutifully. 'About it straight. Do this last errand and the rest of the day is your own.'

Given such an incentive, Dart went scampering off down the hall with a mixture of haste and reverence. Nicholas went after him at a more leisurely pace, savouring the beauty of the frescoes and the subtle artistry of the statuary. Wherever he walked, there were new wonders to capture the attention. The royal palace was a continuous marvel. It seemed to him like a fairy-tale creation. Then he remembered the man who was locked up in one of its dungeons. The plight of Doctor Talbot Royden gave him a more critical view of the opulence all around him. He quickened his pace towards the exit.

As Nicholas left the palace, he saw two figures standing on the steps of the cathedral and recognised one of them immediately. Hugo Usselincx was deep in conversation with a priest. The Dutchman was gesticulating with both hands. The priest was nodding solemnly. When he caught sight of the book-holder, Usselincx excused himself from his companion and trotted across to Nicholas. The diffident smile appeared.

'How was your play received?' he asked eagerly.

'It was much admired, Hugo.'

'And so it should be. Westfield's Men are superb.'

'We strive to give pleasure.'

'My dearest wish is to watch you again somehow. Is *Love and Fortune* to be staged, by any chance?'

'Tomorrow.'

'Then I will do all I can to be here.'

'You will be most welcome.'

'What of *Cupid's Folly?*'

'A decision has not yet been made about that.'

'Please let me know when it has been. I would not wish to miss the joy of seeing Master Gill at his finest.'

Usselincx fell in beside him and they walked into the second courtyard together. Chatting pleasantly, they left the castle and made their way down the hill. Nicholas noted how quickly the Dutchman seemed to have settled into the city. It was clearly not his first visit there. Half-way down the hill, Usselincx came to a halt and took in the view with a gesture.

'What do you think of Prague?' he asked.

'I like it.'

'How much have you been able to see so far?'

'Enough to fill me with admiration.'

'Has it been worth the effort of getting here?'

'We think so.'

'The city is blessed by your presence.'

'It has saints enough to give a proper blessing,' said Nicholas, smiling as he looked at the profusion of church spires. 'What has surprised us is the number of foreigners here. Italians, Poles, Hungarians, French and Spanish.'

'Do not forget the Dutch and the English.'

'Prague is truly a meeting-place of nations.'

'That is one of the things which drew me here.'

'What are the others?' asked Nicholas with interest.

Usselincx gathered his thoughts before replying. As soon as he began to speak, however, he was interrupted by the sound of running feet. Panting stertorously and white with fear, George Dart was struggling up the incline towards them. There was no sign of the costumes he had been sent to fetch.

When he reached them, he fell into Nicholas's arms.

'Slow down, George,' said the latter, supporting him. 'What means this haste?'

'I have just been to the Black Eagle,' he gasped.

[173]

'That was your commission.'

'I went up to Mistress Hendrik's chamber.'

'And?'

'She was not there.'

'Haply, she has stepped out for some reason.'

'She would never leave the costumes in that state.'

'What state?'

'You told me they were being repaired,' said Dart, trembling under the weight of the news that he bore. 'Yet those costumes have been torn to shreds and scattered over the floor. And that is not all,' he added, as he gulped in more air. 'The whole room is in disarray. There has been a violent struggle.'

The Black Eagle was in turmoil. Nicholas sprinted all the way there and burst in through the door to find the rest of the company engaged in a frantic search of the premises.

'Has George Dart told you?' asked Firethorn, rushing across to him. 'Anne has disappeared. We have looked everywhere for her, Nick, but she is not here.'

'Let me see the chamber,' said Nicholas.

'Prepare yourself for a shock.'

Firethorn followed him up the stairs and into the little room where Anne Hendrik had slept alone. Nicholas looked around in consternation. The stool and table had been overturned, the jug of water smashed, a tapestry torn from the wall and Anne's belongings scattered everywhere. The costumes on which she had been working were in tatters on the floor, but it was another garment which made him shudder. Lying on the bed, slit open from top to bottom, was Anne's white night-dress. Nicholas snatched it up involuntarily and clutched it to him.

It was Firethorn who first saw the letter. It had been hidden beneath the night-dress. He picked it up and read the name scrawled across it in a spidery hand.

'It is addressed to you, Nick,' he said.

'Let me see it.'

'Do you wish to read it alone?'

'No. This concerns us both.'

Putting the night-dress aside, Nicholas took the letter and opened it. The message was short and unequivocal.

Bring the documents to the Town Square this evening. Stand beneath the clock when it strikes seven. Come alone or she will sleep tonight with Adrian Smallwood.

Nicholas blenched as he took in the full import of the demand. Anne had been abducted. Because of the pouch that he carried in his jerkin, her life was now in immediate danger. His mind was an inferno of guilt and apprehension. He blamed himself for what had happened to her. The man who had murdered Adrian Smallwood had not given up the hunt. He had simply been biding his time until he could strike at the most vulnerable point. Nicholas had no doubt that he would carry out the threat in his letter. His temples pounded.

'What does it say, Nick?' asked Firethorn.

'See for yourself.'

Nicholas held it out so that his friend could read its blunt demand. Firethorn was so enraged that he immediately snatched out his dagger.

'Meet with him there and I will follow you.'

'No,' said Nicholas.

'I'll cut out his black heart!'

'That is not the way. I am to go alone.'

'You will only put yourself in danger, Nick.'

'If it will save Anne, I will happily do that.'

'It is unjust,' said Firethorn. 'I was asked to carry those documents and not you. It was wrong of me to shirk my duty thus. Let me make amends now. I will meet him at the appointed place instead of you. He will get much more than the documents, I warrant you.'

'We must comply with his orders or Anne will die.'

'You must let me do something.'

'Keep the contents of this letter to yourself,' said Nicholas as he thrust it inside his jerkin. 'Our fellows need know nothing of this. It is private business of mine.'

'And mine, Nick!'

'Only I may go.'

'But you are dealing with a ruthless killer here,' argued Firethorn. 'We both saw what he did to Adrian Smallwood. He may be planning to murder you in the same way. What trust can you place in his word? Anne may already be dead.'

'She is more use to him alive.'

'You may be his next victim.'

'That is a chance I am ready to take.'

'Why?' said Firethorn, searching for a way to protect him. 'We are guests of the Emperor. Let us take this to him. He will send a whole army to comb the streets of Prague until they find Anne.'

'Then would she certainly be killed.'

'Use all the strength at our disposal.'

'No,' asserted Nicholas. 'He has set the terms. I must abide by them. Let us call off the search and calm our fellows down. We are being watched.'

Firethorn eventually accepted his advice. While the actor-manager went off to round up the company, Nicholas looked down again at the night-dress. It was a message in itself. The dagger which had rent it apart would be used on Anne Hendrik without compunction. That could not be allowed to happen.

When he went back downstairs, Nicholas saw that George Dart was seated at a table weeping piteously, and being comforted by Hugo Usselincx. The book-holder's first task was to confine the problem to the company. Though trying to help, the Dutchman was an intruder. Nicholas bore down on them.

'Calm down, George,' he soothed. 'There might yet be a simple explanation for all this.'

'Might there?' sobbed the other.

'I think that you were misled.'

'Was I? How?'

'What has happened?' asked Usselincx solicitously.

'Nothing that we cannot deal with ourselves,' said Nicholas, guiding him to the door. 'I am sorry that you were caught up in this wild excitement. It was a misunderstanding on George's part.'

'Why all this commotion?'

'Unnecessary panic.' They were back in the street now. 'Actors thrive on drama. On- and offstage. It is all over now.'

'Are you certain?'

'Yes, Hugo. We do not need to keep you.'

'But I want to offer what help I can.'

'None is required.'

There was a pause. 'I see that I am in the way,' said Usselincx, moving away. 'Forgive me. It was wrong of me to trespass on your privacy. Adieu!'

He turned on his heel and scuttled apologetically away.

Nicholas went back into the inn. Firethorn had gathered the whole company into a room at the rear where they could be alone. A tearful Dart joined them to hear Nicholas. The book-holder spoke with far more confidence than he felt.

'There is no cause for alarm,' he said firmly. 'Mistress Hendrik is indisposed. We have the matter well in hand. She will be back with us very soon. Meanwhile, you may rest easy. This confusion was unfortunate and took you away from a more proper purpose. We performed at the Imperial Court today with resounding success. You should be celebrating that triumph. Go to it now and forget this unwarranted agitation.'

It took time to persuade the actors, but they eventually began to trickle back into the taproom to compare their theories over a mug of beer. George Dart hovered, wanting to believe Nicholas but prevented from doing so by his memory of the ravaged bedchamber. When he began to gibber his dissent, he was lifted bodily by Firethorn and carried off to join the others. Only Owen Elias and James Ingram stayed behind. Neither of them was convinced by the book-holder's attempt at reassurance.

'Where is she, Nick?' asked the Welshman.

'You have heard what I had to say, Owen.'

'We are more interested in what lay behind your words.'

'Yes,' added Ingram. 'You must have your reasons and we respect them. But do not forget us. You may not need us now, but our swords are always there at your command.'

'Thank you, James.'

'Swords, daggers and bare fists,' emphasized Elias, as he held up both hands. 'Put them to some use.'

'If the bare fists could sew a fine seam, I would. We have costumes to repair and another play to stage tomorrow. Think on those problems. Leave all else to me.'

'As you wish,' said Elias, 'but Anne will be ever in our minds. Sooner or later, we must learn the truth, Nick.'

Nicholas gave a soulful nod. As the two men went out to join the others, Firethorn came back into the room. He knew that they had only bought themselves a temporary respite. If Anne was missing for much longer, the company would be asking more urgently about her.

'What of the hostess?' wondered Nicholas.

'She has been no use at all to us.'

'Did she see nothing, hear nothing?'

'Who knows?' asked Firethorn. 'The woman has no English and we have less than one word in Czech between us. Anne was the only person who could get a coherent sentence out of her and that by dint of talking in German.'

'The servingmen?'

'Complete idiots!'

'Do any of them understand English?'

'Not a jot.'

'Someone at the inn must be able to help us.'

'They are all blind and deaf, Nick. They saw nobody go up to Anne's chamber and they heard no struggle. You saw the condition of the room. She must have fought like a demon. The noise would have been heard all over the inn.'

Nicholas gazed pensively up at the floor above.

Doctor Talbot Royden used one of the fresh candles to take a full inventory of his cell. It was an uninspiring task. The walls were stained by the passage of time and scored with marks from previous guests. Names had been scratched in the stone. A date had been patiently gouged out. Parallel lines of dried blood on one wall suggested that someone had tried to claw his way out of his prison. Royden wondered how long it would be before he sank to the same level of desperation.

No natural light came into the dungeon and the bars on the door were the only means of ventilation. Royden was forced to inhale the stink of his own excrement along with the foul stench left behind by his predecessors. There was no way out. Caspar was his only ambassador. He had great faith in his assistant but he knew how perverse the Emperor could be. It would take more than Caspar's plea to instil some mercy in the wayward Rudolph.

Royden sank down into the straw and wondered what was to become of him. He had been brought to Prague as a brilliant astrologer with the gift of foretelling the future. Even his dreams had borne a mystic significance. Yet now he could not even foresee what would happen in the next hour. The symbols on his gown merged with the stifling gloom. His powers had been taken away from him.

A distant noise concentrated his mind. Someone was unlocking a door to descend the steps. Blowing out the fresh candle, he concealed it in the straw again and relied on the guttering illumination of the candle they had given him. He scrambled to the door in the hope of seeing Caspar again but the gaoler was alone. Torch in one hand, he carried a pitcher of water in the other. He was a slovenly man with a ponderous walk. It took him some moments to find the right key for the lock.

Opening the door, he thrust the pitcher at Royden without comment. The prisoner took it, then jabbered loudly.

'I should not be here!' he protested. 'I am Doctor Talbot Royden and I demand respect for my achievements. Remind the Emperor that I have been his devoted servant. I have cast horoscopes, I have cured diseases, I have set bones. My skills have been of untold value in Bohemia. They have earned me the right to defend myself. Tell him!' he insisted. 'Tell the Emperor what I have said. He must hear me.'

'He does hear you.'

The man looked at him for the first time and Royden saw the familiar face under the soiled cap. Rudolph gave him a sinister smile and stepped back. Before the prisoner could even express his horror, the door slammed inexorably shut.

Firethorn looked on in fascination as Nicholas set the pen, parchment and ink on the table. They were alone in the room from which Anne Hendrik had been kidnapped. Having first set the table upright, Nicholas now sat before it on the stool. He unhooked his jerkin to slip a hand inside. When he extracted the pouch, he heard Firethorn step up behind him to peer over his shoulder. Both men were anxious to see what it was that had caused them such tribulation on their journey to Bohemia.

Nicholas broke the elaborate seal and unfolded the sheets of paper. A letter was enclosed with four documents, but all were totally incomprehensible. They looked at the strange words and the mixture of numbers and symbols.

'Is this some kind of jest, Nick?' said Firethorn.

'Far from it.'

'The letter is not even signed.'

'I believe it is,' decided Nicholas. 'That number at the bottom of the page discloses the sender. Everything is in some kind of code. It will be known to the recipient.'

'Can Talbot Royden make sense of that gibberish?'

'I think so.'

'And was it those squiggles which got Adrian Smallwood killed and Anne Hendrik abducted?' Firethorn scratched his beard. 'What does it all mean?'

'That Doctor Royden is a spy.'

'For whom?'

'I do not know,' admitted Nicholas, 'but I wager that there is espionage afoot here. Hidden in these documents is vital information.'

'About what?'

'That will emerge in time.' He picked up the quill. 'At least, we know what we are dealing with here.'

'Arrant nonsense!'

'Secret orders. Valuable intelligence. Couched in a private language to ensure its safety. This did not come from Lord Westfield. We were couriers for a much higher authority.'

He dipped his pen in the ink and began to copy the letter. Firethorn watched in silence until all the documents had been transposed to the blank parchment. Having completed his task as a scrivener, Nicholas used the point of his dagger to ease off the seal. He melted some wax in a candle flame, folded the original documents, then dropped the hot wax over the marks left by the seal. Firethorn applied the signet ring he had worn in the play that afternoon and their work was complete. Who had sent the documents they did not know, but they now bore the seal of the Duke of Mantua.

'What will you do now, Nick?' asked Firethorn.

'Exchange these for Anne.'

'Let me come to guard your back.'

'Stay here and guard these instead,' said Nicholas, giving him the copies he had just made. 'We will peruse them at our leisure and see what we can deduce from them.'

'Nothing! This language is worse than Czech.'

'That is perfectly lucid to those who understand it.'

'Who is this fiend?' demanded Firethorn.

'I will tell you when I have met him.'

'How did he know we were bearing those documents?'

'That is one of many things I hope to ask him.'

When the seal had dried, Nicholas put the documents into the pouch and slipped them back inside his jerkin. He removed his sword but kept the dagger at his belt. Firethorn embraced him warmly.

'Take care, dear heart!'

'I will.'

'Give Anne my love.'

Nicholas nodded, then went swiftly out through the door.

The Town Square was enormous. Tall, proud, well-maintained burghers' houses ran along all four sides of it, each house given colour and individuality by its elaborate decorations. The Town Hall itself lent civic authority, while the Church of Saint Nicholas and two monasteries showed the spiritual face of the city. Looming over one side of the square were the massive twin towers and the arresting facade of the Týn Church. Power and prosperity were reflected in the square, which lay on the eastern bank at the very centre of Prague. Hundreds of people were abroad, standing in small groups or crossing in all directions, but there was no sense of clutter or discomfort. The Town Square seemed big enough to accommodate the entire population of the city.

Nicholas arrived well before the stipulated time and strolled around the perimeter of the square to show that he was completely alone. That he was under observation was quite certain but he could not begin to guess from where. Countless windows looked down on the square and there was an endless choice of streets, lanes and alleys in which to lurk unseen. His enemy might be any one of the dozens of people whose shoulders brushed him in the great market-place of Prague.

As the hour approached, Nicholas walked across to the huge tower crowning the Town Hall. The astronomical clock was one of the most celebrated sights in the city, and visitors came from far and wide to view the extraordinary and complex device. It consisted of three distinct parts. The large calendar dial was flanked by statues of the philosopher and the angel on the left side and the astronomer and the chronicler on the right. At its centre was the Prague coat of arms.

Even though he was there on such a grim errand, Nicholas was struck by the twelve turning circles around the edge of the dial. The astronomical clock above was even more intricate. Flanked by figures of the Miser, Vanity, Death and a lute-carrying Turk, it consisted of a series of rings, the outer one bearing Arab numerals, and the inner ones, the signs of the zodiac.

Nicholas was not alone. A small crowd gathered to hear the clock strike and to watch figures emerge from the two doors above the clock. At the first stroke, Nicholas swung round to look more closely at his companions. Some were local inhabitants who stopped out of habit but most were curious visitors. None even spared him a glance. He could not compete with the horological masterpiece.

Detaching himself from them, he scanned the square for a sign that did not come. As the astronomical clock finished its performance, the crowd drifted away and Nicholas was left alone beneath the tower. When fifteen minutes had rolled past, he began to wonder if he was the object of some unkind jest. Had someone brought him there simply to mock him? Another fifteen minutes sapped his patience.

He was about to move away when a figure appeared in a corner of the square diagonally opposite. Clad in a dark gown and a large hat, the man was unidentifiable at that distance but he was able to send a clear message. He put a hand to his breast and brought it away again, as if removing something from inside his doublet. Nicholas understood. He took out the pouch from inside his own doublet and held it up. The man beckoned him forward, watching carefully to make sure that nobody was with him.

As Nicholas got closer, the man slipped into a lane and gestured for him to follow. Their transaction would clearly take place in a more private venue. Walking with a steady gait, Nicholas kept one hand close to his dagger. He left the bustle of the crowd and plunged into the lane. Three people were strolling towards him. Over their shoulders, he could see the man waiting for him some thirty yards away. Nicholas continued to follow him until his guide turned down a narrow alley-way. Instinct made Nicholas slow down and slip the dagger into his palm.

He put his head cautiously around the corner and saw two figures waiting for him now. One was the man who had led him there and the other was a woman, wearing a cloak with its hood up. From the grip which the man had on her wrist, Nicholas decided that it was Anne. The bargain had been kept. He hurried forward with the pouch held high, eager to trade it for her safe return. But he never got anywhere near her. As he went past a shop doorway, someone stepped out behind him and clubbed him to the ground with a heavy stone.

Nicholas sank into oblivion. The man who had enticed him into the alley-way paid the woman for her help before sending her quickly on her way. Then he sauntered towards the inert body of Nicholas Bracewell and, with a grin of triumph, took the pouch from the hands of his accomplice.

Anne Hendrik sat in a high-backed chair with her hands tied to its arms and her feet to its legs. A blindfold blocked out all vision and a gag prevented her from calling out for help. She had no idea where she was but the room felt large and warm. Distant voices drifted up to her but she could not pick out what they were saying. For the first few hours, her main problem had been to fight off hysteria.

At least, they had now left her alone. She was no longer being looked at and gloated over by the two men who had brought her there. They had said nothing but she could sense their eyes caressing her. Anne could still feel the hot breath of the one as he had bent over her to check her bonds before quitting the room. When the key had turned in the lock, she had felt a measure of relief for the first time. But she knew that it was only temporary. They would be back.

Her chances of rescue depended entirely on Nicholas Bracewell. She could imagine how disturbed he would be by her abduction and how determined to track her down, but the city was a complete enigma to him. Nicholas would not know where to begin. Anne had no doubts about why she had been kidnapped. She was the weak point in his armour. Unable to wrest the documents from him directly, they had opted for a different means. Fear for her would persuade him to hand over the secret pouch, but what would happen then? Hysteria threatened again and she shook her head vigorously. For her own sake, she had to remain calm.

Anne went back over the series of events that brought her to the room, searching for any clue that might give her some indication of where she was and who was holding her captive. Were the voices coming up from a street or from the river? How far had they brought her from the Black Eagle? Why had she been foolish enough to open the door of her chamber to them? As she assailed herself with questions over and over again, one came to dominate all the rest.

Where was Nicholas Bracewell?

The sound of a key in the lock banished all other thoughts from her mind. She heard the door open, shut and get locked again. Only one man had come this time. Anne counted his footsteps as he walked towards her. The door was at least fifteen yards away. He tested her bonds and adjusted her blindfold. His breath was hotter than ever but he had not come to gloat over her this time.

Something far more important claimed his attention. She heard him sit down and unfold some parchment. He gave a low chuckle and talked to himself in German.

'Now, then. Let's see what we have here, shall we?'

Anne's blood congealed. It was the voice she had heard on the *Peppercorn*. She was held captive by a murderer.

[CHAPTER TEN]

Nicholas Bracewell slowly regained consciousness to find that he was surrounded by a clutch of sympathetic faces. Someone had propped him up in a sitting position and was dabbing at the wound on the back of his head with a damp cloth. A blood-stained cap lay on the ground beside him and it took him a moment to realise that it was his. The pain then hit him with the force of a blow and he reeled. His kind surgeon steadied him with both hands.

Memory gradually returned. He recalled looking up at the astronomical clock, waiting for half an hour, responding to the signal from the man across the square, following him down a lane, seeing Anne in the man's grasp. Beyond that, there was nothing, though the seriousness of the wound and his position on the ground told him what must have happened. He did not need to feel for the pouch or for the dagger. Both had obviously gone. Along with the woman he had foolishly taken for Anne Hendrik.

He had been duped. A stage manager had himself been tricked by some adroit stage management. Nicholas had lost the documents and gained nothing in return apart from scuffed apparel and a throbbing headache. The sense of failure was excruciating. Anne was still captive. The only consolation he could take was the fact that he had simply been knocked unconscious when he might just as easily have been killed. Adrian Small-wood had been bludgeoned, then daggered. There had to be a reason why Nicholas had been spared.

The man who had been bathing his wound sent his wife back into the house for more water and some fresh linen. The circle of onlookers showed great concern for the stranger and offered their solace in Czech or German. Most lived in the alley-way or the adjacent lane. The others were passers-by. When fresh water arrived, the man cleaned the wound more carefully, then put a pad against it to stem any further bleeding. His wife tore the linen for him to bind around Nicholas's head. When the bandage was tied, the injured man struggled to his feet with the aid of several hands. He rocked unsteadily.

A man handed him his cap. A woman seemed to be asking if they could take him anywhere. The amateur surgeon was gesturing an invitation for the patient to go into the tiny house to rest. Nicholas thanked them all with a weary smile, then dipped his hand into his purse to take out money. But his self-appointed physician waved it away. He had been only too glad to tend the wound. Nicholas looked around and tried to take his bearings. He was about to stagger off when two figures came running down the alley-way towards him.

'Nick!' yelled Lawrence Firethorn.

'We searched for you everywhere,' said Owen Elias.

'What happened to you, man?'

'Look at the state you are in!'

'I am fine now,' said Nicholas. 'Thanks to these kind people. They must have found me lying there.'

'Who hit you?' asked Elias, eyeing the bandage and the sodden cap. 'He all but took your head off.'

Nicholas did not want to talk to them in front of the curious audience. He waved a general farewell to them and went off down the alley-way with his two friends. Only when they had entered the square did he feel ready to explain what he felt had happened. They listened with a mixture of concern and irritation. Firethorn put his hand on the hilt of his sword.

'I told you to let me guard your back,' he reminded.

'You would have been seen.'

'I was the man for this task, Nick,' said Elias. 'I know how to hug the shadows and melt into walls. That is how I come to be here. I trailed Lawrence from the inn because I knew that he must be looking for you. He had no idea that I was on his heels. I only revealed myself when I saw him searching the square.'

'True, Nick,' confirmed Firethorn. 'I did not seek Owen's help. He sensed that you were in trouble.'

'Why did you not use my skills to protect you?' said Owen.

'This was something I had to do on my own,' replied Nick.

'With what dire result?' said the Welshman with a surge of emotion. 'It grieves me that you did not confide in me, Nick. We are friends. We have been through so much together. I have always been ready to share my troubles with you—and there have been plenty of those to share. Why do you lock me out when you need help? What is going on here?'

Nicholas traded a glance with Firethorn, then sighed.

'We sought to keep the matter between us, Owen,' he said. 'We did not want the company to become unduly alarmed.'

Elias was incredulous. 'Anne disappears and you think that nobody will notice? She is one of us, man. If she is in danger, we are entitled to know how and why. We have grown to love Anne. Trust your fellows.' He was hurt. 'At least trust *me*.'

'You have earned the right to know what is happening.'

'Then tell me.'

'I will.'

Nicholas gave him a brief account of all that had taken place since the discovery of Anne's disappearance. Firethorn added his comments. As the pain from his wound eased, Nicholas was able to think more clearly. Action was needed. He first retraced his steps to the alley-way and searched with his companions for any clues as to the direction in which his attacker and his accomplice had fled. They found none. The alley-way led to a street off which there were several other streets and lanes, each one of them a possible escape route.

The search was not entirely fruitless. Close to the spot where he fell, Nicholas found the stone which had been smashed against his skull. When he picked it up, his fingers only covered half of it. His attacker must have had a broad hand. But it was the shape and colour of the stone which interested Nicholas. He had seen something very similar before.

'Where do we go from here, Nick?' asked Firethorn.

'I am not sure.'

'I am,' said Elias. 'We press the whole company into service and let them join the hunt for Anne.'

'No,' said Nicholas. 'A hundred people could search and we would still find nothing in this rabbit warren of a city. We are strangers here, Owen.

The men who hold Anne are not. They know where to hide.'

'Close to the inn,' argued Firethorn. 'They could not have taken her far. She would have put up a struggle and attracted too much attention. You saw how she must have fought back in her chamber.'

Nicholas shook his head. 'We saw what they wished us to see. A stark warning, left to frighten us. I do not believe there was any struggle, or it would certainly have been heard by someone. That bedchamber was arranged as carefully as any setting in a play,' he said. 'My guess is that Anne had already been taken away.'

'She is a woman of spirit,' said Elias. 'She would fight.'

'With a knife at her throat?'

'Nicholas is right,' agreed Firethorn, mulling it over. 'She went quietly. That must be how it happened.' He gave a hopeless shrug. 'Where does that leave us? We have nothing.'

'We do,' reminded Nicholas. 'We have the most important clue of all. A copy of those documents. They at least will tell us what lies behind all this. Stakes must be high if murder and kidnap are used. The documents will be our guide.'

'Then are we completely lost,' cried Firethorn. 'Those documents are nothing but inane scribble. How can we be guided by something we do not understand?'

'The code must be used to unlock the meaning.'

'But we do not know what that code might be.'

'Then we must turn to the one man who can help us.'

'Who is that?'

'Doctor Talbot Royden.'

Royden smiled for the first time since the nightmare of imprisonment had begun. Caspar Hilliard had not been idle. By writing a letter of supplication to the Emperor, and by speaking persuasively to the Chamberlain, he had won some important concessions for his master. Fresh straw was put in the cell and several candles were supplied. By their light, Royden was able to study the books he was now allowed to have. Reunited with some of his beloved tomes, he could continue his scientific research. He was still incarcerated, but the loss of freedom was now more tolerable.

'I cannot thank you enough, Caspar,' he said.

'Would that I could have done more!'

'These are wonderful improvements.'

'Your release is the improvement I work for,' said his assistant earnestly. 'Then we may resume our work in the laboratory. I keep it in good order.'

'Simply to have a book in my hands again is a joy,' said Royden, holding a volume on alchemy. 'How on earth did you wrest these mercies out of our mad Emperor?'

'My letter explained how close we had been to success and how unjustly I felt you had been treated. The argument that swayed him was this, Master. That news of your imprisonment would make other scholars and scientists think twice about coming to Prague. If they know they may be locked away in the dark of a stinking dungeon, they may offer their services elsewhere.'

'If only I had, Caspar.'

'That point, too, was made,' said the other. 'The Emperor is proud of his reputation as a generous patron. It brings in the finest minds in Europe. But that reputation will be badly sullied if he is known to deal so callously with his guests.'

'You are a cunning advocate.'

'All I am I have learned from you.'

'Your loyalty has kept me sane down here.'

'That contents me.'

Royden opened the book to flick through the pages. When he closed it, he hugged it to him with a cry of pleasure. Caspar smiled fondly. His master's spirits had been revived.

'What is happening up there?' asked Royden.

'Wedding preparations continue. Guests are pouring in at the castle every day. The bridegroom himself is due to arrive later today. The wedding will be a magnificent occasion.'

'I was to have been there to share in it.'

'That is no longer possible, alas.'

'What of the players from England?'

'They are closely involved,' said the other. 'Westfield's Men are to perform a play at the wedding banquet itself. I am told that they are actors of high quality.'

'And this book-holder you mentioned?'

'Nicholas Bracewell?'

'He was asking after me, you said.'

'That is so. To what end, I do not know. But I believe he has a message from Doctor Mordrake.'

'Mordrake!' echoed the other with a shudder. 'I wish I had never met that sorcerer. He was the one who brought me to this Bohemian bedlam, and look how it has ended. But for John Mordrake, I would be free to do my work. Not caged down here like some wild beast in the Emperor's menagerie.' He put his book aside. 'What business can Mordrake have with me?'

'We may never find out,' said Caspar sadly. 'No visitors are permitted down here. Even I could not worm that concession out of the Emperor. There is no means by which this Nicholas Bracewell can reach you. Whatever message he carried to Prague will have to return to England with him.'

'**I**mportune me no further,' said the Chamberlain. 'What you ask of me is not in my power to grant.'

'You have the ear of the Emperor,' urged Firethorn.

'It is deaf to my entreaties.'

'This is very important to us.'

'I am not able to help you.'

'But you are the Chamberlain.'

'Yes,' replied the other, rising to his feet with dignity. 'I am responsible for the government of Bohemia. I help to raise taxes, draft new laws and keep the peace in this kingdom. I summon the Bohemian Diet, I hold a respected place at any Diet of the Empire and have a strong voice in its affairs. Yes, Master Firethorn,' he said with a touch of exasperation. 'I am the Chamberlain and I enjoy all the powers of that high office. But I can still not authorise you to visit a prisoner in the castle dungeon.'

He slowly resumed his seat behind the desk. Nicholas and Firethorn were in his apartment again, trying to gain access to Talbot Royden without disclosing their reasons for wishing to do so. They had sent Owen Elias back to the Black Eagle with orders to say nothing of the attack on Nicholas. The latter's wound was attracting an offhand interest from their host. The Chamberlain was no more helpful than on their previous visit. Nicholas tried to appease him.

'We are sorry to disturb you again on this matter.'

'It is out of my hands, Master Bracewell.'

'Now that you have explained it to us, we understand that. Why should a man in your exalted position bother with a mere prisoner? You have far more weighty matters to consider. I know little of Prague but I could not fail to notice so many churches.' He watched the other carefully. 'And so many different denominations.'

'It creates many problems,' admitted the Chamberlain.

'It must,' continued Nicholas. 'We know full well how bitter religious dissension can be. England is a Protestant nation now but only after much bloodshed. The troubles have not ceased. Unrest still simmers.'

'Your difficulties are small compared with ours.'

'I disagree,' said Firethorn. 'London is beset by crawling Puritans. They are trying to close the theatres. What would become of us then? Puritans are a menace!'

'We have our share of menaces here.'

'Yet Bohemia is more tolerant,' observed Nicholas.

'That is the Emperor's wish,' sighed the other.

'You have Roman Catholic churches, Lutheran, Calvinist and others whose names I do not recognise. Prague also has a Jewish Quarter. The Josefov.'

'The Emperor has granted Jews many privileges.'

'Freedom of belief is a fine ideal.'

'Yes,' said the Chamberlain. 'But, like most fine ideals, it does not work in practice. We have too many faiths here, too much latitude. Everything from Jesuits at one extreme to Hussites at the other.'

'Hussites?' repeated Firethorn.

'Yet another of our problems.' He stared at the bandage around Nicholas's head, then became brisk. 'But you did not come here to discuss the religious policy which we pursue. You have a request. I must turn it down.'

'Is there nothing you can do for us?'

'On this matter, alas—no.'

'All we ask is that you speak to the Emperor.'

'He would not even listen to me.'

'Why not?'

'That is irrelevant.' The Chamberlain lifted the bell. 'I will ring for someone to show you out.'

'Is there nobody who can help us?' implored Firethorn.

'Nobody at all.'

'You are wrong, sir,' said Nicholas, as a face popped into his mind. 'I believe that there is.'

Sophia Magdalena walked into the gallery on the arm of her great-uncle. Emperor Rudolph had always been fond of her and he would be sad to lose her when marriage took her north to Brunswick. While she was still at the palace, he wanted her to be present at the little ceremony which was about to take place. The Milanese painter was waiting for them beside his easel. An embroidered cloth hid the completed portrait. He was presented to Sophia Magdalena and studied her beautiful face with the concentrated admiration of an artist. He turned to the Emperor and spoke in Italian.

'Such loveliness belongs upon a canvas,' he said.

'One day I will let you paint her portrait.'

'Thank you!'

'If Sophia Magdalena agrees.'

'That goes without saying.'

'But she has come to see the portrait of me unveiled.' He lapsed into German. 'Are you ready, my dear?'

'Yes,' she said, hands held tight. 'I am very excited.'

'I hope that you like it.'

'I'm sure that I shall.'

'Then let us bring the portrait into the light of day.'

The Emperor inclined his head and the artist lifted the cloth from the gilt frame, standing back to give both of them an uninterrupted view of his work. Rudolph giggled with delight and clapped his hands, but Sophia Magdalena took more time to appreciate the painting. Expecting to see her great-uncle staring back at her with an imperious gaze, she was disconcerted to find herself looking at a face that was composed entirely of pieces of fruit.

The nose was a banana, the eyes were grapes, the cheeks were apples, the chin was an orange. Eight other fruits were cleverly incorporated into the portrait. Shocked at first, she came to see that there was a definite resemblance to Rudolph. The symbolic significance of the painting also began to emerge. A ruler of a vast empire was an emblem of nature, a source of health and sustenance to his peoples. Some of the fruits used were imported from other countries, a visual reference to the cosmopolitan nature of the Bohemian Court. And there were many other values in a portrait which had the most striking colours and definition.

The two men waited patiently until her smile of approval came. While the Emperor embraced her, the artist sighed with relief. Her ratification was vital to him and to his employer. Sophia Magdalena began to enthuse about the work and the artist begged the Emperor to translate for him. The praise was soon cut short. A liveried servant came into the room and bowed before delivering his message.

'Someone is asking to speak with Sophia Magdalena on a matter of great urgency,' he said. 'He waits without.'

'Who is the man?' asked Rudolph.

'Lawrence Firethorn.'

'The actor? No, tell him that she is indisposed.'

'But I wish to see him,' she said. 'He and his company have given me so much pleasure. I will not turn him away.'

'What about my portrait?'

'I will come back to view it again very soon.'

Rudolph flicked a finger and the artist replaced the cloth over the painting. The servant led the way along a corridor until they came to the hall where Westfield's Men had performed *The Three Sisters of Mantua*. With the stage still erected, Firethorn could not resist strutting around it and declaiming some verse. Nicholas rested against the edge of the platform. As soon as Sophia Magdalena appeared, both men moved across to meet her and the Emperor. She was taken aback by the sight of the bandage around Nicholas's head. The exchange of greetings was complicated by her ignorance of their language. Rudolph was pressed into service as an impromptu interpreter.

'What is this matter of such urgency?' he asked.

'We need to see Doctor Talbot Royden,' said Nicholas.

'Out of the question!'

'Why is that, your Highness?'

'He is permitted to see nobody but his assistant.'

'Your Highness,' pleaded Nicholas. 'We beg you to make an exception in our case.'

'What is he saying?' asked Sophia Magdalena, frowning when the request was translated to her. 'Why must they see him?'

'They will not,' vowed Rudolph.

'Our petition was to your great-niece,' said Nicholas with a polite bow to her. 'We have come a very long way at her behest and withstood many trials to be here. Please explain that to her, your Highness. We hoped that she might be willing to help us.'

Under pressure from her, Rudolph translated reluctantly. Sophia Magdalena nodded vigorously at the two Englishmen then rounded on the Emperor. She argued with him in voluble German and waved her arms expressively. Having seen her before as a poised and silent madonna, the two visitors were surprised at how animated she had become. Sophia clearly had a mind of her own and a forceful way of expressing it.

Rudolph resisted her appeal but she did not give up. Throwing a glance of sympathy at the two men, she spoke so powerfully and persuasively on their behalf that the Emperor's intransigence began to weaken slightly.

'What harm can it do?' she urged. 'Doctor Royden was a good and loyal servant to you. Can you not allow him this one small concession?'

'He let me down, Sophia. That is unforgivable.'

'I implore you to think again.'

'No!'

'It is such a simple request.'

'I will not grant it, Sophia.'

'Not even to me.' She saw his resolve flicker. 'Can I not wrest this one small favour from you? Think what I have done at your bidding. Surely that deserves some recompense.' She threw another glance at the visitors. 'These are my personal guests. They have made a huge effort to be here for my wedding. I wish to reward them. They would not make such a request unless it was very important to them.' She took the Emperor's arm. 'Help me to thank them for coming to Prague. Please. Let them see Doctor Royden. For my sake. Grant them permission. It is not much to ask.'

The Emperor scowled and grew pensive.

The food was welcome but the manner in which it was served was very distasteful. After warning her what would happen if she tried to cry out, the man with the hot breath removed the gag. He spoke in English but his accent was German. She was grateful to be able to move her mouth freely again and took several deep breaths. Something was held against her lips.

'Eat it,' he ordered.

'What is it?'

'You will find out.'

She bit into the dried fish and found it dry but edible. When the food was swallowed, he held a cup of water to her mouth and she drank it. Anne was still deeply frightened but she took the meal as a hopeful sign. If they intended to kill her, it was unlikely that they would bother to feed her first.

'Why are you keeping me here?' she asked.

'We need a hostage.'

'For what reason?'

'To keep your friend, Nicholas Bracewell, at bay,' he said with a chuckle. 'As long as we have you, he will not bother us. He cares too much for Anne Hendrik.'

He stroked her hair and she pulled away in disgust.

'How do you know my name?' she said.

'I made it my business to find it out.'

'Who are you?'

'That does not matter.'

'What do you want?'

'I already have that,' he said complacently. 'Nicholas was kind enough to hand it over to me. He thought he would be getting you in exchange.'

'How long must I stay here?'

'As long as I deem it necessary.'

'Will you release me then?'

'If you behave yourself.'

'Nicholas will find you,' she said boldly.

'He does not even know that this place exists.'

'He will track you down somehow.'

'No,' said the other. 'He will not need to, Anne. When I am ready, I will go after Nicholas Bracewell.'

'Why?'

'Because I have to kill him.'

Her scream of fear was muffled by the gag as he tied it back in position. She struggled hard but her bonds were too tight. He caressed the side of her face with his finger.

'Forget Nicholas,' he advised. 'You will never see him alive again.'

As his cell door was unlocked, Talbot Royden peered at his two visitors in astonishment. The gaoler stepped well back from the trio but stayed within earshot.

'Who are you?' asked Royden.

'My name is Lawrence Firethorn,' said the actor, 'and this is Nicholas Bracewell.'

'We are pleased to meet you at last, Doctor Royden,' said Nicholas.

'I am not sure that I can say the same about you, sir.'

The prisoner eyed them both suspiciously and wondered how the taller of them had come by his head wound. They had a chance to appraise him. His gown was soiled, his face blotched and his hands filthy. He had removed his hat to reveal short spiky brown hair. Both his ears had been cropped. Royden saw the two of them reaching the same conclusion.

'Yes, gentlemen,' he confessed, 'I was arrested in England for coining and had my ears clipped in punishment. It was a false charge, like so many brought against me, but I bore my adversity. I was also accused of digging up dead bodies for use in my experiments but I was never brought to trial for that. I fled from England and came to Bohemia instead.'

'We expected a more flattering pedigree,' said Firethorn.

'Had you come last week, you would have got it from the Emperor himself. He doted on my work. Then.'

'We need your help,' said Nicholas.

'I am hardly in a position to offer that.'

'We think you are. Before we left England, we were given documents to bring to you in secret.'

'From whom? That old charlatan, John Mordrake?'

'No,' said Nicholas. 'From an unknown source. I hazard a guess that it may be someone in the Privy Council.'

Royden stiffened. 'Why did you act as couriers?'

'That is what we hope you can tell us.'

'Have you brought the documents with you?'

'They were taken from me here in Prague.'

'Nick was attacked and they were stolen,' explained Firethorn. 'Someone was extremely anxious to lay hold of those documents. They have already claimed the life of one of our fellows. He was mistaken for Nick and murdered.'

Royden's face was composed but his eyes darted about.

'Without the documents, I cannot help you,' he said.

'I made a fair copy of them,' said Nicholas, taking them from Firethorn.

'We have risked a great deal to get these to you and we insist on knowing what they contain.'

Royden searched both their faces before he took the sheets of parchment from Nicholas. He unfolded the first one.

'A short letter,' said Firethorn. 'In gibberish.'

'This will take time.'

The visitors stood shoulder to shoulder to block Royden from the view of the gaoler. The prisoner held the missive close to the candle and scrutinised it with care. They saw his lips moving as he attempted to translate the code in which it was written. When he had finished, he passed it over the top of the flame, then realised what he was doing and checked himself.

'This is of no great moment, sirs,' he said airily. 'It is a greeting from a friend at Court. He begs me for news of life here in Prague. I thank you for delivering this to me.'

'Then divulge its contents to us,' ordered Nicholas.

'I have just done so.'

'A letter from a friend does not need to be written in code. Nor does it require secret delivery.'

'There are some private enquiries in it, which my friend sought to keep between the two of us.'

Nicholas bristled. 'You forget, Doctor Royden,' he said, 'we belong to a theatre company. We stage plays on this theme. The spies in our dramas also write in cipher code and wave their missives over a flame. You thought, for a moment, that the letter was the original, did you not?'

'No, sir,' denied the other vehemently. 'If you wish to know the truth, I was about to burn it. What have I to say about life in Bohemia when I am locked away down here?'

'Enough of this!' said Nicholas, grabbing him so tightly by his throat that he could not move. 'Invisible ink can be made with a preparation of milk and lemon juice. Warm the paper and the secret message appears. That is what you were looking for, but it was not there on the copy.'

'You are imagining all this,' said Royden evasively.

'And am I imagining *this*,' demanded Nicholas, pointing to the bloodstained bandage with his other hand. 'Was it for a letter from your friend that I was attacked and that another man was brutally murdered?' He pulled him close. 'Because of these documents, a lady whom I hold dear has been taken as a hostage. You are the only person who can help to rescue her. I will ask you once more, Doctor Royden. Lie to us again and I swear that I will dash your brains out against the wall!'

'No,' pleaded the other, recoiling in horror.

'What is in that letter?'

'And who sent it?' hissed Firethorn.

Royden was cornered. There was no means of escape. He had to trust them. He read the letter again, then flicked through the four sheets of parchment with it. He licked his lips.

'Well?' said Nicholas. 'The code used in the first few lines is number substitution. Thirteen occurs three times. What does that number stand for? London? Prague?'

'Flushing,' admitted Royden.

'What of six?'

'Bohemia.'

'What about those signs of the zodiac?' asked Firethorn.

'They represent people.'

'Which people?' pressed Nicholas.

'You will not know them. They were agents of mine.'

'What sort of agents?'

'They gathered intelligence for me.'

'And where did that intelligence go?' As Royden hesitated, Nicholas shook him hard. 'There is a number at the bottom of the page. One hundred and eighty-three. The sender. Who is he, Doctor Royden? Who used us as his unwitting couriers?'

'It is more than my life is worth to tell you.'

'Deny us this and you will have no life.'

'I'll call for the guard.'

'You would be dead before he reached you,' vowed Nicholas, clapping his hand over the prisoner's mouth. 'Which is it to be? Do we get the name or do you want your skull cracked open?'

'From what we hear,' said Firethorn, reinforcing the threat, 'we would be doing the Emperor a favour. He would probably knight us for services to Bohemia.'

'What was the name?'

More hesitation. Nicholas pulled his head forward as if to crack it hard against the wall. Royden's nerve broke. Unable to speak, his eyes rolled and he nodded vigorously. The book-holder let go of him but stood very close.

'One hundred and eighty-three,' he said. 'Who is he?'

'Separate the numbers and you may work it out for yourself,' bleated the other. 'Eighteen and three. What is the eighteenth letter of the alphabet? What is the third?'

It took them a moment to count through the alphabet.

'R.C.,' said Nicholas at length.

'Roman Catholicism!' announced Firethorn. 'That must be it. R.C. Roman Catholicism.'

'The Popish religion is involved here,' decided Nicholas, 'but these letters stand for a name. R.C. Who is high enough to maintain a network of agents on the Continent? Only one man answers to that description. R.C. Robert Cecil.' He saw the prisoner wince. 'We know the sender at last. Sir Robert Cecil. Spymaster to the Queen. At least, we have learned that you are working for the right side, Doctor Royden.'

'But what is the message?' asked Firethorn.

'A grim one, sirs,' said Royden, electing to confide fully in them. 'My role here is discovered, my reports intercepted. My agents listed here have all been killed. Someone in Prague has betrayed me and sent good men to their death.'

'Add the name of Adrian Smallwood to that list,' said Nicholas. 'He was an innocent victim of all this. But what of the documents we brought?'

'Details of a new and more complex code,' explained the other. 'Sir Robert Cecil has devised it. He instructs me to memorise it and destroy the pages. See here, on this page,' he said, holding it out to them. 'That *T* stands for Tuesday. Sir Robert himself. *W* is for Wednesday. Balthasar Davey. An agent in Flushing. And so on. I am to gather up all the intelligence I can and send it back to London in the new cipher code.'

'Who will carry it?'

'Westfield's Men.'

'Not us!' said Firethorn. 'We've had enough of your cloak-and-dagger work. Deliver it yourself.'

'That was the intention.'

'What do you mean?'

'Master Bracewell was very observant,' he confessed. 'I was trying to read the message in invisible ink. There is no need now. I think that I know what it will say.'

'Well?'

'Now that I am revealed here, my work is done. Sir Robert is ordering me to quit Prague and return to London with you. Westfield's Men would be my passport home.'

'Do not trade on that hope,' warned Firethorn.

'How can I? When you leave, I will still be here. Locked up at the discretion of the Emperor. I may never reach London.' He sagged against the wall. 'Tell Sir Robert Cecil why.'

'That lies ahead,' said Nicholas. 'Let us look at the immediate situation. Someone has betrayed you. Your agents have been identified and killed. Who was responsible?'

'I have no idea.'

'You must have. Name those you suspect.'

'It could be anyone.'

'Take us through your day.'

Coaxed by the visitors, Doctor Talbot Royden talked about his work in Prague and the people with whom it had brought him into contact. Several names were mentioned and Firethorn made a mental note of them all. An actor who could learn a twenty-line speech at one reading had no difficulty remembering eleven names in sequence.

Nicholas was satisfied. Much was still obscure but a great deal had been learned. Adrian Smallwood's death and Anne Hendrik's abduction had now been put in context. The names in Firethorn's memory were a starting point. It was time to go.

'One fear has gone,' said Royden with a nervous laugh. 'I was afraid that you had brought word from John Mordrake.'

'I did,' said Nicholas, remembering his errand. 'It is not so much of a message as a gift.'

'He has no cause to send me a gift. What is it?'

Nicholas took the wooden box from his purse and handed it over. Turning it over in his hands, the prisoner examined it quizzically. He seemed as baffled by it as Nicholas.

'It lacks a key,' noted the latter, 'but Doctor Mordrake said that you would know how to open it.'

Royden held it nearer the flame to study it. There were some Arabic symbols on it in miniature and he had difficulty reading them. The riddle was at last solved. By placing his thumb-nail at one end and pressing hard, he activated a spring. The lid of the box popped open and Royden took something out. Firethorn looked at what he was holding.

'Two small white feathers? Is that all it contained?'

'They are enough,' groaned Royden.

'What do they betoken?' asked Nicholas.

'Worse news than I can bear to tell you, sirs. Have no fear about my travelling with Westfield's Men.' He put the feathers on his palm and blew them into the air, watching them float slowly to the ground. 'I am done for. After this, I can never go near London again.'

Barnaby Gill strolled around the Town Square in the fading light of a balmy summer evening. Back at the Black Eagle, the rest of the company were in a sombre mood. They worried about the disappearance of Anne Hendrik, ordered beer to subdue their anxieties, felt guilty that they were not out searching for her and drank even more heavily to sedate that guilt. But it was not only the prevailing sadness which drove Gill to parade around the city on his own. Westfield's Men, working actors with simple needs, clung together because they had so much in common. A long tour only intensified their togetherness.

Gill soon wearied of their habits and their rituals. With them during performances, he preferred to shun them in private. He sought companionship of another kind. In a city as big and as cosmopolitan as Prague, he felt, he would be certain to find what he was looking for, but an hour of preening himself in the square brought no reward. The fashion and bright colours of his doublet and hose attracted immense curiosity from those who passed, and several women pointed with interest at his purple hat with its long ostrich feather. But nobody spoke, nobody signalled. It was a barren pilgrimage.

After pausing beneath the astronomical clock for the fifth time, he decided to search for a congenial inn and walked back across the square. The Týn Church was directly ahead of him, its sixteen spires silhouetted against the darkening sky to give it a ghostly quality. As he got nearer, someone came out of the street ahead and hurried across his path. Gill recognised him at once.

'Hugo!' he called. 'Hold there!'

Hugo Usselincx stopped in his tracks and smiled when he saw Barnaby Gill bearing down on him. Before the latter could even speak, Usselincx had showered him with more praise for his exquisite performance in *Cupid's Folly*. The actor revelled in the flattery.

'But what brings you here, Master Gill?' he said.

'I was looking at the sights of the city.'

'It will soon be dark.'

'Then I must find other sights to interest me,' said Gill casually. 'Can you commend any to me?'

'What sights did you have in mind?'

'Come, sir. You have travelled Europe and worked in many churches. Even celibate clergy have desires at times. Where might a lonely man satisfy those desires in Prague?'

'I do not share that predilection myself,' said the other with a sheepish grin, 'so I am no sure guide. But I have heard an acquaintance of mine mention an inn that lies behind the Týn Church. It is called the Three Kings and you will know it by its yellow sign. I fancy you will be made welcome there.'

'I am obliged to you, Hugo.'

'It is small payment for all the pleasure you have given me. Westfield's Men have made my journey to Prague a delight.'

'That is good to hear. The name again?'

'The Three Kings.'

'I remember. The yellow sign.'

Usselincx bobbed his head and moved away. Gill strode off in the other direction and turned down the street that led to the Týn Church. Imposing from a distance, it was overwhelming at close quarters and he paused to take in its splendour, staring up at its multiple spires until his neck ached. Since the front door was open, he was tempted to take a peep inside. The interior was dark and gloomy, with pools of light created by a series of altar candles. His eye fell first on the ornate pulpit but a loud noise took his attention elsewhere.

Scaffolding was set up in the chancel and workmen were scrambling over it. He went down the aisle to make a closer inspection. One man was hammering nails, another was winching up some large pipes. Two more were carrying in lengths of wood. When Gill realised what they were doing, he was quite alarmed. The Three Kings did not enjoy his custom that night.

Nicholas and Firethorn spent a long time discussing what they had been told by Doctor Talbot Royden. The latter's position at the Bohemian Court was a convenient cover for his other activities. Royden was at the centre of a web of Protestant agents who reported back to Sir Robert Cecil in London. Prague was a centre for Catholic exiles and Jesuit extremists. It was Royden's task to observe who came and went, to recruit and train new agents, and to keep his master informed of any suspicious developments. Nicholas now understood where the money had come from to fund their travels.

'What did you think of him, Nick?' asked Firethorn.

'I thought he was odious,' said Nicholas, 'but that does not mean he failed in his work. Sir Robert Cecil is too astute a man to employ someone who could not discharge his duties properly. Doctor Royden is a peculiar mixture.'

'Forger, fraud and downright liar.'

'He has a high reputation as an astrologer.'

'He did have until the Emperor found him out. And what was all that business with the two white feathers? Why should a paltry gift from this Doctor Mordrake vex him so?'

'It obviously had great significance for him.'

'But what, Nick?' complained Firethorn. 'Number codes, ciphers, white feathers, German and Czech. This city is a complete riddle to me. I can understand nothing.'

'It all comes down to translation.'

'Anne served us in that office.'

'And will do again when we find her,' said Nicholas with confidence. 'To do that, we may need the help of someone else who can speak both English and German.'

'What of Hugo Usselincx? He can give us Dutch as well.'

'So could Anne.'

'Shall we try to engage him?'

'I think not. There is somebody closer at hand, here in the castle itself. All we have to do is to find him.'

'Who is that?'

'Caspar Hilliard.'

'Royden's assistant. Is he more than that, I wonder?'

'More?'

'Sorcerer's apprentice *and* spy.'

'No,' said Nicholas firmly. 'I do not believe he was involved in that aspect of Doctor Royden's work at all. We would certainly have been told if he had. Caspar will probably have no idea of his master's secret mission. All he wishes to do is to work with a man he reverses. Keep him ignorant of the truth. And say nothing of our visit to his employer.'

'Why not?'

'We must let Caspar do all the talking. He was willing enough to do so when he called on us at the Black Eagle. He resides here at the castle—but where?'

'Royden spoke of his laboratory.'

'Let us start there.'

During the long search, they got completely lost on more than one occasion but they stuck to their task and finally managed to get directions from a servant with a smattering of English. Under his guidance, they came at last to the laboratory where Doctor Talbot Royden had laboured with such distinction until the Emperor's patience had snapped. The door was locked but a faint light under it suggested that it might be occupied. Firethorn banged on it uncompromisingly with his fist but got no response. A second, louder attack on the timber produced no result.

The two men made their way back down to the courtyard. Firethorn had a list of names in his head but those people were beyond their reach until they had an interpreter. It made them feel Anne's loss even more keenly.

'Why are they still keeping her hostage, Nick?'

'To retain a hold over us.'

'We need to widen the search. Bring in more people to help. Owen spoke true. The whole company loves Anne. Let us call on them to help to save her.'

'No,' said Nicholas. 'This must be done privily or we will imperil Anne. Stealth must be our watchword.'

'They have the documents,' said Firethorn bitterly. 'Why did they not release her? What else are they after?'

'Me.'

As they stepped into the courtyard, they heard a voice from above and looked up to see Caspar Hilliard descending the steps at speed. His manner was as amenable as before.

'Good even, good sirs,' he said. 'Did you knock upon the door of the laboratory a few minutes ago?'

'We did,' said Firethorn. 'Were you within?'

'Yes, sir. But I dare not answer. I have sworn to my master to protect his laboratory at all costs. It contains his books, his materials, his equipment. Thus far—thank God—it has been left alone. But when I heard that thunderous knocking, I feared it might be soldiers sent from the Emperor.'

'Is he still so angry with Doctor Royden?'

'He shifts between rage and remorse,' said Caspar with a sigh. 'Emperor Rudolph is at the mercy of his moods. This morning, he relented enough to let my master have light, books and fresh straw for his cell. This evening, he could just as easily order the laboratory to be ransacked.'

'Why?'

'What exactly was Doctor Royden's crime?' said Nicholas.

Caspar pondered. 'I can give no details,' he said. 'The process must remain a secret between myself and my master. But this you may know. Doctor Royden has realised the alchemist's dream. He has found the way to turn base metal into gold. The Emperor extracted a promise from him. When the first piece of pure gold came out of the furnace, it was to be fashioned into a wedding gift for Sophia Magdalena. A small casket, surmounted by figures of the bride and groom. The goldsmith has been standing by for weeks.'

'But the gold was not forthcoming,' guessed Nicholas.

'We were almost there,' said Caspar in exasperation. 'Another day and all would have been well. But that was too late for the Emperor. The goldsmith would not have had time before the wedding to make the casket.'

'Had the Emperor set his heart on this gift?'

'Yes, Master Bracewell. He is man of deep obsessions. If his wishes are flouted, he will turn vengeful. That is how my master came to be humiliated thus. For failing to provide a wedding gift for Sophia Magdalena.'

'Is he so besotted with her?'

'I know that I am,' murmured Firethorn.

'She has always been his favourite,' explained Caspar, 'but there is more to it than that. Or so I have gathered from the gossip that I pick up. Rudolph has a vast Empire but it is very restive. Many battles have been waged in the past and more turbulence is feared. If you travelled through Germany, you will have seen something of the problem.'

'We did,' said Nicholas. 'Religious differences abound. We saw Catholic cities, Lutheran communities and principalities where Calvinism held sway. There was uneasiness between them all. How does the Emperor hold them all together?'

'He does not,' said Caspar with some asperity. 'He turns his back on it all and busies himself with his Court. The Emperor has failed to give a lead. Until now.'

'Now?'

'This wedding, sirs. It was all his doing. And it has caused no small upheaval.'

'In what way?'

'Many people are offended by the marriage. I cannot say who they are,' he added quickly, 'but I hear there has been disquiet. Soɼhia Magdalena comes from a Roman Catholic family. Conrad of Brunswick is a Protestant. The Emperor hopes that a marriage of the two will be an act of reconciliation.' He shrugged sadly. 'We were set to make our contribution. The gold casket was to have been a symbol of the union.'

They began to understand the significance of the wedding. Sophia Magdalena was marrying less out of love than out of policy. She was obeying Emperor Rudolph's command. To show his profound gratitude, he had not only commissioned a unique wedding gift—a beautiful casket, made from gold which had been provided by his own alchemist—but he had acceded to her request to have an English theatre company as part of the wedding celebrations. In their own small way, Westfield's Men were a factor in the attempted reconciliation. As a result, they had been caught between two hostile factions.

'Does that answer your question?' asked Caspar.

'One of them,' said Firethorn, 'but we have several more.'

'They can wait,' decided Nicholas.

'But we need an interpreter.'

'At a later date.'

'Call on me at any time,' offered Caspar. 'I have only a menial position at the castle, but I have come to know everyone of consequence here. If you need information, I am here.'

'Thank you,' said Nicholas.

Firethorn was baffled by the change of plan but he had the sense to keep quiet. He took his cue from Nicholas and traded farewells with Caspar. The two men strode towards the exit. Firethorn waited until they were outside the main gate before he spoke in a baffled tone.

'Why did you tear us away like that?' he asked. 'He was keen to help. He could have told us something useful about the eleven names on Doctor Royden's list.'

'Twelve.'

'Eleven, Nick. I memorised them.'

'Twelve.'

'Who is the twelfth?'

'Caspar Hilliard. His master forgot his own assistant.'

'Surely, he is above suspicion.'

'I wonder,' said Nicholas thoughtfully. 'As he was talking, I called to mind a remark he made to us at the inn.'

'What was that, Nick?'

But the answer had to wait. A volcano of sound erupted. Hooves drummed, harness jangled and wagons creaked as a long cavalcade came surging up the hill. Riding at the head of it was a big, broad-shouldered young man with a fair beard. Conrad of Brunswick had arrived with his train. Beside him, attired in a cloak and hat that matched his dignity, was his father, Duke Henry-Julius of Brunswick-Wolfenbüttel.

Flaming torches held by outriders lit up the faces of the newcomers. Sophia Magdalena's bridegroom sat upright in the saddle and gazed around with a fearless eye. He rode through the castle gates with an almost proprietary air. His entourage was so large that the two friends were forced to step swiftly out of the way. Firethorn protested loudly and Nicholas had to reach out a hand to steady himself. As it made contact with the wall, it dislodged one of the loose stones in the neglected rampart. Nicholas caught it in his palm to stop its falling.

When the whole cavalcade had thundered past, he looked down at the stone. It was almost dark now and he could barely pick out its colour but he knew instinctively what he was holding.

[CHAPTER ELEVEN]

Anne Hendrik was in considerable discomfort. She had been tied to the chair for several hours now and cramp was setting in. Her arms were aching, her wrists were chafed and she had shooting pains in both legs. Yet the physical pain was small compared with her mental anguish. She was terrified that they might never release her. They would certainly have no qualms about killing her. Anne shuddered when she recalled how easily she had been abducted.

Sewing in her chamber at the inn, she had heard the gentle tap and opened the door out of curiosity without even taking the simple precaution of asking who was there. Two men had rushed in with their faces muffled from view. Anne had been overpowered in a matter of seconds. The gag had stifled her cries and the rope tied her hands immovably behind her. She was shown no courtesy. A dagger robbed her of all resistance.

The blindfold made her helpless. She could neither see her kidnappers nor move of her own accord. They had come prepared. A cloak was slipped over her shoulders and its hood pulled up to conceal much of her face. One of them hustled her down the back stairs and out into the street. They walked arm in arm, the knife pressed unseen against her ribs. To passers-by, she must have looked like an ungainly wife being helped along by a caring husband.

Panic deprived her of common sense. Instead of trying to work out how far from the inn they went, and in what direction, she was dizzy with apprehension. Instead of listening for clues as to her whereabouts, she heard only the pounding of her own heart. Had she crossed a bridge? Climbed or descended a hill? Walked over earth or cobbles? Anne could not remember. It was only when she was bound in her chair that she began to ask such vital questions.

Fear for her own safety was compounded by her concern for Nicholas Bracewell. She knew how shocked he would be by her disappearance and how frantic his efforts would be to trace her. But he was up against clever adversaries, who held all the advantages. The thought that Nicholas was marked out as a murder victim made her break out in perspiration. To avoid the trap they might set for him, she almost wished that he would not come looking for her. Anne was horrified at the idea that she might be used as the bait for Nicholas.

Her recriminations came to a sudden end as she heard the door of her prison open. The two men came in, turned the key in the lock and stayed at the far end of the room to continue their conversation. Their voices were subdued and she was only able to hear certain words clearly, but they were enough to cause her even more alarm. Not realising that she was proficient in the language, they talked in German as they finalised some sort of plan.

She heard the last exchange all too distinctly.

'What of Nicholas Bracewell?' asked one.

'I am saving him until afterwards,' replied the other. 'I have promised myself the treat of killing him very slowly.' He strode across to Anne and she felt his hot breath once again. 'Still here, Mistress Hendrik?' he teased in English. 'I thought you might have been rescued by your knight in shining armour. Where is he?' He removed her gag. 'Doesn't he care enough about you?'

'What are you going to do with me?' she asked.

'I know what I would like to do,' he said, running his hands freely over her body and making her recoil. 'But other work preoccupies me tonight. However, I will be back. You will not be alone. My friend will look after you. Guard you. Feed you. Fetch a chamber-pot when it is needed.' Anne convulsed with shame at the very notion. 'I am sure that you will both have a happy night together. I am sorry that I shall not be here to share in it.' He sniggered into her face. 'Yes, I can see why Nicholas Bracewell is so eager to have you back. He is a man of taste.'

'Why do you hate him so?'

'He got in my way.'

'Nicholas was only a courier.'

'He should take more care which messages he carries.'

'He did not even know what this message was.'

'That is his misfortune.'

'Spare him!' she pleaded.

'I could never do that.'

'Why not?'

'Because I have a score to settle with him,' said the man. 'Nobody obstructs me so and then walks free. Your beloved Nicholas made me change my plans. I will chastise him roundly for it before I make him pay full price.'

Barnaby Gill had plenty of time to meditate on his findings. When the two of them returned to the Black Eagle, he was waiting for them with twitching impatience. Westfield's Men reacted with surprise at the sight of the blood-stained bandage around Nicholas's head, but in his excitement, Gill did not even notice it. He leaped up from his seat to accost Firethorn and the book-holder.

'I must speak with you both,' he insisted.

'Another time, Barnaby,' said Firethorn dismissively. 'We have other things on our mind.'

'This will brook no delay.'

'I have already told you. We are not going to indulge you again. I refuse to play *Cupid's Folly* just to satisfy your vanity. Enough is enough.'

'It is nothing to do with that, Lawrence.'

'Then why do you ambush me like this?'

'To tell you about my visit to the Týn Church.'

'Why should we have the slight interest in that?'

'Because of what I learned about Hugo Usselincx.'

Firethorn was about to wave him away but Nicholas sensed that Gill had something of consequence to say. It was so unlike the latter to consort with his fellows in the same inn that there had to be a sound reason why he was even still at the Black Eagle. Nicholas motioned both men to an empty table and they settled down on the benches.

'Well?' he prompted.

'Earlier this evening,' said Gill in a conspiratorial whisper, 'finding the atmosphere in here too stuffy, and the companionship too dull, I decided to view some of the sights on the other side of the river.'

'Spare us the excuses, Barnaby,' said Firethorn cynically. 'We know why you went and what you hoped to find.'

'I was in the Town Square when I met Hugo Usselincx. He was still full of admiration for my performance as Rigormortis in *Cupid's Folly*.'

'That accursed play again! I knew it.'

'Meeting him was no surprise,' commented Nicholas. 'Hugo Usselincx is the organist at the Týn Church, which is nearby.'

'But that is the point, Nicholas,' said Gill. 'He is not.'

'How do you know?'

'Because I went to the church and ventured in. There is scaffolding up and a deal of rebuilding is taking place. One of the things they are putting in is a new organ.'

'But Master Usselincx told us in Frankfurt that he had to hasten here in order to take up his duties. Perchance he was expecting to play this new organ.'

'It will not be ready for a week or more. I took the trouble to ask. Besides, the church already has a resident organist. He has been in the office for a number of years.'

'What of Hugo Usselincx?' wondered Firethorn.

'They had never heard of him.'

There was a pause as the two men absorbed the impact of the news. Nicholas was first to see how valuable a piece of intelligence it was.

'You have done well, Master Gill,' he said, as his mind raced ahead. 'This explains much. He was always too ready to befriend us and to find out the innermost workings of the company. I begin to suspect why.'

'One moment,' said Firethorn. 'If Hugo had nothing to do with the Týn Church, why was he in its vicinity?'

'My guess is that he may have a lodging nearby. That might explain why he was there earlier.' He indicated the bandage. 'When he or his accomplice was responsible for this.'

Gill blanched. 'What happened, Nicholas?' he said, seeing the wound for the first time. 'Were you assaulted?'

'Close by the Týn Church.'

'Why?'

'I am only now beginning to understand that.'

'That two-faced Dutchman!' exclaimed Firethorn.

'We have no proof that he *is* Dutch. That is merely what he wanted us to believe. Supposing,' said Nicholas, remembering the voyage on the *Peppercorn*, 'that he is a German who can speak Dutch. We could tell no difference between the accents. Hugo Usselincx—I doubt that is his real name—gulled us all. There is only one reason he could wish to do that.'

'The rogue! Let's go hunt the villain down.'

'Where?'

'We begin at the Týn Church.'

'No, Lawrence,' said Gill, 'that is the one place he will not be. Besides, night has fallen. We cannot search for anyone in the dark. It will have to wait until morning.'

'I will not leave Anne in peril a moment longer than I have to,' vowed Nicholas. 'We may not be able to find Hugo Usselincx—whoever he is— but his accomplice could be a different proposition.'

'You have found the man?'

'Not yet, Barnaby,' said Firethorn. 'But we will.'

Nicholas rose to leave. 'Pray excuse me.'

'Where are you going?'

'Back to the castle.'

'But we have only just come from there, Nick.'

'No matter,' said Nicholas. 'We twice met Hugo in the courtyard of the castle. The stone which struck me down was from the castle fortifications. The man who has shed most light on this business is in the castle dungeon. That is where the answer lies,' he concluded. 'And that is where Anne may be held.'

Rudolph knelt alone at the altar rail in the Cathedral of Saint Vitus. In the soaring majesty of the vast edifice, he was a tiny and insubstantial figure. It was symbolic, he felt, of his relation to his Empire. He was dwarfed by religion. Unlike the cathedral, the colossal structure that was his Empire was in danger of crashing down about his ears. Too many rivals' hands had helped to build it. The Pope had laid the foundation stone, but Huss, Luther, Calvin, the Ultraquists, the Bohemian Brethren and others had been involved. Its pillars were unsteady, its massive roof too heavy and its services too controversial.

The Empire was a travesty of its original design. Its constituent materials clashed, its proportions were distorted and it rested on shifting sands. It was architecture without artistic merit or common purpose.

Rudolph quailed in its shadow. Having received absolution, he did not feel absolved. Having bared his soul, he had no sense of being cleansed. Prayers circled endlessly inside his febrile mind but they could find no way up to God. After an hour on his knees, an hour of pain, humility and penance, he was still unable to connect with his Maker.

The priest eventually walked over to him. Fearing the Emperor had either gone to sleep or been taken ill, he put a gentle hand on his shoulder. Words finally forced their way out of his tormented mind.

'I know that I am dead and damned,' confessed the Holy Roman Emperor. 'I am a man possessed by the devil.'

'No, no!' he protested vehemently. 'I refuse to believe it.'

'At least, consider the possibility,' said Nicholas.

'There is no need. Caspar has been like a son to me.'

'Sons have been known to rebel against their fathers.'

'Not him. He is the epitome of loyalty.'

Doctor Talbot Royden was studying one of his books when the visitor descended on him and the heavy tome still lay open across his knees. Surprised to see Nicholas Bracewell for a second time, he was even more astonished by the proposition that had been put to him.

'I would stake my life on Caspar Hilliard,' he affirmed.

'That is exactly what you have done.'

'How do you mean, sir?'

'Look where you have ended up,' said Nicholas, gesturing at the cell. 'Entombed down here. Is this not a kind of death?'

'Worse than that.'

'And who was responsible for your imprisonment?'

'Emperor Rudolph.'

'The blame is not entirely his. He could not have had you arrested without cause. And you told us what that cause was.'

'We failed.'

'Why?'

'Because we ran short of time.'

'Could there not be another reason, Doctor Royden?'

'Another?'

'Base metal into gold,' said Nicholas. 'You would not have promised the Emperor such a wonder unless you knew that it was within your compass. You had been conducting experiments for years.'

'We had,' admitted the other, 'and we finally achieved success. There are twelve stages in the alchemical process. The first six are devoted to the making of the white stone. That involves calcination, dissolution, conjunction, putrefaction and forms of distillation I may not disclose.'

'What of the other six stages?'

'That is where science and magic go hand in hand.'

'In what way?'

'They are designed to turn the white into the red stone. The true philosophers' stone, Master Bracewell. And we did it.' He referred to his book. 'It is all here. The two final stages of the process are the crucial ones. The augmentation of the elixir and the projection or transmutation of the base metal by casting the powder of the philosophers' stone.' His eyes glinted. 'And we did it. Caspar and I actually did it.'

'When?'

'A month ago,' said Royden, aflame with the memory. 'We created the philosophers' stone. It transformed heated mercury into gold. Only a minute amount, it is true. But it was a triumph. Caspar deserves his share of the credit for it.'

'Should he then not also take his share of the blame?'

'For what?'

'Your failure.'

'It would simply not come right somehow.'

'Who devised the process?'

'I did.'

'Who was in charge of the work?'

'I was!' said Royden defensively.

'Who heated the furnace?'

'Caspar did.'

'Who provided the materials?'

'Caspar did.'

'Who made notes of each of the twelve stages?'

There was a long pause. 'Caspar did.'

Nicholas waited while the alchemist finally came to accept that his assistant might not have been as blindly loyal as he appeared. Instrumental in the successful experiment, Caspar had also occupied a key role in the failed one. Royden was so profoundly shaken that he could not even speak for a moment.

'You have been betrayed, Doctor Royden,' said Nicholas softly. 'By the one person whom you would never suspect. The only one in a position to discredit his master.'

'But why? Why? Caspar loved me.'

'He loves something else more and that made him act with such calculation. He knew that the Emperor would turn on you if you failed and he made sure that you did. With what result? Caspar still has his liberty. You do not.'

Royden was perturbed. 'He *wanted* me imprisoned?'

'He contrived it.'

'But I was his master!'

'His true allegiance is to the Pope,' insisted Nicholas. 'Caspar Hilliard was set on you deliberately. Under the guise of being your assistant, he was able to divine your other activities. He is the one who intercepted your letters and identified your agents. It is at his feet that the deaths of your spies must be laid.'

'So young and yet so callous?'

'His task was to destroy you. That argues how effective you must have been here in Prague. Intelligence sent back to London by you led to the arrest of Catholic spies and no doubt saved Her Majesty from falling victim to a conspiracy. Doctor Talbot Royden, the alchemist, was ruined in order to render him useless as an intelligencer.'

Royden slumped back against the wall and the book slipped off his lap. The betrayal left him paralysed.

'How did you guess?' he croaked.

'A number of things came together,' explained Nicholas. 'He offered to deliver any message I had for you. At first I thought him helpful, but he was only trying to relieve me of the documents I had brought. How did he know that I had them? Only Master Firethorn and I knew of their existence.' He gritted his teeth. 'We two and Mistress Hendrik.'

'What else drew you to suspect Caspar?'

'A remark he made about you. When I pressed him on the subject of your relationship with Doctor Mordrake, he grew evasive. He told me that he was your assistant and not your father-confessor. The phrase slipped out,' said Nicholas. 'I think we know why.'

'Caspar is a covert Jesuit.'

'Working on behalf of Rome. That was another clue. He told me that he had studied medicine at Padua.'

'One of the finest universities for the subject.'

'What else was he taught there?'

'How to cheat a credulous fool like me,' groaned Royden.

'How to win his way into your affections.'

'Caspar was so conscientious and sincere.'

'He was well-trained in the arts of spying. One more thing,' added Nicholas. 'When Caspar could not get the documents from me by deceit, they abducted Mistress Hendrik to force my hand. You see this wound? I was struck down with one of the loose stones from the castle rampart. That pointed to a culprit here.'

'Caspar Hilliard!'

'Do you believe me now, sir?'

'I do, indeed!' yelled Royden, hauling himself to his feet. 'Let me at the traitor! I'll murder him for what he has done!'

'You are trapped down here,' said Nicholas, restraining him. 'This is work for me. I, too, have a personal stake in this. Caspar will not go unpunished, I assure you. What I need from you, Doctor Royden, is your help.'

'Help? What help can I give?'

'The key to the laboratory.'

'Caspar has it.'

'There is no duplicate?'

'None.'

'Could the door be easily forced?'

'No,' said Royden. 'It has been strengthened. The laboratory contains things of great value. They need to be protected. A battering ram would be needed on that door.'

'Is there no other way in?'

'Not without that key.'

'Think hard, sir,' urged Nicholas. 'If that key were lost, if you and Caspar were locked out and had somehow to get back into the room—how would you do it?'

Royden ran a pensive hand through his spiky hair.

'There is one way, I suppose. But only a brave man would even attempt it. A very brave and very foolish man.'

His silence was disconcerting. In its own way, it was as frightening as the other's speech. Anne Hendrik knew that her captor was in the room but she could not draw a single word out of him. He had given her food and left the gag off her mouth. Was he himself eating? Was he close? Was he at the far end of the room? Or was he simply watching her?

'I know that you're there,' she said.

No answer. Was he sitting or standing?

'Don't you understand English?'

Still no response. Had he been ordered to say nothing?

'Where am I?' she asked. 'At least, tell me that.'

There was a creaking sound as he shifted his position on a chair. It was barely a yard away. Anne was unsettled by the idea that he was so near to her, then a new thought struck her. The other man had done all the talking. His accomplice had been careful not to speak to her directly. The conversation between the two men had taken place some distance away, so that she could not hear him properly. There was a reason for that.

'Do I know you?' she challenged.

Words at last came but they were not from him.

'What ho! Within there!'

It was the voice of Lawrence Firethorn, accompanied by a banging on the door. Before she could cry out, the gag was back in place, tied tighter than ever. Firethorn knocked harder.

'We need your help, sir! Are you there?'

She heard him walk down the room towards the door. There was a third shout from Firethorn, then he seemed to give up. A full minute passed before the door was unlocked, opened and locked again from the outside. Anne was in despair. Help had been within reach and she had been unable to call for it. She struggled hard against her bonds, but the ropes were too secure. A scraping sound drifted into her ear. She stopped to listen. It was coming from outside the room and getting closer.

Nicholas Bracewell had borrowed the rope from one of the ostlers in the castle stables. The bribe had been too generous for the man to refuse.

Up on the roof of the palace, Nicholas tied one end to the pole which bore the Bohemian flag and let the rest of the rope hang down the front of the building. He was at the highest point in the city. A fall would mean certain death, but he did not hesitate. Taking the rope in both hands and pushing himself out with his feet, he began the perilous descent.

The secret, he knew, was not to look down. Three years at sea with Drake had taught him how to swarm up the rigging and stay aloft even in bad weather. There was no swell to contend with here, no rocking movement of the mast to make a climb more hazardous. At the same time, he realised, there was no sea to break his fall if he was hurled off, no swirling waves from which he could be retrieved by helpful shipmates. As he inched his way down the front of the building, there was no margin for error. Darkness was an enemy.

When his foot slipped, he was left dangling in mid-air for a few moments and had to adjust his position quickly. Sweat broke out on his brow and his weight began to tax his muscles. The slow descent continued. As befitted a man who, among many other things, was a skilled mathematician, Royden's instructions had been extremely precise. He had told Nicholas where to tie the rope and exactly how far down the window of the laboratory would be. After hanging in space for what seemed like an age, the climber was relieved when one foot made contact with the sill. It allowed him to pause, to rest, to take stock.

Reaching the window was only half of the battle. He still had to gain entry. The shutters were locked firmly from the inside. With both feet on the sill, Nicholas kept one hand on the rope and used the other to take out the dagger which had been lent to him by Firethorn. Its blade was long and thin but it could still not be inserted between the shutters to flick up the catch. There was only one means of entry and that was by brute force.

Nicholas slipped the dagger back into his sheath and took a firm grip on the rope with both hands. Then he pushed himself off and swung away from the building. For a split second, he was suspended in the middle of a black void, then he swung back towards the window and kicked hard at the moment of impact. The catch broke, the shutters burst open and he was into the laboratory in a flash. Candle-light illumined the captive.

'Anne!' he exclaimed.

She wriggled in her chair and made what sound she could.

Nicholas moved quickly. Checking that they were alone, he raced across to embrace her before tearing off the blindfold and the gag. His dagger started to cut through her bonds.

'Thank God!' she said through tears of relief.

'Have they harmed you?'

'Only by taking me away from you. Where am I?'

'In Doctor Royden's laboratory.'

'Why here?' she said, looking around.

'I will explain later,' he said, slicing through the ropes around her ankles. 'There—you are free.'

Anne tried to stand but almost keeled over. Nicholas held her in his arms, then lowered her gently back into the chair. He looked furtively around.

'How many of them are there?' he asked.

'Two. One was left to guard me.'

'Caspar Hilliard.'

'That young man we met?' she said in disbelief.

'I fear so, Anne.'

'But he was so pleasant and helpful when he met us.'

'What better way to throw suspicion away from himself?'

'The other man is German,' she said. 'I recognised his voice. It was the one I overheard on the *Peppercorn*.'

'Let us worry about Caspar first,' said Nicholas, as he moved to the door. 'He will be back soon. Lawrence Firethorn was to distract him while I found a way in. He will not be able to keep him away for long.'

Even as he spoke, they heard the scrape of the key in the lock. Waving Anne away, Nicholas darted across to the door and stood behind it. Caspar came in and gaped when he saw the open shutters. Nicholas was on him at once, grabbing him by the shoulders to run him across the room and dash him against the opposite wall. All the breath was knocked out of him. Before he knew what was happening, the young assistant was turned around and flung down on his back. Nicholas pinned him to the floor and held a dagger at his throat.

'Remember me?' he asked.

Even the joy of knowledge could not hold him. Books which had offered Talbot Royden an escape for his mind were now cast aside. He paced his cell in a frenzy. The visit from Nicholas Bracewell had opened his eyes to the full horror of his position. Caspar Hilliard, his trusted assistant, had betrayed him in every way. As a man, as a Protestant agent, and as an alchemist, he had been the victim of calculated treachery. The assistant whom he had loved and schooled had ruined him. Royden had lost his position at Court and his reputation. If the Emperor became more vengeful, worse might follow.

He threw himself at the iron bars in the door and tried to shake them, but he was far too puny. His energy was soon spent. He flung himself to the floor in despair, but even that worked against him. As he hit the straw with a thud, the sudden displacement of air made two white feathers rise up and float teasingly. Royden saw them out of the corner of his eye and groaned. Even in a dungeon, he was not safe from Doctor John Mordrake.

An explosion of noise brought him to his feet again. A door opened above, voices were raised, many feet descended. This was no social visit. When he heard chains clank, he feared the worst. Rudolph had ordered his execution. The prisoner would be fettered and dragged off to meet his fate. Royden buried his face in his hands and awaited damnation. When the door of his cell was unlocked, he began praying furiously. But the touch on his arm was light and courteous.

'Come this way,' said Nicholas, 'you are released.'

'Released?' Royden lowered his hands. 'Can this be so?'

'You are set free and exonerated.'

'By whose order?'

'That of the Emperor.'

'But he put me in here in the first place.'

'He repents of that folly,' said Nicholas. 'Besides, the cell is needed for another occupant.'

Nicholas gathered up his books for him, then led him out. When Royden saw who would replace him in the cell, his anger returned. Caspar Hilliard was manacled and held between two soldiers. Before his former master could attack him, he was hurled into the cell and the door was slammed behind him. Royden yelled at him through the bars until his throat was hoarse. He turned to Nicholas for enlightenment.

'What happened?' he asked.

'I found a way into your laboratory.'

. . .

The marriage between Conrad of Brunswick and Sophia Magdalena of Jankau was an event of great diplomatic and religious significance. Eminent guests converged on Prague from every part of the Empire. Archdukes and dukes, electors and princes, margraves and landgraves, archbishops, bishops and counts would be there to witness what Rudolph hoped would be part of a healing process in his ailing dominions. Protestant and Catholic were to be joined together in holy matrimony.

Such an important ceremony could not be improvised. Careful rehearsal was needed. On the eve of the wedding, therefore, the couple went into the cathedral to be instructed in how they should conduct themselves during the long and complicated service. The couple harboured no illusions. Theirs was not a love match. They were marrying out of duty and expediency. They had met only once before. Conrad marvelled at her beauty and Sophia Magdalena was impressed by his forthrightness, but neither sought the other as a partner throughout life. Obedience was all. For the good of the Empire, they were doing what they were told.

As they entered the Cathedral of Saint Vitus, their footsteps echoed in the cavernous interior. Sepulchral music played. Apart from the Archbishop, the organist and the two monks who attended the couple, the bride and bridegroom were alone. They neither touched nor looked at each other. Conrad wore his finery with great poise but Sophia Magdalena was not in her wedding gown. That would be saved until the morrow. She was dressed in blue for the rehearsal, with the veil shielding her face from her future husband.

They had come in through the Golden Gate, the main entrance to the cathedral, walking beneath the mosaic which depicted the Last Judgement. Ahead of them was the organ, a massive structure whose pipes cascaded down from above like a waterfall and whose sonorous notes reverberated around the entire building. Bent over his instrument, with his back to them, the organist coaxed deeper notes still to mark their arrival.

They turned right and paused at the entry to the chancel. The monks took up their position several paces behind them. There was no hurry. Dignity and ostentation went side by side. A slow procession would enable all to see and savour. Far ahead of them, the Archbishop waited at the steps of the main altar in his cope and mitre. On the following day, Sophia Magdalena would be led to the altar rail on the arm of the Emperor, but he was absent from the rehearsal. Conrad was allowed the privilege of walking beside his future bride to the archbishop.

The music stopped and there was dead silence. When the couple began to walk off again, Hugo Usselincx slipped gently off the organist's stool and glided up to the bridegroom. When he took him by the sleeve, it seemed as if the organist was about to offer a word of congratulation, but a dagger was now in the palm of his other hand. He struck quickly.

Nicholas Bracewell was ready for him. Garbed as Conrad of Brunswick, he had walked with the measured tread of a nobleman. He now burst into life. He grabbed his attacker's wrist and twisted with such power that the knife fell from Usselincx's grasp. Nicholas punched him hard but took some solid blows himself. As they grappled, Usselincx tried everything to dislodge him. He kicked, spat, bit at Nicholas's cheek and went for his eye with a thumb. The frenetic scuffle turned the cathedral into a gigantic echo chamber.

Usselincx was a strong and experienced fighter, but Nicholas burned with a deeper passion. He remembered the murder of Adrian Smallwood and the abduction of Anne Hendrik. Those memories put extra power in his muscles and greater determination in his mind. When Usselincx finally began to tire, Nicholas had a surge of energy, lifting him bodily into the air above his head and spinning around several times before hurling him to the marble floor. Usselincx was dazed by the force of the impact.

By the time he began to recover, he found himself surrounded by four drawn swords. Owen Elias and James Ingram had shed their monastic habits, and Archbishop Lawrence Firethorn had joined them to produce a weapon from beneath his cope. Nicholas had also drawn a sword. Even Richard Honeydew—in a dress borrowed from Sophia Magdalena—was armed. His trembling hand held a poniard.

Firethorn stood over the cringing figure and gloated.

'You praised Westfield's Men so much,' he said, 'that we decided to give you a private performance. It will be something for you to think about on your way to your execution.'

'How ever did you know?' hissed Usselincx.

'From your hostage,' said Nicholas. 'Mistress Hendrik was blindfolded and gagged, but you did not stop her ears. She understands German. When you talked with Caspar Hilliard, she heard enough to know that a plot was being hatched. We guessed the rest.'

'Yes,' added Firethorn, 'your sense of theatre gave you away, Hugo. We knew that you would strike during the wedding. Since escape would have been more difficult at the actual ceremony, it had to be during the rehearsal.'

Usselincx sat up and grinned. Without irony, he started to clap his hands. It had been a convincing performance. Intent on playing his own role as the organist, he had not had time to look closely at the principals in the tableau. They had made him show his hand and caught him. He got up on one knee.

'What is your real name?' asked Nicholas.

'Christian Dorsch.'

'We can see why you changed it,' said Elias. 'Murder sits ill with a name like Christian.'

'I have several names,' boasted the other. 'Usselincx has been useful before and, as you see, I can play the organ.' He looked around. 'Well done, gentlemen. A fine performance. I own myself privileged to have had a play written for me by so famous a company.'

He began to chuckle, then put his head back to laugh his fill. Nicholas was not fooled. Without warning, the prisoner suddenly produced another dagger from under his surplice and lunged at the book-holder. The latter moved even swifter and raised his swordpoint at precisely the right moment. His adversary's surge was his own downfall. Impaled on the weapon, he could only scream in agony and squirm impotently. When Nicholas extracted the sword with a decisive pull, the German fell dead at his feet.

Richard Honeydew burst into tears at the shock. Firethorn took the boy in his arms to comfort him. He looked across at Nicholas's resplendent attire.

'Next time,' he said. '*I* will play Conrad of Brunswick. It is the only way I will marry my fair maid of Bohemia.'

Restored to favour and clad in a new gown, Doctor Talbot Royden was permitted to attend the wedding after all. He had a seat at the very rear of the cathedral and could see nothing of the ceremony itself, but that did not matter. He was there. Honour had been satisfied. When the organ swelled in celebration and the couple came down the aisle as man and wife, Royden got only the merest glimpse of them, but it was enough for him to make his prediction about their marriage.

[223]

Floating on the wishes of the Emperor and the goodwill of the congregation, Conrad of Brunswick and Sophia Magdalena of Jankau were filled with happiness and optimism at that moment. Royden wished that he could share it. But his work as an agent had given him too close an insight into the lethal religious undercurrents in the Empire. Rudolph had contrived to wed a handsome Protestant with a beautiful Bohemian maid, but it would achieve little in the way of permanent reconciliation. A man who had alternately ignored or exacerbated the schism in the Empire could not really hope that a two-hour ceremony in the Cathedral of Saint Vitus would solve the problem.

During the magnificent banquet in the Vladislav Hall, Royden kept his cynical reservations to himself. The Emperor was beaming, Sophia Magdalena was an angel in white and her husband was lovingly attentive. Rich wine and plentiful beer achieved a temporary amity between Protestant and Catholic. Every stage of the endless repast was accompanied by some kind of entertainment. Singers, dancers, musicians, tumblers, clowns, performing animals and conjurers were brought in to delight and divert. The portrait of the Emperor as a selection of fruit was borne aloft proudly by its artist. Royden at last understood the meaning of the fruit basket sent to his cell.

Westfield's Men were given pride of place. Saved until the evening, when the celebrations were at their height, they were given a standing ovation as soon as they were announced. Without the bravery of the theatre troupe, there would have been no banquet. Westfield's Men had foiled an assassination attempt on Conrad of Brunswick, designed to rescue Sophia Magdalena from marrying into a Protestant family. She had unwittingly become a symbol of Catholic defiance. Had the bridegroom been murdered during the rehearsal for the wedding, the consequences would have been hideous. The guests preferred not to contemplate them. Disaster averted, they now wanted to put it behind them, but they had not forgotten that Westfield's Men were their saviours.

The Fair Maid of Bohemia was given its debut in the largest secular hall in Prague. Its size intimidated some of the company, who feared that their voices would not be heard. Built at the end of the previous century, the Vladislav Hall had the most remarkable ceiling they had ever seen. Its reticulated stellar vaulting covered a huge expanse, yet had no supporting pillars. Some of the actors could not understand how the ceiling stayed in position.

'It is a miracle,' said George Dart, gazing up.

'So is our play,' reminded Nicholas. 'Edmund has written while we travelled across Germany in our wagons. Yet it holds together every bit as well as the ceiling.'

'Thank you, Nick,' said Hoode, 'but you helped me to fashion the piece. Its lustre is partly due to you. We can but hope that Sophia Magdalena will like it.'

'She will adore the play,' said Firethorn confidently. 'And dote on my performance as the Archduke.'

'What about my role as the jester?' asked Gill sniffily.

'An ill-favoured thing, Barnaby, but we'll endure it.'

'My comic skills are the joy of this company.'

'Yes. We never stop laughing at your absurdity.'

'My Rigormortis in *Cupid's Fool* was the shooting star of Frankfurt. Everyone loved it.'

'None more so than Hugo Usselincx,' noted Elias with a grin. 'He has aped your performance and now plays rigor mortis himself.'

The laughter was mixed with groans of distaste. They were in the tiring-house, an ante-chamber off the hall. A high stage had been built up against the door and screened at the rear with curtains. To mount the stage, actors had to skip up five steps. Once there, they held a commanding position over the entire audience. After feasting for the best part of a day, that audience was in the most receptive mood possible.

Nicholas called the actors to order, then gave the signal for the play to begin. The quartet went out to set the mood with music, then Elias swept onto the centre of the stage to deliver a Prologue, which Hoode had kept deliberately short and simple. It began with one of the three German words he had mastered.

> *'Willkommen, friends, to our new-minted play,*
> *A humble gift upon this wedding day*
> *To Brunswick's Conrad and his lovely bride,*
> *Sophia Magdalena, Beauty's pride.*
> *Our theme today is Happiness restored,*
> *A long-lost child, remembered and adored,*
> *Is on her sixteenth birthday found again*
> *And reunited with her kith and kin.*
> *In Prague's great city is our action laid,*

Prepare to meet Bohemia's fairest maid.
To help your understanding ere we go,
Our play, its theme, we here present in show.

Elias bowed low and the tidal wave of applause carried him off the stage. When the sound finally faded, the musicians struck up again and the cast came on to perform the play in dumb show. It held the entire hall spellbound.

The Archduke and his wife were seen doting on their baby daughter. The girl is stolen by an unscrupulous lady-in-waiting and sold to childless peasants. Blaming the court jester, the Archduke banishes him and he commits himself to a search for the missing child. Sixteen years pass. She is now a gorgeous girl with a nobility of bearing that marks her out from the peasants. A prince falls in love with her but is forbidden to marry her because of her lowly station. The jester eventually tracks her down, identifies her, reunites her with her parents and is reinstated at Court. The play ends with the marriage of the fair maid and her prince.

Having seen the play in mime, the spectators had no difficulty in following its story in verse. Songs and dances were used in abundance. Eager to find his daughter himself, the Archduke disguises himself as a troubadour and goes among his people for the first time in his life. Firethorn extracted enormous pathos and humour out of his scenes and sang like a born troubadour. Richard Honeydew blossomed as the fair maid, with James Ingram as her handsome prince. Barnaby Gill added yet another mirthful jester to his collection, and Owen Elias displayed his comic touch as a drunken hedge-priest who keeps marrying the wrong people to each other. Edmund Hoode was the kind old peasant who brings up the fair maid as his own.

The rustic simplicity of the narrative enthralled the sophisticated audience. Emperor Rudolph clapped with childlike glee. Conrad of Brunswick laughed heartily and thumped the arm of his chair. Sophia Magdalena was overwhelmed that a play had been written specifically for her and she was in ecstasy throughout. Alone of those present, Doctor Talbot Royden saw the true worth of *The Fair Maid of Bohemia*, and he applauded the way that Westfield's Men had taken the base metal of their drama and turned it into pure gold. They were the true alchemists.

Vladislav Hall echoed with cheers when the actors came out to take their bows. Firethorn and his company were exultant. All their setbacks and sufferings melted away in the heat of the acclamation. They had entertained an Emperor and his Court. Westfield's Men had reached a new peak of achievement in their erratic history. During two magical hours on stage, their love for Sophia Magdalena, the fair maid of Bohemia, had been gloriously consummated.

The remainder of their stay in Prague was an uninterrupted idyll. They rehearsed every morning, performed at Court every afternoon and caroused every evening. Their work was revered and their purses were filled. They knew that it could not last and, in their hearts, they did not wish it to do so. The more admired they were in Prague, the more homesick they became for London. The more they played at their lavish indoor theatre, the more they yearned for the shortcomings of the Queen's Head. They even began to miss Alexander Marwood.

Handsome offers flooded in from distinguished guests. They were invited to perform at the respective courts of the Elector Palatine, the Elector of Saxony, the Elector of Brandenburg, the Duke of Stettin, the Duke of Wolgast, the Landgrave of Hesse-Kassel, the Landgrave of Hesse-Darmstadt and even that of the King of Poland. All were reluctantly turned down, though the company promised to return at some future date to take up the invitations.

On their journey home, the only place at which they consented to play was at the court of the Duke of Brunswick-Wolfenbüttel in the presence of the newly-weds. At the request of Sophia Magdalena, they agreed to give a second performance of *The Fair Maid of Bohemia* in the city which would become her home. The company would then make their way to London, pausing at Flushing on the way to pay their last respects to Adrian Smallwood.

'We have one consolation,' noted Elias. 'Adrian's killer also lies in his grave now. Thanks to you, Nick.'

'You played your part as a monk, Owen.'

'What about my Archbishop?' reminded Firethorn. 'I gave off the authentic odour of sanctity in that cathedral.'

'That was the incense, Lawrence,' teased Hoode.

They were outside the Black Eagle, loading up the wagons for departure. Doctor Talbot Royden was to ride part of the way with them. His pack-mule was laden with his books and equipment. Nicholas strolled across to him for a private word.

'Are you leaving Prague with any regrets?' he asked.

'Several,' said the other. 'But my work is done here and it is time to move on. I need to get well away from memories of Caspar Hilliard and his Popish conspiracy.'

'Why will you not travel all the way to London with us?'

'Because of John Mordrake.'

'Do you fear him so?'

'I do not fear him at all, Master Bracewell. But I am in terror of his wife.'

'His wife?'

'Yes,' confessed Royden. 'After all the services you have rendered me, you deserve to know the hideous truth. Do you recall those two white feathers?'

'Very well. What did they signify?'

'Unwanted fatherhood.'

'I do not follow.'

'Almost a year ago, I returned to London and stayed with John Mordrake and his wife in Knightrider Street. Mordrake is old, his wife is young. My flesh was weak. I told them I had received an injunction from the spirit world to lie with the wife if I wished to divine the secret of the philosophers' stone. The wife resisted, but Mordrake was so eager to learn the secret which all alchemists search for that he compelled her to share their bed with me. A featherbed.'

'I begin to see the consequence,' said Nicholas.

'I possessed her,' admitted the other, 'then fled before Mordrake realised that the command from the spirit world had really arisen inside my breeches. That night of madness between the thighs of Sarah Mordrake has returned to haunt me.'

'She is with child?'

'Worse, sir. Those two feathers were taken from the bed on which I gave my lust full rein. It was Mordrake's way of telling me that his wife had given birth.' He grimaced in pain. 'Doctor Talbot Royden is the father of twins.'

Nicholas smiled. He could not condone what Royden had done and his sympathy went out to the wife, but he could understand why his companion felt unable to return to London. Exiled from England and driven out of Bohemia, the homeless Royden was doomed to roll around the Continent for the rest of his days.

By contrast, Nicholas had somewhere to go and someone with whom to go there. He clambered up onto the first wagon and took his seat beside Anne Hendrik. She was slowly recovering from her ordeal at the hands of the kidnappers and had more pleasant memories to take away from Bohemia. As the rest of the company climbed aboard the two wagons, she took a last look around the city.

'I am sorry to leave,' she sighed, 'but I will be glad to get home to London.'

'It will seem a rather quiet place after Prague.'

'That will suit me, Nick. I am ready for quietness.'

'I still feel guilty that I brought you here.'

'But you did not,' she pointed out. 'I made the decision to come. So I must bear some of the blame for what happened. I should not have inflicted myself on Westfield's Men.'

'You were our inspiration, Anne.'

'No, that role fell to Sophia Magdalena. She brought you here, not me. Tell me, Nick,' she said with a teasing smile. 'What did you really think of her? Everyone else in the company fell madly in love with her. What of you? What is your true opinion of the fair maid of Bohemia?'

Nicholas grinned and gave her an affectionate squeeze.

'I am taking you home with me,' he said.